...Novels of 2017

"Like Tom Perrotta, Mehta digs into suburban angst and household secrets with insight and humor. . . . A family saga for the twenty-first century, *No Other World* journeys into daunting horizons to discover the familiar."

—*Shelf Awareness*

"Mehta uses vivid, memorable imagery to present likable, complex characters . . . and shimmering descriptions of emotionally resonant moments."

—*Booklist* (starred review)

"*No Other World* is deeply satisfying, a novel so moving that I worried about its main characters for weeks after I finished reading it. Rahul Mehta is a writer with astonishing emotional subtlety and generosity; I loved this beautiful book."

—Lauren Groff, author of *Fates and Furies*

"What a compelling, magical, big-hearted, lyrical book. Rahul Mehta is an expansive and mesmerizing talent—he sees things generously, from all angles, and makes the reader care, and feel, deeply."

—George Saunders, author of *Tenth of December*

"*No Other World* is a luminous novel about desire and disloca-
tion, about the lives we lead within the privacy of our homes
and the secrets we guard even there. Rare is the book that
explores so compassionately how the love within families can
fail; rarer still is one that shows so movingly how, and against
what odds, it can survive."
—Garth Greenwell, author of *What Belongs to You*

"*No Other World* is a tough and touching master class on being.
Kiran's life is a remarkable catalogue of the many brands of
love, some painful, some nourishing, all of them necessary."
—Brian Leung, author of *Take Me Home*

"*No Other World* is a profound and engrossing family saga
about the immigrant experience. Mehta is a confident, em-
pathic storyteller, his rendering of brutal scenes of pain, lust,
and love on two continents is fearless but forgiving, and this
is just his début novel. I impatiently await his next."
—Bharati Mukherjee, author of *Jasmine*

No
Other
World

ALSO BY RAHUL MEHTA

Quarantine

No Other World

A Novel

Rahul Mehta

HARPER PERENNIAL

NEW YORK • LONDON • TORONTO • SYDNEY • NEW DELHI • AUCKLAND

HARPER ● PERENNIAL

A hardcover edition of this book was published in 2017 by
HarperCollins publishers.

HarperCollins books may be purchased for educational, business,
or sales promotional use. For information, please email the Special
Markets Department at SPsales@harpercollins.com.

Epigraph from *The October Palace* by Jane Hirshfield. © 1994 by
Jane Hirshfield. Courtesy of HarperCollins Publishers.

FIRST HARPER PERENNIAL EDITION PUBLISHED 2018.

Designed by Fritz Metsch

The Library of Congress has catalogued the hardcover
edition as follows:
Names: Mehta, Rahul, author.
Title: No other world : a novel / Rahul Mehta.
Description: First edition. | NewYork : Harper, 2017.
Identifiers: LCCN 2016032306| ISBN 9780062020468 (hardback) |
ISBN 9780062199119 (ebook)
Subjects: | BISAC: FICTION / General.
Classification: LCC PS3613.E4258 N6 2017 | DDC 813/.6—dc23
LC record available at https://lccn.loc.gov/2016032306

ISBN 978-0-06-202047-5 (pbk.)

18 19 20 21 22   LSC   10 9 8 7 6 5 4 3 2 1

Every book is for Robert Bingham.

This one is also for Susan Morehouse.

WITHIN THIS TREE

Within this tree
another tree
inhabits the same body;
within this stone
another stone rests,
its many shades of grey
the same,
its identical
surface and weight.
And within my body,
another body,
whose history, waiting,
sings: *there is no other body,*
it sings,
there is no other world.

—JANE HIRSHFIELD

No
Other
World

WESTERN NEW YORK, 1985

Kiran—twelve, almost thirteen—stood in the tall grasses on the edge of Sherman Road, which rose in a steady incline, climbing past fields, a dairy farm, an evangelical ministry called Ray of Light housed in a large, boxy building that looked more like a storehouse for farm equipment than a place of worship, and a section of woods he and the other neighborhood kids had always called the Cathedral because of the firs and pines that towered like spires and the way the light on a sunny day (when they were lucky enough to have one) shot down in beams. At the top of the hill was a T, and you could turn left or you could turn right, but either way you ended up in the same place, back at the main road that headed into town.

It was early fall, the leaves had not yet turned. They fluttered in the breeze like winking eyes in day's last light. Fall so suddenly became winter in these parts, winter itself stretching endlessly like an enormous gray carpet being slowly unfurled.

Kiran stood midway up the hill, his back to the woods, and across the street was a house, an A-frame, an anomaly among the old wooden farmhouses haunting the lane. The newer houses were farther downhill where Kiran lived, in the small subdivision that pooled off Sherman Road.

It didn't occur to Kiran how similar the A-frame was to a dollhouse his older sister, Preeti, had when they were younger, and which Kiran loved but wasn't allowed to play with since it was Preeti's and he was a boy. When she wasn't hunched over playing with it, she kept it on a high shelf she had to stand on her bed to reach. It didn't occur to him as he looked at the A-frame, and yet the image must have been there—the high shelf, the bed he wouldn't dare step on—sloshing around in his head in a sea of other images.

It had been over two weeks now that he had been stopping here, each evening before dusk, just as the light outside was disappearing but before anyone had thought to draw the curtains, not that there was much of a need, there being no real foot traffic on this road and no houses on the opposite side.

This was what he would see:

Amy Bell standing at the kitchen window, washing dishes. Another time, at the stove, stirring a pot.

The children doing homework in their bedrooms. Or watching TV. Or in the backyard on the trampoline. Who would guess—watching them fly one by one into the air—that in the future one would become a BMX champion, another a large-animal veterinarian, a third would marry very young and struggle her whole life with alcohol addiction, and Kelly, the oldest, the smart one, the *ambitious* one, just one year younger than Kiran, would be class president and then study at Duke and then take a job in investment banking in New York and would die when the towers were attacked and her mother would be very angry for a very long time and would spit unscripted at

Kelly's memorial service the following words: "No one knew my daughter. No one. If you think you knew her, you're wrong."

And finally, Chris Bell in the living room with a tool in his hand, hunched over something broken. Or at the kitchen table, sorting through mail, the light from the pendant lamp making his blond hair glow in the same way his hair glowed that day, four years earlier, when Kiran spotted him on the far end of the skylighted food court at the Elmira mall, a day that would change everything.

Kiran had stopped boarding the bus after school. He'd also quit Odyssey of the Mind. Instead, he walked. Two hours. Three hours. Sometimes four. He wandered. He walked in circles. Sometimes he stopped at home. But he always ended up here. Outside this house.

Slowly dusk brushed its murky gray wash across the landscape. Shapes around Kiran became fuzzy, indistinct, crispening by contrast the illuminated rooms of the A-frame house. Tonight, Chris was upstairs in the bathroom, washing away the dirt that his long day as a building contractor had left on him. Kiran had seen him go in there, had watched him unbutton his blue shirt, toss it on the floor, unbuckle his pants, slide them down, move into the shower. Steam clouded the window. Several minutes passed.

Images from the fated summer and fall four years earlier flashed through Kiran's memory. A four-armed monster in silhouette, a demon come to life from the Ramayana, emerging from the woods, only to reveal itself to be not a monster at all but his half-naked sister swimming in a man's sweater. Days later, Kiran's sister holding a brick, barking, "Look away, Kiran! Look away!" Another day, Chris Bell's damp, flannel-sleeved arm slung across the back of his pickup truck's seat, hovering behind Kiran. And the look on his mother's face. He'd see that look twice that summer and fall and then never again, not quite the same look in all the years that followed.

In Kiran's mind, the events of that summer and fall were all connected, and they all came back to this: Chris.

The bathroom window turned a steam-blurred beige as a figure approached, curled its fingers under the cracked window, and slid it halfway open. For a second Kiran could see a strip of Chris's bare, clean skin. And then Chris—aware of the darkness, perhaps even aware of the boy who stood within it—pulled the curtain closed.

WESTERN INDIA, 1998

They were not expecting it, even though they had heard the commotion coming toward them on the quiet lane in the afternoon heat. They heard two voices—one deep and strong, the other more tentative—warbling a bawdy call-and-response folk song. They heard rhythmic clapping, crowds laughing, the ruckus coming closer and closer until it sounded as though it were just outside their house. Still, it had not occurred to them that it was all intended for them until they heard the sudden silence and then four sharp raps at the door.

When Kiran's older cousin, Bharat, opened the door—leaving the iron security gate shut—what Kiran noticed first was not the woman directly in front of them, and not the girl behind her, but rather the crowd that had formed, that must have followed them, first one curious onlooker, then another. Kiran hadn't been in town long, but he recognized many of the faces, or at least thought he did. He knew firsthand how quickly crowds could form. He'd already experienced it, his first day: the children who lived on the quiet lane spilling out of their houses to gawk unabashedly and unreservedly at the long-haired, brown-skinned, but unmistakably American oddity, and the women and men hovering in doorways or porches, being slightly more discreet, but gawking nonetheless.

When his attention finally did turn to the woman at the door, he noticed how she was leaning possessively with her fore-arm propped against the doorframe, how dirty she was, how dirty she and the girl both were, the oily film on their faces, the heavy makeup, the cheap outfits in shiny, stained synthetic fabrics, inferior versions of the chaniya cholis his mother and sister wore to special family occasions. The woman was about fifty, he guessed, a little heavy in the hips, and the girl was maybe fifteen, maybe a little younger, slender and flat-chested despite presumably passing puberty.

Kiran couldn't have known that Guru Ma was leaning against the doorway not in some show of dominance but out of exhaustion. He couldn't have known how she and Pooja had traveled all day, how they had left early that morning, hoping to arrive by noon, but how at the station where they were to switch buses, the driver of the second bus had refused to let them board—"Your kind is not welcome"—even though they had purchased tickets, and despite their protestations, which started off calm, then escalated. By the end of it Guru Ma was clutching, in tight fists, the cloth of her lehenga, threatening to lift her skirt, to expose her mutilated genitalia, to curse the driver. "I'll show you," she had said, "and once I do, you will never be the same." But the driver's eyes had been red, he called them "disgusting" and spat on the floor of the bus and reached behind his seat for some heavy object—a tire iron or a large wrench, Guru Ma didn't see it clearly—and she thought to herself, *It's not worth it*, and unclenched her fists and took Pooja's hand and led her away. Kiran could not have known how they had walked the rest of the way in sandals during the hottest part of the day, or how, when they got to town, they had to perk up, regardless of how withered they felt; they had to sing, they had to dance. They were hijras—everyone expected a show.

Later, Kiran would keep coming back to this moment: the opening of the door, the woman and the girl on his cousin's doorstep. At the time he didn't notice their Adam's apples. But when he photographed Pooja days later—after the two had told each other their stories, not that they needed to; kindred souls, they had known each other immediately, the way one accustomed to standing outside knows another—it was the feature he focused on most. Pooja in profile, her neck elongated, the setting sun behind her, an arc of light along the mound of her throat, the sharp edge of a crescent moon, that heavenly body ancient and honest and brave.

Part
One

Part

One

WESTERN NEW YORK, 1985

D id the boy think they couldn't see him?

Amy, from the kitchen window, watched him watching them, as she had for several evenings in a row. Today was an unusually frigid evening for early fall, and, seeing him—his skinny, awkward frame in baggy shorts and a rugby shirt, though it was obvious this boy didn't play rugby, probably didn't play any sports—the mother in Amy wanted to bring him something warm, a sweater or a barn jacket from Chris's closet, clothes she understood would never fit him.

She knew him from the neighborhood and from around town; everyone knew everyone. And while she had never spoken to him, she had seen him just days earlier at the dollar store. She had stopped at the end of an aisle when she spotted him halfway down, thumbing through neon poster boards. He saw her and looked quickly away, and then turned back toward her when it was clear she wasn't leaving. She wanted to confront him. "We see you," she would say. "We know you're out there. This has to stop." Maybe she'd even accuse him of being a pervert, a voyeur—"It's disgusting what you're doing"—though she knew that wasn't what this was about. But seeing him under the fluorescent lights—his mop-cut hair, the braces on his teeth as he smiled, clearly terrified, the beginnings of acne along his jawline, acne that would get much worse in the coming years, so much so that when his orthodontist removed his braces two years later, leaning in close, Kiran would see him wince in revulsion, and Kiran would come home and spend a full four minutes in the garage staring at the electric sander, wondering what would happen if he took it to his face, would he be given a transplant? some beautiful, smooth new skin?—seeing all of this, and remembering what her daughter had said when she asked her what Kiran was like at school ("He's a loser, Mom." "Kelly, we don't use words like that." "Fine, he's . . . *weird*"), she decided to leave it.

She and Chris had not spoken about it, though she felt sure he had noticed, too. It was a delicate topic to broach. Besides, she could barely admit this, even to herself, but there was a tiny part of her that liked that Kiran was out there, that liked being watched by him. She was proud of her home, proud of what she and Chris had created together. She was proud of everything. The house itself. The furniture, each item with a story. The sideboard, a family heirloom. The couch from an upscale furniture store in Rochester they bought just after they got married and which they could barely afford, even on a monthly payment plan. The occasional tables they'd found at an estate sale two towns over after a pancake breakfast at a place high in the hills that featured its own homemade maple syrup, outside aluminum buckets hanging on tree trunks; they'd literally stumbled into the sale, hand in hand, full and happy, syrup on their lips. They had painted all the rooms and picked the colors so carefully. They had done it all themselves and had laughed and fought and spilled paint. She was proud, too, of her children, *beautiful* children, and of her husband. It made perfect sense to her that someone would want to see, would yearn to be inside that house. A boy like Kiran: he would always be on the outside looking in. And yet she knew that was not why he was out there. That wasn't the whole story.

"I'm going to talk to his mother."

Chris didn't respond. They were lying in bed in the dark, the room quiet. They had just had sex. They had been particularly loud, loud for them, so much so that in the midst of it he had wondered if their children could hear them. Amy had been loud. She had climbed on top of him and arched her back and thrown back her head in a way he wasn't sure she'd ever done before.

Ever since Kiran had started standing outside, Chris had experienced the sensation of being watched even when he knew he wasn't. He had been thinking about it just then, as they were having sex, imagining that they were being watched. He wondered if Amy had been thinking about it, too, if that was why she had arched her back in such a way, if that was why she was mentioning Kiran now.

"It's gone on long enough," she said. "I'll call his mother tomorrow."

It wasn't only when he was home that Chris experienced the sensation. He felt it at work, and even while driving his truck the forty-five minutes to Olean to his current construction project. It had made him sit a little straighter in the seat of his cab. It had stopped him from singing along off-key to the Supremes song he had landed on while switching through stations. Chris remembered a sermon his brother had given several Sundays earlier at Ray of Light about how God was always watching. It was meant to be both a warning and a comfort: even when we thought we were alone, we were not.

"No," Chris said. He put his hand on Amy's shoulder. "I'll do it." He felt Amy's body tense and turn the slightest bit away from him. "I'll go see his father at his office. I'll do it tomorrow."

Chris didn't go see him the next day. He called. He told the receptionist he wanted to talk to Dr. Shah directly. It was personal, he said, and of some urgency. When he got Dr. Shah on the phone, he repeated those words: *personal, urgent.* He did not say, *It's about your son.*

"Today is impossible," Nishit said. "Tomorrow? Lunchtime?"

Chris could have easily cleared his schedule, but he said, "No, that won't work," and suggested the following day. Nishit said, "No," and they settled on the day after that, which in fact wasn't particularly convenient for Chris, but he'd already shot down the day that *was* convenient for him, and he didn't want to draw things out any longer.

Nishit's haggling over the date baffled Chris. If someone called you and said he had a "personal" and "urgent" matter to discuss, Chris wondered, would you wait three days, allowing your imagination to run wild with possibilities? Wouldn't you want to know immediately?

But in fact Nishit did not want to know, not immediately, maybe not ever. He of course did not know why Chris wanted to meet, but he had a theory, and if his theory was correct, he had no interest in discussing such matters with Chris.

That evening he and Shanti arrived home at the same time: he from the office, Shanti from the bank. They had been trying to sort through old items; their garage was in disarray, so they parked their cars side by side in the driveway. Nishit kissed Shanti on the cheek.

The house was empty. Nishit went upstairs to wash. Given all the germs with which he came into contact, he was fastidious about washing. He'd first developed the habit when the children were born. He'd worried about what he was bringing home, what microscopic organisms might have hitched a ride on his tie or his shirt cuff or might have nestled in the web of skin between his fingers; he'd worried about how fragile his children seemed, these new lives, how desperately they were in need of protection.

These days, Preeti was almost never home in the evenings. She had just gotten her driver's license, and if she wasn't at cheerleading practice she was at the ministry up the road at a Bible study group or helping to serve a beef-on-weck dinner to raise money to build a church in Haiti or to send some boys on a mission to Uganda or Uruguay. He and Shanti had not been thrilled when Preeti had said, two years earlier, she wanted to convert, but they hadn't stopped her. It occurred to Nishit just then that maybe his theory was wrong. Maybe the reason Chris wanted to see him wasn't what he imagined. Maybe it had something to do with Preeti. After all, they did belong to the same church.

Either way, he wasn't going to tell Shanti, not until he had spoken to Chris, and perhaps not even then. He looked at her in the kitchen. She looked tired. He remembered her once describing the particular exhaustion she sometimes felt after a day of dealing with other people's needs. Nishit said, "I deal with people all day, too," and she said, "It's different. In those relationships you have the power. I have no power. Your patients may want something from you, they may even need something, but they know better than to demand it. With the customers at the bank, you should see them, you should see the impatience in their eyes, the entitlement. They're not all like that, and not always. But enough, and enough of the time. I'm there to serve them."

Now she was preparing dinner—cheese enchiladas—moving slowly. He watched her slice jalapeño peppers paper-thin. He thought to offer help, but knew it would be an empty offer. He had no skills in the kitchen. He would wash dishes later.

He went downstairs into the family room. He gazed out the window, idly wondering when Kiran would be home. Kiran had been coming home late, keeping himself busy with Odyssey of the Mind after school. Or perhaps he was out playing with friends in the neighborhood, though, thinking about it now, Nishit realized he had no idea who Kiran's friends were these days. He wasn't still playing with that tubby boy Greg he spent so much time with when they were younger, was he?

The house was a split-level construction, and the bottom floor was partially underground, so that several of the windows, positioned high on the walls, were exactly at ground level. It was only September now, but before they knew it the first snowfall would swoop in, and then there'd be snow on the ground for the better part of four, maybe five, months. Every morning he would come downstairs and open the blinds and look across the eye-level snow and feel buried.

And then there were the spiders. And spiderwebs. Everywhere. In every corner, in every window, under every side table, behind the black faux Chinese cabinet. (Shanti never told him about the dreams she'd had those first few weeks in America in this house, when Nishit was spending long hours at the office and she was alone. Dreams in which spiders wove tight webs that covered all the windows, all the doors, trapping her.)

It was almost eight when Kiran finally arrived home. Nishit and Shanti were sitting at the dinner table, eating already. They heard the front door open and shut, heard Kiran kicking off his boots (actually *kicking* them; they thudded against the scuff-marked beadboard in the split-level foyer), heard him stomp up the stairs, click the bathroom door shut. A few minutes later he came down the hall and sat down at the kitchen table, a knit cap pulled low on his head, a loose sweatshirt two sizes too big ("That's the style, Mom," he'd said at the store). Nishit looked at his son. His hair was too long and it stuck out from beneath his cap. He slouched, not looking up from his plate. Nishit tried to remember himself at that age. He remembered being a schoolboy, being a good student, working hard. He would fill his notebooks, and at the end of the term, when all his exams were finished, he'd bring them to the chana vendor on his street corner, who used the sheets of paper to make narrow cones in which he served his roasted chana. As payment for the notebook he would rip out a page and fill it with chana for the young Nishit. Nishit hadn't considered it at the time, but thinking about it now, he wondered whether any of the chana vendor's customers ever opened up the cones and read his schoolboy notes—algebra equations or Indian history timelines or English vocabulary words, not just from school but from his own personal lists of words he'd encountered in books or in conversation, words he wanted to someday know.

When Nishit asked Kiran where he had been, Kiran shrugged and said, "Nowhere." Nishit didn't press him. He understood, of course, that Kiran was being insolent, but it also occurred to him that on another level Kiran was telling the truth: there was nowhere to go in this town, not without a car. The whole town, in a way, was nowhere. That's how Nishit had felt when he first arrived almost twenty years ago, after landing a job at the regional hospital before eventually opening his own practice. That's how he assumed Shanti had felt when he first brought her from India, from her home—a large, bustling, joint-family bungalow in

Pune—and they made the two-hour drive south from the airport in Buffalo, no direct highway, only winding country roads. Her body made her thoughts transparent; he could sense her muscles tense with each tiny town they drove through—dingy, sagging clapboard houses; rusting junk on the front lawns—wondering each time if this was where they would stop, if this gray town was the one in which she was expected to make her life. And even if they had never come to love living here, they had become comfortable, and there were things they did love. Shanti had taken up cross-country skiing after a coworker from the bank introduced it to her, and Nishit was proud of his status in the community, his invitations to serve on boards of various civic organizations. But even as Nishit found the town suitable for his own desires, he didn't want his children to feel too comfortable. He wanted them to want more, and when the time came, to seek it.

Chris had to be at the site that morning. His men were putting on the roof, and he wanted to be there. He left so that he'd have time to run home, wash up, and change; he didn't want to show up at Nishit's office in dirty boots or with grime on his face. He'd swap his truck, too. He had the Mercedes convertible in the garage. He'd bought it used from a client in Corning who had wanted to unload it and was so thrilled with the addition Chris built that he was willing to part with it for a song. Chris hadn't driven the car in weeks and forgot that the top was down. He had to crank open the rag top and wrestle the bolts into their fasteners and then tighten them into place using the special ratchet in the glove box, and somehow, even though it was a cool day, he'd managed to work up a brand-new sweat that soaked the pits of the fresh shirt he'd donned. He stood back a moment, wiped the sweat from his forehead with his sleeve, and looked at the car. It was beautiful, sleek, powerful. But not him.

"Screw it," he said out loud. He was going to take the truck. He had nothing to prove, no one to impress. He owned his own business, made good money, great money, probably as much as Dr. Shah, if not more. Nishit should be the one sweating, not him. After all, it was Nishit's son that they were meeting to discuss. Although Chris, of course, had his own reasons for feeling anxious about their meeting. It had happened four years ago, and in the end it had come to nothing, but he didn't know what Nishit knew about it, or what he thought he knew about it.

At the office, the receptionist told Chris that Dr. Shah would be with him in a few minutes. But Chris wasn't going to sit in the waiting room. He wasn't a patient. He'd be in the parking lot, he told her. He sat in the truck, windows open, enjoying the slight chill in the air. He was glad he hadn't brought the Mercedes. Zeppelin was on the radio. He closed his eyes, leaned back into the seat. It wasn't until he felt a hand shaking him and opened his eyes and saw Nishit mouthing, "Chris! Chris!" that he realized just how loud he'd cranked the volume.

Nishit was wearing a cheap-looking shirt and tie, the kind you buy already matched up and packaged together in crinkly cellophane. It didn't fit him right, Chris could see that. Nishit's shoulders were narrow and his arms too long. His proportions were all off. Looking at him, Chris couldn't help thinking of Kiran, who shared his father's awkward outward appearance.

Earlier on the phone, Nishit had suggested the sandwich shop across the street from his office, but now Chris turned down the radio and said, "Hop in," and Nishit walked around to the passenger side and climbed up. Nishit didn't ask where they were going, he only said, "I need to be back in an hour," and Chris said, "That won't be a problem."

Once they'd made a few turns and hit a stretch of open road, Nishit said, "So, what did you want to talk about?"

"Not here. Let's wait until we're sitting."

We are sitting, Nishit thought, but didn't say so; he knew what Chris meant. Some people liked to talk face-to-face. When he had difficult news to tell patients, he made sure to look them in their eyes if the patient allowed it—not everyone did. But with Shanti, it had always been different. They liked to talk in the car. There was something about the enclosed space, the sitting side by side, the forward motion, that allowed them to say what was difficult but which needed to be said, even if they themselves hadn't realized it until that very moment.

Chris had taken Nishit up one of the back routes he traveled when he had a job in Rochester; the back routes could be faster than the highway if you knew which ones to take. He pulled the truck over at a roadside barbecue, a small, dirty white wood structure, not more than a shack really, mostly a takeout place but with a couple of picnic benches inside and a few more outside for when the weather was warm. They ordered at the counter inside. Chris ordered first and he already had his wallet out and was handing the cashier a twenty, saying, "I'm getting both of ours," before Nishit had even said anything.

"Your son has been standing outside our house," Chris said after they'd sat down at a picnic table outside. It was chilly, but the sun was bright and Nishit was shielding his eyes with a hand. "We've seen him there. Several times. He's out there for twenty, thirty minutes, standing across the road at the edge of the woods."

"Why would he do that?"

Chris looked at him but didn't answer.

Nishit dragged his plastic fork through the baked beans in the cardboard boat. When he ordered, he had decided not to ask if the dish was vegetarian; he didn't want to know.

"Listen, it's not a big deal, but it needs to stop. It's not right for a boy his age to be doing that. Amy . . ." Chris searched for the right words, then trailed off.

"Are you suggesting something, Mr. Bell? Are you trying to say he's a Peeking Tom?"

Chris laughed and looked down at his food, trying to control his smile. "*Peeping* Tom. No, I don't think so."

"Then what *are* you suggesting?"

"Nothing. Honestly, we just want it to stop."

Nishit watched Chris take an enormous bite of his pulled pork sandwich, wincing at the smear of barbecue sauce at the corner of his mouth.

"Do you own the road, Mr. Bell? This is a free country. Anyone can stand on a public road."

"Just talk to your boy," Chris said.

In the truck, heading back into town, Nishit kept remembering how Chris had laughed at him, smirked, corrected him. Why wasn't it called peeking tom? Tom was peeking.

Nishit thought about all the words he knew, the lists he had kept even as a twelve-year-old, Kiran's age, lists with words like *equanimity, prodigious, epistolary, spiriferous*. Did Chris, a native speaker, know what *spiriferous* meant? Had Chris even been to college? Who was he to correct or to criticize anyone? Who was he to point a finger?

Nishit's anger continued to build as the truck tore down the back roads. Nishit glanced at his watch. He would be late for his next appointment. He was not going to be back within the hour, as Chris had promised. Chris had lied.

In the parking lot, Nishit stepped out of the cab, and without having planned it, found himself pointing his own finger—rigid and shaking—and spitting out words he couldn't recall ever having said in his entire life: "Fuck you."

* * *

That evening, Kiran was outside, just as he had been for the past two weeks. Amy remembered that today was the day that Chris was to have had lunch with the boy's father. It made sense to her that Dr. Shah had not yet been able to speak with his son. The fact that Kiran was out there again this evening didn't mean anything.

Chris had said that he would take care of it, and she trusted him to do so. They had grown up together in this town, had been sweethearts since high school. Their families had known each other since long before they were born. Hours of her childhood had been spent sitting in the pew directly behind Chris in Ray of Light, the church Chris's father had founded. Week after week she charted the ebb and flow of his hair on the nape of his neck, inhaled the scent of his Sunday-morning boyness, equal parts cheap soap and grape gum.

Amy remembered the specific moment she first knew she loved Chris. It was eighth grade. She was with a group of kids, eight of them or so, boys and girls, all popular—she and Chris were always part of the popular crowd. They were sitting on the bleachers outside. There was a lull of some sort, they were waiting for something, idle for some reason, she couldn't re-member the details. What she did remember is that one of the girls pulled out her makeup bag and squeezed in close to one of the boys and went to work: applying foundation, lipstick, eye shadow, mascara. The other girls followed suit. The boys were happy to comply. They liked having the girls press up against them. They liked smelling the girls. They liked being touched.

Amy remembered making up Chris. How quietly he sat for her, how big his eyes were when she told him to open them big, how sweetly he gazed at her as she held his chin in her hand and swiped the eyeliner across his bottom lid. It took Chris another three and a half years to ask her out, but Amy had loved him ever since that moment. It had even been immortalized in the yearbook; someone from staff had happened by, snapped a photo. Sometimes, when she saw him on the football field or, years later, playing with the children in the yard, or when she caught a glimpse of him across Kmart greeting a buddy he'd run into, slapping him on the back, she'd think of that boy— the red lips and blue eye shadow, bobby pins holding back his shaggy blond hair—looking up at her, smiling.

Later that night, in bed, Amy lay next to Chris. He still hadn't said anything about his conversation with Dr. Shah. What had transpired? Surely they talked about Kiran, but had they talked about anything else? Amy decided she wasn't going to ask. She didn't need to know, she didn't need to dredge up the past any more than it already had been.

Not long after they were married, when Amy was eight months pregnant with their first child, Kelly, she saw in Chris's eyes a particular fire that scared her, a fire that she would see once more, many years later. They were sitting in the bleachers in the unfamiliar gymnasium of a neighboring town (unfamiliar even though surely she had been there at least once at some point during their youth, cheering from the sidelines as Chris raced up and down the basketball court). They were there for a special presentation; the flyers photocopied on goldenrod stock had been distributed two weeks earlier at Ray of Light. Amy had known Chris would volunteer to stand onstage even before he did it, raising his hand not in the eager rocket-launch of a reedy schoolboy but in the smooth, confident motion of a man who knows what he wants. They hadn't exchanged glances, the way some married couples might have; he hadn't wordlessly asked for her permission or warned her. But she had felt the energy build in his body as he watched the men on stage, had known, perhaps even before he had, that he longed to be up there with them.

As he made his way down the bleachers, Amy couldn't help admiring his ass in his jeans. She felt her cheeks get hot remembering the weekday evening a month earlier when they'd bought them, when he stood in front of her, outside the dressing room, and she asked him to lift his untucked shirt and to turn around. She was surveying the fit, yes, but she was also surveying him, the parcel of land she had conquered for herself.

They had asked for someone strong. "Who wants to test his mettle? See what he's made of?"

The audience applauded as Chris hustled his way toward the stage on the floor of the gymnasium. His heart was racing. One of the men stood very close to him, held a microphone between them, and asked loudly, "You think you got what it takes?" His breath was hot on Chris's face.

"I'm willing to give it a shot," Chris said. The crowd erupted in cheers.

The man handed Chris a length of pipe. "See if you can bend it."

Chris strained. His arms bulged. His face squeezed tight. He shut his eyes, remembering what Amy, in her sweet voice, sometimes said to him: "You're my Superman." But the pipe remained rigid.

The man standing next to him smiled, satisfied. "Can't do it, can you? Hand it over."

Chris, still breathing hard, watched the man, barely breaking a sweat, bend the rod. The audience went wild. The man, pacing lion-like across the stage, roared, "How did I do it? I'll tell you." He paused for effect: "I didn't." He pointed upward. "God did. And this is *nothing*. God's powers are limitless, impossible to even begin to imagine. He works through us in amazing ways. And when we believe, when we truly believe, we are capable of miracles. Now I'm not saying that all of you, if you believe, can bend steel. But what I am saying is if you relinquish your self to God—mind, body, and soul—He will give you strength you never knew you had. Let Him in! Let Him transform you!"

Somewhere up in the bleachers was a young girl eating Crackerjacks, mesmerized. Somewhere was a single mother of three who came with her boys because she saw that goldenrod flyer posted on a bulletin board outside of the library and the event was free and it was hot out and she knew the gymnasium would be air-conditioned. Somewhere was a man, mid-thirties, who saw behind him only miles of missteps stretching to the horizon, who heard in the word *transform* a hope he thought had long ago passed him by.

It was hard not to be seduced. The men in their tight white T-shirts emblazoned with "Gladiators for Christ," looking themselves like gods, like young Apollos, acting like superheroes. *Capable of miracles.* Their bodies themselves were evidence of the divine.

Lingering after the show, Amy and Chris found the man who had bent the steel.

"That was some trick," Chris said.

Amy was holding Chris's hand, her other hand on her belly. Her body had transformed in its own way over the past eight months, as it would again three more times.

The man looked at Chris. "It wasn't a trick." A few seconds later he added, "You know, *you* could do this. You've got what it takes. We could train you." His eyes drifted toward Amy. "But it's not an easy life. We're on the road much of the year, a hundred shows a year, spreading the Word of God. Like I said, it's not an easy life. But it's a good life, a life with purpose. Think about it. If you want to join, contact our office down in Virginia. Tell them Gabe sent you."

Seeing the light in Chris's eyes, Amy knew that, were it not for her pregnancy, were it not for *her*, Chris would have gone. It wasn't that he didn't want the life he had, it was just that he also wanted something else. Wasn't it natural, the desire, if only fleeting, to live another life, to be able to capture one more of the infinite versions of oneself floating around in the ether like so many fireflies?

Now, in bed, having decided not to ask Chris about his meeting with Dr. Shah earlier that day, Amy listened to Chris breathe. She knew he was awake, but he was pretending to be asleep; she was doing the same. For just a moment, just two or three breaths, their inhalations-exhalations were exactly the same. She strained to extend the moment, to keep their breaths synchronized. She felt if she could do that, if she could just keep their breaths in sync, everything would be all right.

WESTERN NEW YORK, 1981

Later, in their family shorthand, they would refer to this time as the Year of the Mouse, even though most of the memorable events (not that anyone wanted to remember them) happened over the course of just a couple of months during late summer and early fall. Still, the events were momentous enough that they would loom, for each of them—Shanti, Nishit, Preeti, and Kiran—over the entire year, and unspeakable enough that they needed a euphemism to contain and to neutralize them. They might just as easily have called it the Year of Prabhu, since it was also when Nishit's elder brother was living with them, visiting from India. But Prabhu was complicated; the mouse was not. The mouse was only a minor annoyance. It could be exterminated.

It was early August when she first appeared. "She" because Shanti was the only one who'd actually seen her—although Preeti had noticed the chewed-through Saltines sleeve and they had all seen the tiny, torpedo-shaped droppings in one corner of the kitchen counter—and Shanti had decided she was female. "Her body was misshapen," Shanti said. "I think she might be pregnant."

The children begged their parents not to kill her.

"If you kill her, you'll kill the babies," Preeti said.

Kiran said, "We're not going to murder Minnie, are we?"

"Darling, it's dirty," Nishit said, pulling his son close to him. "We can't just let strange creatures live in our house."

Kiran glanced sideways at his uncle Prabhu. His kaka had just arrived a week earlier, and Kiran was suspicious, both children were. They had never met him before; they'd only heard stories, or rather, overheard stories. And then, of course, there was the portrait of Neela Kaki, Prabhu's deceased wife, which hung at the top of the stairs and, positioned as it was, seemed to float over their lives. It was a framed and garlanded photograph in an alcove, illuminated by its own recessed lights, which were always on, even at night, a place of prominence, never mind that Neela Kaki was no blood relative, only an in-law, and only for two years at that. Both the photo—black and white and blurry—and the woman in it seemed to belong to another world, one that felt very far away to the children, a world in which women could die in childbirth, which was in fact how she had died, giving birth to a son named Bharat.

Kiran returned his attention to his father. "What about Kroncha?"

"Yeah, Dad," Preeti said, "What's the difference between Minnie and Kroncha?"

"Stop calling her Minnie. *It*. Stop calling *it* Minnie. *It* is an *it*. *It*s do not have names."

"You haven't answered our question," Preeti said.

"They're not the same," Shanti said, trying to help out her floundering husband. "Kroncha is a pet. Minnie is wild."

"A mouse is a mouse," Kiran said.

"You didn't see Minnie," Shanti said. "She looks nothing like Kroncha. She is dark and ugly with beady eyes. Not cute like Kroncha. If you had seen her . . . *it* . . . if you had seen *it*, you would want *it* gone."

The children huffed and crossed their arms.

"*Babies*, Dad." Preeti turned to her mom, looked up at her with big, pleading eyes, enunciating each syllable: "*Ba-bies.*"

Nishit found the live catch traps at the hardware store. Frank, at the counter, was skeptical. "You can try them, but the mice around here are smarter than you'd think. At best, you might catch a couple of the young ones, the ones that haven't learned yet. But the adults, you're going to need something else. Snap traps. Or better yet, poison."

"We've only got one mouse," Nishit said. "We only have to catch the one."

Frank wanted to tell Nishit he'd only seen one; there were more. But he knew better than to contradict him. He could tell that Dr. Shah was not the type to listen to men behind counters. And, judging from the tassels on his loafers, he was not the type who could catch a mouse.

At home, the children wanted to see the traps—they didn't trust their father—so Nishit showed them: gray plastic boxes with doors that shut automatically. "Just like garages," he said cheerfully. The trap operated a little like a seesaw. It was on a fulcrum, the back end pitched slightly up, the front end down. When the mouse ran inside the weight was supposed to shift, the back end falling, the front end rising, then the door was supposed to snap shut. The whole thing looked cheap to Nishit, and he was beginning to see Frank's point: no mouse would be so stupid. But the children seemed hopeful.

"What should we use as bait?" Nishit asked.

"Oreos," Kiran said. "Or licorice."

"The instructions recommend cheese or dry cereal."

"Froot Loops."

"I think they mean uncooked oatmeal. Or we could use granola?"

"I heard mice like peanut butter," Preeti said.

"Frosted Flakes. They're *grrreeeeeeaaat!*"

In the end they settled on a crumb of Parmesan cheese in one trap and a smear of peanut butter in the other. Nishit wore rubber gloves so his human scent wouldn't rub off onto the traps. But if the mouse was so afraid of human scent, he wondered, what was it doing on the kitchen counter in the first place?

Kiran ran in circles. "I'm cuckoo for Cocoa Puffs! Cuckoo for Cocoa Puffs!" As his father laid the traps, Kiran fetched the crinkly bag they kept beneath the kitchen sink and refilled the food pellets in Kroncha's cage.

Before Kroncha, the pet mouse, there had been a pet bird, and before the pet bird another bird: two birds—first Shilpa, then Deepa—both ill-fated. Ostensibly they were for the children, who had wanted a dog, or a cat, though Nishit and Shanti had been firm: they were too much trouble, a cat would scratch up the furniture, a dog would have to be walked, who would scoop the poop? and what would they do when they visited relatives who, even more so than they, would never allow such a filthy creature in their houses? *Pets for the children*, that's what they had said about each of the birds in turn, and yet somehow they had become Shanti's, both of them. She was the one they fell in love with. It wasn't her fault, she couldn't help that the birds loved her more—more than they loved Nishit, more than they loved the children—and she couldn't help how much she loved them back. She doted on them. In the winter, after Nishit had gone to bed, Shanti, worried that Shilpa was cold in her cage, secretly nudged the thermostat higher. Shilpa loved to be bathed. Shanti let her sit on the edge of the kitchen sink and used her own fingers to gently drip water in between her feathers. Then there was Deepa, whose tiny bird heart ached when she was apart from Shanti, her homing instincts always tugging her Shantiward. She perched on Shanti's shoulder at all times, even in the morning as Shanti sat on the toilet, as she brushed her teeth, even in the evening as they ate dinner, or afterward as she warmed her back just inches from the glowing space heater.

And it was this love, perhaps, that ultimately did them in, because, loving them so much, and knowing firsthand—though she never would have admitted this, not even in the deepest recesses of her consciousness—what it was to have clipped wings, Shanti wouldn't hear of clipping theirs.

One summer afternoon when Shanti walked into the subterranean family room, she saw that the sliding door that led out into the backyard was wide open and that the children were upstairs after having played all day in the yard and that Shilpa was gone. A year later, Deepa flew across the house into the kitchen where Shanti was standing at the stove, cooking. But Deepa, whose name meant light, just like Kiran's name, misjudged the distance, missed Shanti's shoulder, landed, instead, in a skillet of hot oil. Shanti rushed her to the vet and for a week afterward rubbed ointments and salves into Deepa's claws, but they didn't heal. Finally Shanti took the bird back and held her in her cupped palms as Dr. Paulson plunged the needle into the creature and depressed the syringe. When Preeti, who was old enough to want to know about such things, asked her mother what it was like to hold Deepa as she died, Shanti described having the sensation that her spirit was flying to heaven, just like in cartoons when someone gets hit by a train, and then a faded miniature version with halo and wings flies out of its body. But that wasn't what it was like. It was an indescribable loss, a sudden darkness. It was a light going out.

In the months after Shilpa disappeared but before they'd gotten Deepa, Shanti often thought she could hear Shilpa calling her from the woods at the end of their yard. A few times she had even gone to look, trudging into the thicket, emerging later, a leaf in her hair, a twig in her sweater. But then after almost a year had passed, she was still hearing Shilpa's voice, and how could that be, how could a tropical house bird survive a Western New York winter? And besides, Shanti reminded herself, she had never been one to know things by their names, to know trees by their leaves, flowers by their blooms, birds by their calls. She would not have known one hurt creature calling out from the woods from any other.

For someone else it might have meant something, it might have been a deliberate choice, a symbol of something larger. But for Nishit it was an accident, or at the very least not a choice he was conscious of making. He hadn't even noticed it until this particular Thursday night, during their weekly puja. ("*Cheers* is on!" the children would complain in years to come, in screeches grating enough that Nishit would eventually switch puja night to Tuesdays, but for now it was still on Thursdays.) They were all sitting on the floor in his and Shanti's bedroom, Prabhu was sitting next to him, and Nishit looked down and saw that the bell Preeti was ringing—the bell they always rang while singing the aarti, Preeti and Kiran alternating weeks—was a replica of the Liberty Bell, crack and all. They huddled around a makeshift mandir consisting of a few pictures and statues of gods Nishit brought carry-on aboard Air India and held in his lap ("Bagwan does not travel baggage class," his mother had reminded him at the airport) and in America arranged on a low platform in the corner of the bedroom. The diya flame was fueled by Crisco, not ghee, and the bell rung during the aarti prayer was, yes, a Liberty Bell—someone else may have seen symbolism here, but Nishit knew none of it was planned.

Nishit was not particularly patriotic. He liked America, even loved it at times, but he also loved India and hadn't entirely ruled out returning one day. Still, he and Shanti had vowed that they would not be like the Yamamotos, who lived next door in the pale green, square-shaped bungalow. They had arrived even before he and Shanti, and yet for all the years they lived in this community they had been a mystery to most of the residents. Without Nishit and Shanti even meaning to pry, neighbors volunteered stories about how, when the Yamamotos first arrived, they refused every dinner invitation, claiming they were still settling in, still unpacking, or sometimes giving no excuse at all; the neighbors were eager to offer these stories, praising the Shahs by comparison. Year after year the Yamamotos skipped the annual back-to-school block party, which happened to take place almost directly in front of their house, so that when people were sliding along the buffet table, loading up their disposable plates with macaroni salad and hot dogs and stuffed peppers, they couldn't help but gaze across to the Yamamotos' house, the door shut, the windows on this particular day each year always closed, even if it was hot and despite the fact that the Yamamotos had no air conditioner. When the boys were old enough, they would come to the block party without their parents. The older one seemed normal enough, but the younger one, who was Preeti's age, was always quiet, barely seemed able to speak at all, and was his brother's shadow.

Every summer, practically from the day the kids got out of school until the day before classes resumed, Mrs. Yamamoto would return with the children to Japan. Nishit had been told by a colleague—though he wondered how the colleague could possibly know this—that Mrs. Yamamoto was just biding time until her husband retired from the hospital, where he read X-rays, and they could return to Japan to live permanently, that she always thought of her life in America as temporary. "Everything is temporary," Shanti said, when Nishit told her what his colleague had said. "What in this life is forever?"

So, despite his not being particularly patriotic, Nishit had to concede he *had* bought the Liberty Bell some years ago when his aunt and uncle were visiting from India and he had taken them on a fast-paced sightseeing tour of the mid-Atlantic— New York, DC, and Philadelphia in three packed days—and had brought it home for the children, along with, come to think of it, an action-figure-size Statue of Liberty, so it must have meant something more to him than he was willing to admit.

It hadn't been Nishit's idea to come to America. His father had suggested it. More than suggested; instructed. Prabhu, the eldest son, would be the son to stay in India and, as tradition dictated, take care of the parents; Nishit, the second son, would be the one to go. Only now did it occur to Nishit that maybe his parents had insisted Prabhu stay not so he could take care of them but so *they* could take care of *him*. It was convenient to blame Prabhu's problems on grief from the unexpected loss of his young wife, but Nishit wondered now whether the problems had started even before then. Perhaps their parents, knowing their son in ways others could not, had seen signs of what was to come.

* * *

The bank was cold. It was always cold, no matter how hot it was outside. Today, being the end of August, was sweltering. The management deliberately kept it freezing, as if the money inside needed to be preserved lest it rot or spoil. Cold cash, Shanti thought, shivering.

Before working at the bank, Shanti had briefly held another job. Shortly after she arrived in America, Dr. Phillips, head of surgery at the hospital, arranged a dinner party to introduce her. Nishit had reminded Dr. Phillips that both he and Shanti were vegetarians. (Shanti had not yet started eating meat; later she would eat chicken and fish, even as Nishit remained a vegetarian: an inverse of most of the Indian couples they knew in America.) When the plates came out, the ones served to Nishit and Shanti looked liked all the others minus the roast chicken and with an extra dinner roll. Shanti pushed around the bland vegetables and creamed corn but was grateful for the warm rolls. In India there were all kinds of flatbreads and there was the packaged Britannia-brand sliced bread, but she rarely experienced the wonderful, fluffy, fresh bread you found everywhere in America.

She was complimented on her enamel earrings. She was told her husband was a real asset to the hospital, to the whole community. She was asked how she liked America so far. (She was tactful. She did not answer, "Well, at least the bread is first-class!")

After a while the conversation turned to the Phillips's house-cleaner, and Nishit, who had been quiet most of the evening, showed great interest. At the time Shanti assumed Nishit was contemplating hiring her.

That night, when Shanti was turning over in her mind all that had happened that evening, what she remembered most was not meeting Nishit's colleagues or their spouses or any of the conversations she'd had, but rather Nishit asking Dr. Phillips about the housecleaner, "How much does she get paid?" She had not noticed it at the time, but now the phrasing seemed significant. He had not asked, "How much do you pay her?" It was not about the paying; it was about the getting paid.

The next evening, after dinner as they were washing up, Shanti said, "Maybe I should work." She knew about the money Nishit had borrowed from an uncle to come to America. She knew about the medical school loans and another loan to buy the house. She knew, too, about the money he had been sending his older brother, although she knew he didn't know she knew. "I can help out in people's houses."

Shanti's family had always had servants. Even in lean times, there was always someone at least to clean floors and toilets and to wash the clothes every few days and to come after dinner and scrub the pots and plates and pans. She was ashamed to think of it now, but she had never known any of their names, had hardly even noticed when one was replaced by another. She had only ever known them as *Bai*, "Woman." It never occurred to her that in America she might become one of these nameless women.

She had wanted Nishit to say, "Absolutely not," but instead he said, "It would only be for a few months."

Two days later Nishit had already managed to line up three clients for Shanti, one of whom was a woman named Mrs. Sharp. Mrs. Sharp was perhaps fifteen years older than Shanti. She was pretty, not beautiful; it was the kind of prettiness that could be purchased. Shanti admired, in the bathroom cabinet (which she sometimes had to open to replace an item—say, tweezers—left out on the counter), small, beautiful glass jars of creams, and in the walk-in closet, silk blouses on padded hangers, hanging not clumped all together but with a sliver of space between each, as though each garment needed room to breathe. Shanti imagined weekly trips to the salon: hair and nails; Swedish massage; feet submerged in a warm salt bath.

The other clients had given Shanti keys to their houses, but not Mrs. Sharp. She was always there when Shanti cleaned, dressed as if she were about to dash off somewhere else, somewhere she might be seen by someone who mattered, someone other than Shanti. Shanti didn't matter. Shanti knew this. She knew by the way Mrs. Sharp greeted her at the door, her thin lips mouthing a curt "Hello." Occasionally she'd have special instructions for Shanti, but beyond that she didn't speak, never asked after Shanti, never asked, in the kind though slightly patronizing voice Shanti was becoming accustomed to, "How are you settling in, dear?" As quickly as she could, she would turn her attention to some other activity: making a telephone call, paying bills at the wooden secretary in the living room alcove, paging through *McCall's* in the breakfast nook.

It happened in the master bathroom, amid the pink wallpaper and the gold-toned fixtures, the countertop shimmering with metallic flecks, those beautiful jars of cream in the cabinet on glass shelves next to bottles of Lanvin Arpège and Chanel No. 5. In the peach-colored toilet bowl, beneath the carpet-covered lid Shanti lifted, there it was: excrement. Not a formed turd, but rather a soupy, putrid stew, accented by shredded ribbons of gray toilet paper. Shanti immediately shut the lid and flushed not once, not twice, but four times, waiting between each flush for the tank to refill. She wondered if Mrs. Sharp, sitting downstairs, would note all the extra flushing, would wonder what was going on, would even perhaps remember, in horror, that she had accidentally forgotten to flush the toilet, had left a mess. Shanti was embarrassed for her, embarrassed for herself. She dumped in double the cleaning powder she would ordinarily use and turned her head sideways as she bent over the bowl, scrubbing.

When Shanti came downstairs, Mrs. Sharp was in the kitchen, standing at the island counter, licking a postage stamp and carefully affixing it to the corner of a greeting-card envelope. She looked up at Shanti. Something about the way Mrs. Sharp smiled, the tightness of her mouth, a certain wildness in her eyes, made Shanti feel sure Mrs. Sharp had deliberately left her shit for Shanti.

Shanti sat for a moment in a kitchen chair, removed her clean white sneakers—her designated indoor sneakers—and pulled on the street shoes in which she'd walk home. She was still getting used to the fact that Americans wore shoes in their houses, that she also was expected to wear shoes in their houses, and, even harder for her, to allow them to wear shoes in hers.

"Will you pop this in the mailbox on your way out?" Mrs. Sharp asked when Shanti stood. "You know how it works, right? You just flip the flag up?"

"Yes," Shanti said. She took the envelope, along with two folded ten-dollar bills. Mrs. Sharp followed her to the back door, her heels clicking across the floor.

In the driveway, Shanti admired the creamy, pale pink envelope, the quality of the paper, the perfect placement of the avian postage stamp. She admired Mrs. Sharp's elegant script, the dips and loops spelling out "Dr. Greta Weingarten, Hollyhock Drive, Sunnyvale, Calif." And yet she couldn't get out of her head the image of what Mrs. Sharp had left for her, and then the wild glint in her eyes. Shanti had the urge to pocket the pink envelope, to toss this beautiful, perfect thing into the filthiest public trash bin she could find. But she knew, without having to look back, that Mrs. Sharp was watching her from the window, that she would want to make sure that Shanti remembered to put the flag up as instructed.

The very next day Shanti put on a white blouse, gray wool slacks, a black cardigan, and black flats, pinned her hair up, and without telling Nishit (and without an appointment), walked into the bank, asked to speak with the branch manager, and walked out with a job as a teller. Over time Shanti would grow to like working there, even if she sometimes felt uncomfortable having such intimate knowledge of the financial accounts of friends and neighbors. She sometimes knew things about people, about their finances, even their spouses did not. Like a hairdresser, a bartender, or, yes, a doctor, she too would become the keeper of secrets.

And the folks at the bank would grow to love her, would think sophisticated her postcolonial British accent (courtesy of a convent education); they would feel fortunate to have her. Later, when she wanted time off to stay home with the children when they were young, her manager said, "Of course," and then, a few years later when she was ready to return, she was welcomed back.

After getting the bank job, Shanti didn't call Mrs. Sharp, as she had her other clients, to tell her she wasn't returning. Instead, using her fanciest stationery, with a floral motif and a lined envelope, she wrote a note, which she slipped the next afternoon into Mrs. Sharp's mailbox, and which read in full:

> *Dear Mrs. Sharp,*
> * I regret to inform you I shall not be continuing my employment with you.*
>
> *   Sincerely,*
> *   Mrs. Shah*

The note took her twenty minutes to craft.

Years later the image still sometimes returned to her, not just when she ran into Mrs. Sharp, as she inevitably did in the small town, but at other times too: when she was waiting in the hallway of her children's school on parent-teacher conference night, or when she was at a dinner party at the house of one of her husband's colleagues. She would remember the swamp of sewage; the hot, putrid smell that lingered in her nostrils for hours; the tight smile, the wildness in Mrs. Sharp's eyes.

Shanti didn't know exactly how or when her feelings had shifted. She knew it must have occurred over time, in tiny increments, like crocuses pushing up, inch by inch, through winter's ground. But when you notice them it is all at once, a splash of impossible purple in the melting snow. That's how it felt that day, sudden and surprising, a light switch being flipped. Shanti looked up from the counter. It was a quiet morning. She had been rolling quarters, a task she liked. Carefully counting the cold coins and tucking them into their paper wrappers, she imagined tucking children into bed (*Good night, quarters*). She saw him across the lobby, and something asleep came alive inside her.

He came in often. He had reason to, since he had both a personal account and one for his general contracting business. But if Shanti was being honest with herself, maybe she had noticed that he'd been coming in a little more often than necessary and that he seemed always to end up at her window regardless of how many of the other tellers were free.

She realized that she had unwittingly picked out a particularly beautiful shawl to wear today. Usually she wore a cardigan. She kept it on a hook in the back, a light blue cardigan with faux pearl buttons. But this morning she had grabbed a Kashmiri shawl in deep purple with delicate embroidery. It was Tuesday. Of course. He always came in on Tuesday mornings.

Even if she wasn't fully conscious of it, she must have known that when she chose the shawl.

When he came to her window, she pushed aside the rolls of quarters.

"Good morning, Mr. Bell."

"Chris."

"*Chris.* How can I help you today, Chris?" Feeling her mouth smile, her cheeks flush, she looked down.

So many years ago, when Nishit was brought to meet her for the first time in the bungalow in Pune—her brothers and all of her uncles and aunts and cousins from the joint household hovering—the only instruction she had been given by her mother was "Don't look him in the eyes." So she looked down, risking only furtive glances at his neck, beautiful and smooth and long and string-thin in the way-too-big, clearly borrowed checked dress shirt.

Chris slid the checks and the deposit slip, already filled out, across the counter. His hand lingered a few extra seconds on her side of the counter, and then he withdrew it.

Much later, when she would hold him, when she would bury her head in his chest, his blue T-shirt sweat-damp against her cheek, it was his size she would notice most. He must have been six-three, maybe six-four, still with the build of the high school football player he once was, and enormous hands, of course she would notice the hands, hands she had seen again and again across the bank counter, hands that would now be touching her hands, her back, her neck, her hair. In India, she had not known men like this. Nishit had such slender fingers, perfect for removing his eyeglasses, folding them, laying them gently on the bedside table, a gesture Shanti loved. Perfect, too, for his duties as a surgeon, for extracting what was diseased or damaged, for suturing what was torn.

When she gave Chris the receipt for his deposit, his new balance printed in small gray digits, she included a lollipop. He smiled, unwrapped it, and popped it in his mouth. Much later, when she would reach up and touch his face and he would take her fingers in his mouth, she would remember this moment.

One day, not long after the school year started, Kiran picked up the kitchen receiver and caught them on the phone together. Kiran had just started using the phone to call friends now and then, but he hadn't yet learned the art of conversation, so his calls were always very brief. *Hello, Greg. What are you doing? I'm doing my math homework. What did you get for number five? Me, too. What are you having for dinner? OK, bye.* Occasionally he'd pick up the receiver even when he had no intention of dialing. He'd walk by and see the shiny canary-yellow contraption on the wall and he'd pick up the receiver on a whim, because he liked the heaviness of the receiver in his hand, liked the way the cradle flipped up, liked even the soothing sound of the dial tone on the other end. He couldn't have put words to it at the time, but part of what drew him to the dial tone was feeling connected to something outside of himself, outside of the house, something far away. With a few rotations of the dial, that tone could turn into anything, anyone, anywhere.

That his sister was talking on the phone to his best friend's brother surprised Kiran. Shawn was two years older than Preeti. He was a freshman in high school. He couldn't possibly have been interested in going with Preeti. (Kiran had only recently learned the term *going with*, had even been asked by Carla on behalf of Staci, on the first day of school, if he wanted to go with her, and he had said yes; but that was three weeks ago, and absolutely nothing had changed except that kids occasionally referred to Kiran and Staci as "going together," and sometimes his friends, mostly Greg, would ask—sometimes over the phone—"Are you still going with Staci?" and Kiran would say, "Yes," and Greg would say, "Cool.")

In the minute or so that Kiran listened to their conversation, Preeti spoke very little, which was probably why he hadn't noticed that she was upstairs on the phone in the first place. Neither of them spoke much. It wasn't so much a conversation as it was a stretch of silence interrupted by brief utterances.

"I'm going to get me a car," Shawn said.

Brief silence.

"What kind?"

"Doesn't matter. But in the next two years for sure. I'm saving up. I'll want it the minute I turn sixteen."

More silence.

"You can ride in it," Shawn said. "We can go anywhere you want."

Kiran listened to them breathe. He hadn't seen *Grease*, but a friend of his had trading cards with stills from the movie, and sometimes they would spread them out on the carpet and spend the afternoon looking at them and listening to the sound track. Kiran pictured Shawn and Preeti as Danny Zuko and Sandy snuggling in the front seat of the hot rod that lifts off into the sky in the final scene. Sweaty-palmed, Kiran fumbled the receiver before recovering it and pressing it back to his ear.

"Do you hear something?" Preeti said.

"Huh?"

"I heard something. Is someone else on the line? Kiran? *Kiran!* Is that you?!"

Kiran quickly hung up.

The next day after school, when Kiran saw Preeti go up to their parents' bedroom, the pompoms on her socks bouncing up the carpeted stairs—socks she'd begged their parents to buy her, along with the Nikes with the powder-blue swoosh, the first pair of name-brand shoes either of the children had ever been permitted ("I know you think it's not fair, Kiran," Shanti had said, "but you can have Nikes when *you're* in seventh grade")—he waited several minutes and then tiptoed into the kitchen and, as quietly as he could, picked up the yellow receiver.

"Cathy Pacofsky is a cunt," Shawn spat.

Kiran didn't know who Cathy Pacofsky was. He had never heard that word before, had no idea what it meant. He suspected that Preeti, still in middle school, might be equally ignorant on both counts. But hadn't they both heard the sharp edge of anger in Shawn's voice? Were they complicit in having overlooked signs of what was to come?

Kiran waited for Shawn to elaborate or for Preeti to ask a follow-up question, but instead there was silence. He could almost hear Preeti holding her breath. When she finally spoke and asked a question, it wasn't the one he was expecting.

"Kiran? Is that you? Kiran, I can hear you. I *know* you're on the line. *Again!* I can't believe it. I'm going to kill you!"

Kiran pressed down on the cradle to disconnect his extension. He held his hand there, while with the other hand he continued to hold the receiver to his ear. After a minute he very gently released the cradle and continued listening.

One afternoon, lying on the bed in her parents' bedroom, talking on the phone with Shawn, Preeti thought she heard scratching at the door. She ignored it, assuming she had imagined it, but a moment later there it was again: scratching.

The door, which was shut all but a crack, creaked open. Kiran came crawling in, his ass pitched high and waving in the air. "Meow."

"What?"

"Meow." Kiran circled the carpet, stretched his front limbs, alternated pressing his paws into the shag.

"Get out! What? Oh, nothing. It's just Kiran. He's in the room. He's being a brat. A *weird* brat."

Soon Preeti got pulled back into the conversation. When she hung up forty-five minutes later, Kiran was curled in her lap, purring. She had been absentmindedly petting his head. She gently tickled his neck. He giggled.

"So you're a cat, huh? What kind? Are you a tiger? Or are you a pussy?" Preeti laughed. "How about catching that mouse?"

The previous spring, Nishit telephoned Prabhu to try to convince him to come to America.

A few days earlier, he had spoken with Shanti about it. "At least he can sleep at night," Nishit said, citing a recent conversation with Kamala Ben, Prabhu's second wife.

(What Kamala hadn't told him was that Prabhu's real problem was the opposite: not that he couldn't sleep but that he couldn't wake up. Many mornings he stayed in bed, only to emerge midday, moving through rooms only half alive. In a rare moment of clarity and honesty, Prabhu had described it as living on a different plane than the rest of the world. It was like the world was a movie and he was sitting alone in the vast theater, watching.)

When Nishit said this, Shanti knew that he meant it, that he was genuinely grateful and relieved that his brother—despite all his problems, despite all they heard about him from relatives recently returned from India, tidbits spoken in stutters and whispers, dropped like slips of paper from pockets—could somehow sleep. She also knew that, without any bitterness and without explicitly saying so, Nishit was contrasting his brother to himself: Nishit could not sleep.

Kiran, overhearing the conversation, knew in his own eight-year-old way what his mother knew. He had heard the footsteps at night, the familiar series of sounds: the door of the cabinet above the refrigerator, where the gin was kept, clicking open and shut; the ice from the automated dispenser on the freezer door tumbling and clinking into a jelly jar; the two-liter bottle of flat Sprite, only ever drunk on these occasions—the children were not permitted to drink soda—being fetched from the shelf on the inside door of the fridge. Kiran could only imagine that this came after an hour or more of his father lying awake in bed, worrying about this or that, or this *and* that, and that this little ritual, not nightly but almost, was the last resort. His father would sit for half an hour in the recliner, watch cable, sort junk mail, until the gin kicked in, taking just enough of the edge off that he could fall back asleep.

When he said, "At least he can sleep at night," Nishit wasn't implying that Prabhu was in any way responsible for Nishit's own sleeplessness, though if he *had* intended that implication, it might not have been entirely untrue. After all, Prabhu's difficulties—financial, mental, emotional—weighed heavily on Nishit, even if Nishit was the younger brother. Nishit sent what money he could, often more than he could; the dollar being strong against the rupee, he knew that a small extra sacrifice on his end would translate to a larger payoff on the other end, and it was penance for not being able to see his brother or comfort him in other ways.

So Nishit and Shanti agreed: they would invite Prabhu to come stay with them for six months, so he could see what it might be like to live in America, and so that they could assess whether he might be better off living closer to them. But Nishit knew that Prabhu would not want to come. He'd have to convince him.

International phone calls were so expensive. You never knew when you would get a line—sometimes you'd wait an hour or more—and when you did finally get one, you didn't know how long it would last. Nishit wrote out everything he wanted to say. He made a bullet point list on the back of one of his business cards—the limited space, he knew, would force him to be brief and to the point. He listed:

- Better opportunities.
- Fresh start.
- Close to family.
- Better for Bharat.
- Nothing to lose.
- Just try.
- If you don't like, go back.

But when the time came, when he actually had Prabhu on the phone, when he knew that every word counted, every word cost money, and the distance those words had to travel seemed so enormous, he said none of what was on the card. What he said surprised him because as soon as he said it he knew—without knowing how or why, as if in a premonition—that it was true: "Big brother, come. I need you."

For many days in a row, Kiran sat with Preeti while she talked on the phone with Shawn. He continued his cat act, strutting around the room, rubbing up against her, and eventually curling up in a circle, his head either in or next to her lap. Kiran couldn't make out the words on Shawn's end of the conversation, but he could hear the murmur of his voice: deep, already dropped; a man's voice. The voice thrummed through Kiran's small boy body, resonating, filling his chest.

Kiran liked hearing his sister's voice, too. The previous year, Preeti, twirling her hair, had told Kiran stories of an upside-down world, a world in which everything was the opposite of this world. People walked backward, soles on the sky, were born old and grew young, kissed their enemies, clobbered their beloved, sobbed when happy and laughed when distraught, said the opposite of what they meant, the words themselves anagrams of their Planet Earth counterparts. Preeti told Kiran that this opposite world was a planet called Narik. She said the word with emphasis, enunciating the syllables with crystal clarity, and looking at Kiran meaningfully, but it was only some days later that Kiran realized the planet's name was his own, backward.

Preeti hung upside down on the edge of the bed, as if to emphasize her point.

Kiran believed, or at least half believed, his sister's stories about the upside-down world, in spite of what he'd learned in school about the solar system and its planets. He understood, as children do, that there was an immense universe out there, unimaginably vast, in which anything, *anything*, was possible. The stories of Planet Narik evoked in Kiran excitement, but mostly terror. The upside-down world was unsettling enough to a young boy just learning the rules and laws of physics of this world, but on top of all of that there was the name. What was he to make of it? What did he have to do with any of it?

But even as he found the upside-down world unsettling, Kiran begged his sister for more stories, and she obliged, spinning wild tales about Planet Narik night after night. Kiran thought the stories were what he wanted from his sister, but they were not. He wanted to hear her voice, to have her close. He wanted to lie in her lap, just as he was now.

Then one day, without warning, the phone calls with Shawn stopped. Preeti wasn't in their parents' bedroom after school, as usual; instead, she was sulking on the couch in the family room. Kiran pushed his head against Preeti, purred.

"Cut it out," she said.

He pushed again, ever more insistent, unwilling to be rebuffed.

"I mean it," Preeti said, taking a throw pillow and slapping him over the head.

As she did this, she noticed the rakhi on Kiran's wrist. She had tied it a few weeks earlier in the middle of August, on Raksha Bandhan Day. It was an annual tradition, when a sister ties the sacred thread for her brother, a sign of her love and blessings in return for the brother's promise to protect her. Their mother had taken her up to the Indian store in Rochester to buy it. The selection had not been huge. She chose the girliest one, pink (an auspicious color in Hindu culture), partly because she hoped Kiran would get teased at school for it, but partly because she knew that he would secretly like it. She had seen the covetous way he eyed her dolls. As for the Raksha Bandhan tradition itself, she didn't know if she really believed in any of it, but she always got a gift out of it: this year, Pat Benatar's new LP, which Kiran had wrapped in last year's Christmas paper.

She and Kiran sat cross-legged, facing each other in front of the mandir. The diya was lit. They said the prayers, mumbling their way through as they always did. Preeti tied the string on Kiran's right wrist and pressed vermilion to his forehead. She pinched a ladoo sweet between her fingers and leaned in to feed him.

Kiran watched the ladoo come toward him, as if in slow motion. Something was not right. Was Preeti smirking? Was there a twinkle of mischief in her eyes? With a sudden swipe, Kiran knocked the ladoo out of her hands, and it went flying across the room.

Shanti was horrified. How many times had Kiran closed his mouth and turned his head away, picky eater that he was, and how many times had she had to tell him, "Absolutely not. You cannot refuse prasad. Take a tiny bite at least"? You did not refuse something that had been offered to God and blessed by Him. Never mind that Shanti had her own doubts about the existence of a Supreme Being. Culture was culture; tradition, tradition. And you absolutely did not throw prasad across the room and let it fall on the floor. And in front of Prabhu Bhai? Visiting from India? Just wait until word got around about Shanti's wild brood. "What are they doing over there in America?" people would whisper.

"She did something!" Kiran said, pointing at Preeti. "The ladoo! She took a bite out of it!"

"Did not," Preeti said, smiling. She was telling the truth; she had done nothing. Still, she was enjoying the scene Kiran was causing and the trouble he was sure to be in.

"She *did*! I *saw* it!"

Because the ladoo had crumbled into pieces when it hit the wall, they were unable to verify Kiran's claim. Kiran insisted.

"But I swear," Preeti said. "I didn't do it."

The children looked at each other a moment and then, almost in unison, cried, "Minnie!"

They'd been checking the live catch trap every few days, but it was always empty. Completely empty. Somehow the mouse had been managing to abscond with whatever goodies had been left there without getting caught. Was the mouse getting bolder? Had she really nibbled on the prasad in the hour or so it sat on the mandir before the rakhi ceremony began?

Now Kiran was on the couch next to Preeti. Unfazed by the pillow-pummeling, he was licking the side of his hand and cleaning the fur behind his ears. She looked again at the rakhi. If anyone was going to protect her, she thought, it would not be this goofball. She would have to do it herself.

Kiran had not told Preeti—had not told anyone—what happened with Shawn earlier that summer when he was over at Greg's house.

Greg only ever wanted to play *Star Wars*, and he had an almost exhaustive collection of every action figure, every spaceship, every landscape, ever released. Birthdays, Christmas, Easter, the only gifts he wanted were *Star Wars* action figures. He also collected baseball cards—organized in two shoe boxes underneath his bed—but his real love was *Star Wars*.

When they played, Greg always insisted on being Luke Skywalker ("My house, my rules") in the same way, a year or two earlier, Greg would demand to be the cowboy to Kiran's Indian ("Because that's what you are, no offense"). Greg's claiming of Luke Skywalker was fine by Kiran; he preferred the dark-haired, complicated, cocky Han Solo. Or R2D2, with his sputtering of clicks and beeps, never a word wasted. Who he *really* wanted to be was Princess Leia, but he knew better than to tell Greg. He'd have to wait some years before he could be her, finally, one year when he was living in New York, dressing as Leia for Halloween and marching in the parade in Greenwich Village, re-creating her iconic hairstyle by affixing cinnamon buns to a headband.

"Kool-Aid?" Greg asked and Kiran said, "Uh-huh," and Greg said he would go make some. A minute later, Kiran pushed himself up from the carpet and went to find Greg. He wanted to remind him about his special Kool-Aid technique. You had to at least quadruple the directed amount of red crystals, so that the liquid would reach a saturation point and some crystals would remain undissolved, settling like silt on the bottom of the glass to be slurped up later. But Kiran was intercepted. Just as he was passing the bathroom, the door swung open and Shawn popped out, freshly showered. He smelled strongly of bath soap: coconut and chemicals. Shawn's straw-colored hair was wet and messy; he hadn't combed it in the steam-streaked mirror the way Kiran always did after a shower. He was naked except for a threadbare, too-small brown towel tied tightly around his waist. Seeing Kiran, Shawn flashed a crooked, snaggletoothed smile. He ducked into his bedroom, only to reappear a second later—in parts. Body parts. First a leg poked out, then disappeared. Then an arm did the same thing. Then a hip. All the while he was whistling and humming Sheena Easton's "For Your Eyes Only." When he was done, Shawn tossed the towel into the hallway and disappeared into his room.

Later, Kiran would tell himself that it was the smell that somehow—almost against his will—drew him down the hallway, the way it happened in cartoons, the wavy lines emerging from an apple pie and forming a long arm, a hooked finger.

He would not be able to admit that a switch had been flipped, that something he couldn't understand and had no name for had come awake, that he had followed Shawn down the hallway because he wanted to. When Kiran entered Shawn's bedroom, Shawn was already naked, lying on the bed. Somehow Kiran knew to shut the door behind him. He scurried across the room and dove under Shawn's desk. He crouched there, knees pulled to chest. Shawn played baseball. In a couple of years he would be named All-State, the apex before a downward slide so precipitous that it would terrify, if not completely surprise, all those around him. Next to Kiran, crumpled on the floor, was Shawn's baseball shirt, number thirty-eight, sweaty and stained from his most recent on-field heroics. A baseball bat was leaned against the closet doorframe; on a shelf, the Jim Palmer–signed baseball Greg and Kiran weren't allowed ever to touch or even to look at, but sometimes, when Shawn was out, they would sneak in and take turns holding it, turning it over in their hands. On the bedside table to the left of Shawn's head, a leather mitt. On the wall above his bed, a Rush poster. Once, while Kiran was waiting for Greg, Shawn tossed a baseball back and forth with him out front of their house. Shawn's pitches occasionally thudded into Kiran's borrowed mitt but mostly whizzed past him; Kiran's all fell short, fizzling into the unmowed grass. "You throw like a girl," Shawn had said.

Lying there, naked, Shawn looked so strange to Kiran. Kiran couldn't quite figure it out. It was like a What's Wrong with This Picture? puzzle, or maybe One of These Things Just Doesn't Belong, because, reflecting on it years later, Kiran would realize it was the thing between Shawn's legs that didn't belong. It was almost comical, the juxtaposition of Shawn's body—skinny legs, skinny arms, the thin chest of a boy—and this enormous, thick, hairy penis of a man.

Shawn began stroking his penis. Head propped on the pillow, he stared at Kiran, his eyes glinting like glass.

"You can touch it."

Kiran stayed under the desk. He hugged his knees tighter, tried to make himself smaller, imagined pulling himself into a small, tight marble, a cat's eye.

"Go ahead," Shawn said. "Touch it."

Kiran unfolded himself and, on hands and knees, crawled over to Shawn's bed. He extended an index finger and poked at Shawn's penis, as if it were an animal lying on a dirt path and Kiran was testing to see if it was still alive, if it was going to snarl and bite him.

Shawn laughed. He took Kiran's small hand, unclenching his fingers, and placed it on his shaft. He held Kiran's wrist, helping him move his hand up and down. Shawn leaned his head back onto the pillow.

It wasn't long before he came.

Kiran was terrified by the way Shawn shuddered and convulsed. Afterward, Shawn laughed a sticky, rank laugh.

"Good job, slugger," he said, smiling his crooked, snaggle-toothed smile, punctuated by the briefest of winks, a single flap of a butterfly's wing.

Kiran washed his hands in the hall bathroom before returning to Greg's room.

"Where were you?"

"In the bathroom."

"I looked there."

"The other bathroom. Your parents'."

"Why?"

"Um . . . you know . . . I had to . . ."

"Oh. I *thought* you were taking a long time."

Greg had already rearranged the action figures. He had

devised a new scenario, but it was really still the same as all the others: Princess Leia, although fierce, is in need of rescue. This time she was being held captive by Darth Vader on top of the bookshelf. Luke and Han would have to climb all the shelves, but—*Be careful!*—there were stormtroopers hiding behind books. One wrong move, and they'd all be doomed.

Kiran kept thinking he still smelled Shawn on him, though he had washed his hands meticulously. He kept seeing his snaggletoothed smile, hearing him say "slugger." He felt sick. Kiran tried to play that afternoon as if nothing had happened. He was in charge here. Well, Greg was in charge, but he was second in charge. This was their world. They could make the action figures do whatever they wanted.

S ome of the boys from Ray of Light are going on a mission," Chris said across the counter. "Calcutta. Do you think you might come to the church and speak to the congregation, Mrs. Shah? Let them know what to expect?"

"I've never been to Calcutta," Shanti replied. Chris may have insisted she call him by his first name, but she had never made the equivalent offer, and she was glad he had not taken liberties. There was the matter of propriety, of course, and not wanting to give Chris the wrong idea. But for Shanti there was also the irritation she felt—still felt—upon hearing mispronunciations of her name. Poor Americans, it wasn't their fault. The problem was the *t* that sounded more like a *th*. There simply wasn't a sound quite like that in the English language. But hearing her name pronounced "shaunty" like *jaunty*, or worse, "shanty," as though she were some third-world shack slapped together from discarded lumber and scrap metal, always made her feel so, well, out of place.

"Yes," Chris said, "but you can at least tell them what India's like."

"Pune and Calcutta are worlds away, Chris. It would be like you trying to tell someone what they'd find in Los Angeles."

"How do you know I've never been to Los Angeles?"

Shanti looked Chris up and down, noting his faded T-shirt and farmer's tan, the dirt under his fingernails.

"I know."

Chris blushed. "Anything you say would be useful. They know absolutely nothing."

Shanti thought of the presentation Preeti had been asked to give to her third-grade class four years earlier when they were studying India in social studies. Preeti had neatly copied out, word for word, passages from the *World Book Encyclopedia* entry on India and read it out loud to the class. It was her first time encountering a semicolon; Shanti had had to explain what it was. Practicing her presentation at home, when she reached that particular punctuation she'd say "semicolon" out loud. Shanti kept telling her it's just a signpost, like commas and periods. No different. But Preeti couldn't seem to break the habit. Shanti didn't know if Preeti said "semicolon" during her presentation to the class, but even so she felt sure the whole thing was not at all what Mrs. Henry had wanted. But honestly, what had Mrs. Henry expected? Preeti didn't know any more about India than any of the other children in class. Well, maybe a little more, but not much. At least Shanti had sent with her a marble replica of the Taj Mahal, and it was Preeti's own idea to bring in a record with her favorite Bollywood song, the disco-tinged "Mehbooba Mehbooba," though afterward Preeti never seemed to want to listen to it, and Shanti wondered if her classmates had snickered. Now Kiran was in Mrs. Henry's class. Would he be asked to give the same presentation? Would he copy the same article out of the same *World Book Encyclopedia*? Would he play *his* favorite Bollywood song—"Aap Jaisa Koi"—

and would his classmates cough "loser" into their fists? Would Shanti allow him to make the same mistakes all over again?

"Hearing from you would put them at ease some. Their parents, too. These boys have never been anywhere."

Shanti remembered what it was like to have never been anywhere. Before coming to America she had barely traveled, and never without her parents. She had sat on the New York–bound flight alone, her first time on a plane, having no idea what would meet her on the other side. She had eaten almost nothing because she couldn't open the cellophane in which the silverware was packed, her hands were trembling.

Across the counter, Shanti looked at Chris. His eyes smiled an honest blue, skin crinkling at the corners. Shanti shivered.

"You're nervous," he said. "Let's have coffee. We can practice. I'll talk you through it."

That his brother hadn't brought a suit infuriated Nishit.

"How could I have known I'd need one?"

It was true that when Prabhu was planning his trip, Nishit hadn't been totally transparent about his plans for his brother, but hadn't Prabhu understood that he was there partly to see if a new life might be possible, and hadn't it occurred to him that a new life might require a good suit?

"You can borrow one of mine, but there isn't time for alterations."

Shanti let out the trouser cuffs—still too short, but at least it didn't look like he was wearing high waters. There was nothing to be done about the jacket, two sizes too small. Prabhu would have to find a way to fit into it.

Growing up, Prabhu had been the smart one, hunched over homework afternoon onward, always top of his class, leaving big footsteps Nishit couldn't fill. Nishit was also smart, but not like Prabhu. Prabhu had graduated top of his class with a degree in industrial engineering from an excellent school in Baroda and immediately landed a coveted position in civil service. True, Prabhu's situation there had started to deteriorate even before Neela's death (Nishit recalled Prabhu's complaints that his coworkers were all idiots, small-minded pencil pushers, provincials really, not an ounce of innovation among the lot of them), but surely he would have eventually sorted it out were it not for his nervous breakdown in the wake of his wife's death, and really who could blame him for that? So even though Prabhu hadn't worked in his field for many years—hadn't done meaningful work of any sort in that time—Nishit felt confident that, given another chance and the right support, Prabhu could thrive somewhere like Eastman Kodak. It was only an informational interview, but Nishit had had to call in favors to get it and was hopeful it might lead somewhere.

Nishit first noticed it when they stopped at the rest area halfway to Rochester. Already irritated that they were stopping at all (Couldn't his brother go an hour and a half without having to pee? Hadn't he thought to go before they left?) Nishit—waiting in the car, tapping the steering wheel—watched Prabhu shuffling into the shelter.

When Prabhu returned to the car, Nishit barked, "Pull up your pant cuff."

"What? Why?"

Nishit leaned over the passenger seat, reached down, yanked roughly at Prabhu's trouser leg. "Pull it up." Prabhu complied, revealing gray tube socks.

"Why aren't you wearing the dress socks I gave you?"

"These are better."

"How?"

"Warmer."

"What 'warmer'? It's not winter. It will be close to seventy today!"

"My feet are always cold. Besides, the way you crank up the AC in the car? I'm sure it will be the same or worse at Kodak. Shouldn't I be comfortable in the interview? Isn't that what you said? Just be myself? How can I be myself if my teeth are chattering?"

"I never said 'Just be yourself.' I wouldn't have said that."

"Somebody said it."

"Somebody was wrong."

For the next half hour, Nishit gripped the steering wheel tight with both hands. When they arrived, he pulled up to the building and reminded Prabhu of the name of the woman he was to ask for. "Listen," he said, "forget what I said earlier. Of course be yourself." He put his hand on his brother's shoulder.

"Silly," Prabhu said, opening the door, "who else can I be?"

Nishit liked to call it *MACK*-Donald's. The children would protest in the backseat of the car, "Dad, c'mon, *McDonald's*, say it right," and Nishit would say, "Yes, yes, *MACK*-Donald's," and the children would harrumph and laugh.

There weren't many options for a vegetarian. Sometimes he'd get an apple pie or a milk shake. Today he ordered a small coffee (he only drank tea at home) and a small order of fries, not knowing (no one knew then) that the fries were flavored with beef. The woman behind the counter had an asymmetrical haircut and blue eye shadow. "Here, hon," she said, handing him the brown tray with the small cup and the fries in their paper wrapper. He collected several ketchup packets and a pile of napkins and retreated to a quiet booth.

He looked at his watch. He'd give himself fifteen minutes and then he'd head back over to Kodak. He'd be early, but he didn't want Prabhu to have to wait. He imagined him sitting in a vast lobby, a leather couch swallowing him, his pant legs hiked high, his gray tube socks showing.

It was nice, Nishit thought, to be in the city, to be anonymous, no one coming up behind him, "Hi, Dr. Shah." It was nice to be called "hon" by an attractive young woman he didn't know. When he'd ordered, he had noticed her smooth neck, the delicate gold chain and glinting pendant nestled in the hollow above her collarbone. He ate his fries slowly, deliberately, holding each one and squeezing a teardrop of ketchup on its tip before popping it into his mouth.

"She was not an engineer. Or a scientist of any sort. She did not know the first thing about research and development, or design, or production. You were aware of this?"

"Your seat belt," Nishit said. Prabhu reached behind him and pulled the strap across his chest, struggling to find the buckle. No one wore seat belts in India; Prabhu was always forgetting. Nishit watched him wrestle with it a moment before sighing, reaching over, and clicking it locked for him.

"You knew who this Mrs. Lee was?"

"I don't personally know her, no, but she's in personnel, right?"

"*Per-son-nel.* What does someone in per-son-nel know about what *I* can do? She has no qualifications to assess my suitability."

"It's just a first step. Big companies always have you screened first. Besides, it was an informational interview. You understood that, didn't you? Just a chance for you to get on their radar?"

"She didn't even have an office. She was in one of those— what do you call them?" Prabhu waved his hand dismissively.

"Cubicles," Nishit said quietly, almost to himself.

Nishit drove. Prabhu looked out the window. After several minutes Nishit asked, "What did she actually say?"

"She had no qualifications to judge me. None whatsoever."

In the days that followed, Nishit watched his brother transform, retreat, drift from room to room like dust riding drafts. He would become ghostlike: there and not. Once, Nishit would find Prabhu paused in front of the alcove at the top of the staircase, where the portrait of Neela hung. Another time, Nishit would be on the couch a full ten minutes reading *Fortune* before realizing his brother was also in the room. Prabhu was sitting in a straight-backed chair he had positioned by one of the windows in the subterranean family room, the eye-level window flush with the ground outside. He was staring across the expanse of grass—now the green-brown of early fall—that separated their house from the Yamamotos'.

Many years later, in the age of Prozac and Paxil and television commercials depicting anthropomorphized balls regaining bounce they thought they'd lost or perhaps never knew they had, Nishit would attempt to put a name to Prabhu's troubles and wonder if there was more he could have done, more he could still do. But by then it would be too late. Prabhu would have settled into darkness, a literal darkness, a light-starved interior room he rarely left, the only illumination a naked low-watt bulb on the bedside table and the flickering diya flame lit during lengthy morning and evening pujas. He spent his days tending to the gods' needs, washing the idols, dressing them in silks: deities having replaced the humans for whom he no longer had need. Prabhu's eyes had adjusted to the darkness. He was the man that he was, he was not a bouncing ball. He was not interested in becoming someone new.

It wasn't Kiran's intention to spy, so if he occasionally heard something he wasn't supposed to, he told himself that wasn't his fault. He crouched in crawl spaces, hid in attics, curled up in closets. Enclosed spaces made him feel safe. It wasn't so different from pulling the covers over your head during a lightning storm. He especially loved the linen closet, the bottle-spring scent of freshly laundered towels and sheets. He liked his parents' closet. Hangered clothes brushing the top of his head reminded him of his father tussling his hair.

Years later, it would become the punch line to a joke. "When I came out of the closet, I *literally* came out of the closet," he would tell friends. And in fact the week before he announced his homosexuality to his friends at college, he had spent three straight days in the closet of his shared dorm room, emerging only to fetch grilled cheese sandwiches and curly fries from the dining hall downstairs and to use the bathroom. His roommate, a track star, told his own friends over the phone, "This isn't even the weirdest thing he's done."

Kiran was not allowed in Preeti's room under any circumstances, and certainly not permitted in her closet, but that's where he was—camped out amid ballet slippers, resting in a nest of shirts and skirts and culottes she hadn't bothered hanging up or folding—when Preeti came in. She was just back from school, and through the wooden slats he could see her sloughing off her backpack, tugging a purple scrunchy from her hair. The LP was already on the turntable. Preeti dropped the needle and there it was, through the speakers, volume on high: Pat Benatar wailing "Promises in the Dark." It took a minute for Preeti to get into it, but soon she was singing along, flailing around. She clenched her fists, hugged her arms to her chest, threw her head back.

At first Kiran found his sister's display of preteen angst comical, but he quickly understood it was deeply felt. He had never seen her like this. Everything about her body indicated to him that she was in pain. He wanted to comfort her, but he had no comfort to give, and even if he did, he knew she wouldn't accept it from him. He wasn't even supposed to be there. Still, he felt proud that Preeti was listening to the album he had bought her for Raksha Bandhan, proud that he had known what she would want.

No one was there to witness it, the shape-shifting way he became liquid, let his body pour through the crack between the wire gate and the plastic tray. No one heard the awful rattling of the cage, or saw the relentless way he chased her and then held her neck in his mouth, held her down as he mounted her. No one heard her shrieks. No one knew anything at all until one morning three weeks later, when Nishit noticed the tiny pink creatures in the cage, wet and barely formed.

It took a few minutes for the family, gathered round, to realize what had happened. Finally Shanti said, "Looks like our Minnie is a Mickey." Kiran thought for a moment, then said, "No, Speedy Gonzalez. Arriba! Arriba! Andale! Andale!"

"And what about Kroncha?" Nishit asked. When they'd given her the name, they'd assumed she was male (isn't that what they were told at the pet store?).

"Kali?" Preeti suggested.

"No way," Kiran said. "Kroncha is Kroncha."

They watched the tiny bodies, each the size of the tip of a baby's finger, wriggling beneath their mother. Fifteen. Shanti knew the number because later that very morning, after the children had boarded the school bus, Nishit had gone to his office, and Prabhu had retreated to the guest room, she lifted them, one by one, with a plastic teaspoon, deposited them into a black plastic bag from the liquor store, and dropped them— along with the spoon—into the garbage receptacle on the sidewalk outside the bank. That evening she told the children she'd taken them to the pet store, that was what was best for them, and when the children whined she cut them off with sounds sharp like slaps—*Eh! Chah! Ouh!*—and they understood there was nothing more to be done.

"You believe in Jesus?" Chris asked. They were at a diner in town, sitting in a booth in back, a full hour after the lunchtime rush. Shanti had been telling him about her convent-school youth: the strict nun who would rap her knuckles with a ruler when she held her pencil wrong; the kind one who once, after Shanti was tormented by her peers for some long-forgotten infraction of whatever social code had been in place back then, spoke softly to her as she braided her hair; Father Torres, jovial and bumbling, with his caterpillar eyebrows and porpoise nose.

"At that time it was very common for girls from good families to go to convent school, regardless of their religion," Shanti explained. "Going to convent didn't mean anything. The curriculum included very little explicit Christianity—morning prayers, chapel on certain holidays, an occasional Bible verse thrown in here or there." What Shanti didn't mention is that the one activity in which she always participated, even though it was not required, was confession. She loved sitting in the confessional across from Father Torres, loved knowing that she was being listened to (no one listened to girls), that there was someone deeply concerned for the state of her soul. She liked being told, in Father Torres's voice—jolly even when he was being his most serious— that God would forgive her, even if she wasn't so sure *this* God, the Christian God, was the one with power to do that.

When she saw that Chris was still waiting for an answer— did she believe in Jesus?—she said quietly, holding her small coffee cup with both hands, "I'm Hindu."

"For Hindus, what is your version of Jesus?"

"Ram? Maybe Shiva? There are many."

"And that's what you believe?"

"It doesn't matter what you believe. Hinduism is not just a religion, it's a culture. When you're Hindu, you're Hindu. You can't not be Hindu."

Chris understood tradition. His father had founded the ministry. From the beginning, it had been inextricably linked to every aspect of Chris's life. It was his home. There was never any question that he and his brother would assume leadership roles. There never seemed to be a space in his life to question anything. He had never considered what he believed independent of what he'd been taught. Still, noting that Shanti had not really answered his question, he pressed her.

"Is that what you believe?"

Shanti didn't reply. She gazed absently into her coffee cup, which was almost empty, which had been almost empty for several minutes. Was their server being neglectful? Or had she sensed they wanted privacy? Shanti had been nursing the last sips, not wanting to empty her cup. Once it was empty, she'd have to put it down. She needed something to hold on to. "I'm not sure what I believe."

Chris reached across the table, taking both of his hands and closing them around hers. Together, like that, they held the cup. Chris was no longer thinking about the question he had asked, no longer thinking about God. He was thinking only of how long he had waited for this moment, how much he had needed to touch her.

She suspected Chris's church was nothing like this one. Still, it was with him in mind that, flipping through channels, Shanti allowed the dial to rest on the program: the huge auditorium, packed to the rafters, organ music droning and steady, the stage strewn with white lilies, the televangelist with his white hair and his white three-piece suit. "Laying on of hands," he called it. "The touch that heals." She watched the men and women crowd the aisles, the ones who wanted their suffering stopped, the ones in wheelchairs or with bent backs or arthritis, or feet swollen from diabetes. Cancer, hearing loss, cysts in wombs. Torn ligaments, shattered elbows. Weak knees. Cloudy vision, irregular hearts, wandering eyes. The litany of ailments was endless. And then there were those who didn't know what was wrong, just knew that something was; like the old man in the plaid shirt who stood onstage shaking his head and muttering, "I'm just not right, Reverend. Can't remember the last time I felt right."

"Jesus will make you whole," the reverend said, the heel of his palm on a supplicant's forehead, the man or woman, held up by helpers on either side, almost always then falling backward. Must be plants, Shanti thought, because invariably they were cured: the chair-bound could walk, the deaf could hear, the blind could see. Shanti, in India, had seen her fair share of fakirs—men walking barefoot across hot coals. *Can't be real.* And yet when the reverend asked the television audience, asked *her*, to put her palm to the glass, to feel the healing power of God through the television screen, she found herself complying, spreading her fingers wide, pressing her hand against the screen, pressing hard, harder than she had intended. She imagined Chris's large hand with its dirty fingernails pressing against hers. Minutes later, she sprayed the television screen with cleaning fluid and wiped it with a dust cloth before heading off to work.

Early that October, Fall Fest made its annual descent upon the village green. Kiran, years later, an adult—nomadic, though always urban-dwelling—remembered it fondly, called it "country quaint," until a trip home, husband and rescue mutt in tow, revealed it for what it was: a dingy assortment of death-trap scramblers and carousels, sour-breathed barkers, talentless cover bands trolling after shows for willing local girls, clowns with smeared makeup handing out balloons that would be found, weeks later, deflated, draped over tree branches, looking obscene.

Preeti and Kiran couldn't get enough.

Their anemic allowances meant they had to be choosy about games and rides, but grounds entry was free, and most afternoons it was enough wonderment simply to wander after school among the fried dough, the bings and bongs, the lights, the merchant booths hawking hand-tooled leather cuffs and belts, crystal pendants promising powers to heal or to ward off unwanted energies, customizable T-shirts with airbrushed arrow-pierced hearts awaiting "Randy-'n'-Suzy 4ever." Preeti's fantasy was this: she'd find Shawn repentant on her doorstep, in his hand an offering, a T-shirt emblazoned "Shawn's Girl." It'd be too big, and she'd wear it to sleep, and during the day knotted at the waist with acid-washed jeans.

But it was Kiran, not Preeti, who Fall Fest week would greet an unexpected guest, not exactly on the doorstep, but close. Chris Bell, stopping in the street in front of their house, pulling a wagon with a nodding-off toddler, two more children straggling behind, four enormous stuffed tigers distributed among the four of them. Kiran was in the yard, crouched beneath the tree, racing Hot Wheels in the dirt. He knew animals—could tell an Indian elephant from an African, a turtle from a tortoise, a rabbit from a hare—and he knew tigers: Sumatran, Siberian, Indochine. These were Bengal, Kiran decided. And not Tigger tigers. *Jungle Book*–obsessed, Kiran dubbed them Shere Khans. He smiled mischievously, imagining the stuffed cats come to life, batting at the fair-haired Bell children, devouring them one by one.

Had anyone been watching—and wasn't someone *always* watching? Mrs. Yamamoto in her kitchen window? Or Mr. Miller across the street, leaning on a rake in the side yard?—they would have thought Chris lingered in front of the Shahs' house to allow young Kelly and Jim to catch up. But Chris had his own reasons.

The Shahs' house had been one of the first Chris had worked on, when he was still a young man, a fresh high-school graduate, a summer hired hand for the Buffalo-based developer. The developer, overzealous and underinformed about the economics of this particular swath of the Southern Tier of New York State, had overbuilt: twelve brand-new houses on one street edging a ridge, all similar, but each a little different, facades of brick and stone fronting cheaper materials; split-levels and modest colonials and two ranches, side by side, with small windows tucked high against the eaves, like tired eyes. Only half the houses sold within a year of their completion, and the Shahs' house, or more accurately, what would eventually become the Shahs' house, had remained empty for many years, until Nishit, seeing this house and only this house—not appreciating that his new bride, arriving from India in less than a month, might want some say in the decision, and knowing, upon seeing the maple cabinets in the kitchen and the beadboard walls in the slate-floored foyer, that this was nothing special, but that it was the best they would find, and that it was a perfectly suitable, even an ideal, blank canvas on which to create their new lives—had made an offer on the spot, which was quickly and gratefully accepted.

Chris knew this house intimately, knew its very bones, had poured his own sweat into its foundation. He had stood on its roof, had spent hours on ladders on every side of the structure and in every kind of light, had, during his lunch breaks, straddled its windowsills inhaling hoagies. Now, from the street, he searched those same windows for a sign of Shanti: a flutter of curtain or a shock of black hair turning a corner.

He didn't even notice Kiran beneath the tree until he'd been standing in the street for more than a moment.

"Hey, buddy."

Kiran, though looking intently, didn't respond. Chris followed his gaze to the huge tiger he held to his chest, its head resting on his shoulder, like a child being burped. "Fall Fest," Chris explained. "Ball toss." He looked behind him. Kelly and Jim had gotten distracted by something on the edge of the road, a small critter or a particularly exotic insect.

"Where's your mother?"

Kiran sat blinking. Chris had asked on impulse and didn't know what he would have done even if Kiran had answered. He looked again at the house. He thought he saw movement in an upstairs window, shifting shadows, a flash of fabric. Then Jim was behind him, poking at the back of his thigh with a twig. He dragged his tiger behind him. Chris looked again at Kiran. "I'll win you one, buddy."

Chris had always been good at games. He'd varsity lettered in three sports—football, basketball, baseball: the Holy Trinity. And perhaps, at least partly, it was this athletic prowess that allowed him so effortlessly to pitch the ball into the narrow-mouthed milk jug. But it was partly something else, too; after all, he didn't have quite the same luck with other carnival games. Standing there that Saturday, sinking ball after ball, he felt that everything was in perfect alignment—his height, the length of his arm, the weight of the ball, the distance to the jug, the thickness of the lip, the diameter of the opening. Nothing in his life had ever been as effortless. It was as though he were made for this game, as if his body had been engineered specifically for this purpose. And yet, if that were the case, wasn't that sad, Chris thought. *This* was what God made him for? *This* was his calling? Throwing a ball into a jug? He remembered the steel bar he'd tried to bend at the Gladiators for Christ show. "You could do this," the man had said. "You've got what it takes. It's not an easy life. But it's a good life, a life with purpose."

So it was a strange relief Chris felt when, the following day—after church, while Amy shepherded the children from Bible study to birthday parties—he found he'd lost his magic. Balls hit the lip of the jug, bouncing out, not in; some missed altogether. "A i r b a l l," a high school teammate might have called, cupping his hands around his mouth, stretching the word out into an admonishing drone. Chris wondered if the jug was smaller, if the man had swapped it out after his winning streak the previous day. Or maybe the ball was different—didn't it feel lighter? Or was it the clouds, or the wind that swept periodically through the fair, unsettling dirt, launching hot-dog boats and food-soiled wrappers into the air? Much later Chris would wonder if these had all been signs he should have heeded. He should not be here. But he had made a promise. He thought of Kiran sitting in the dirt beneath the tree, miniature car caught mid-race clutched in hand. Chris couldn't disappoint a child.

The man sold him three more balls but didn't call them balls, called them "chances," then sold him three again, and again. "Three more chances?" the man asked, and how could Chris say no? Who didn't want more chances? By the time Chris finally won, he had all but emptied his wallet. Peering into it, he was glad he couldn't remember how much he'd started with, what he'd lost. Chris had not walked today, he had driven, and back at the truck he set the tiger upright in the passenger seat, almost buckling it in. But then he thought better of it and shoved the animal down on the floor in the back of the cab, where no one would see.

Neither was being entirely honest—not even to themselves—about their need to be in Elmira that day. Chris said he had a job out that way. Shanti mentioned a gift for an upcoming wedding. Both instinctively understood they wanted to meet somewhere they wouldn't be recognized.

That morning Kiran had insisted so emphatically, and in front of Nishit, that he wanted to go with his mother that Shanti had no choice but to bring him along. Kiran sat in the front seat of the car—thighs sticking to the vinyl seat of the Tercel, their second car, the bare-bones car, the car Nishit said was just for rambling around town, no need for air conditioning—and commandeered the radio. He flipped obsessively back and forth among the three stations they could receive—one country, one oldies, one pop (its tagline morphing over the years from "Lock it in, then rip off the knob" to the not-so-subtle racially coded "All the hits, without the rap")—never settling on a song for more than a minute. Another time Shanti would have slapped Kiran's hand away from the console, but she was glad he was occupied; besides, her mind was elsewhere. Voices from the radio drifted through her head—Crystal Gayle, Perry Cuomo, Rick Springfield (she did love his steamy Dr. Noah Drake on *General Hospital*, though his flawed physician portrayal would surely make Dr. Nishit Shah fume)—mixing with her own internal dialogue with herself (*Aré baap, Shanti Shah, have you gone mad?—What? It's all very innocent. I'm speaking at his church, aren't I? He and I have to prepare, don't we?*). Hot air—an Indian summer, everyone said—rushed past the half-open windows (only half, so Kiran could still hear his radio). Outside: valley fields, cows ruminating, hills rising gently out of the ground, smooth and round as river rocks. For their part, the cows watched idly and without interest but watched nonetheless. They'd seen so much: not just the dramatic—an eighteen-wheeler wiping out, taking half a dozen cars with it, a helicopter landing on the highway to airlift the injured—but the prosaic—countless vehicles racing (to the cows, they were always racing) hither and thither, shuttling folks to births or anniversary parties or lunch with Grandma in the nursing home or just to work, someone's daily morning and evening commute. None of it mattered to the cows. They tugged at the grass and continued their steady ruminations.

Shanti was sitting before the Styrofoam container of greasy noodles when Chris arrived. It had been her idea to meet in the food court at the mall. She really had needed a wedding gift for the wavy-haired, almond-eyed daughter of a Venezuelan surgeon in Rochester who had mentored Nishit when he first arrived in the region.

Earlier, when they first reached the mall, Shanti had given Kiran three dollars for video games and her own slim wristwatch and told him she'd fetch him from the arcade at two o'clock. Then she'd gone to the department store where the couple had registered and bought, off the list, a heavy crystal bowl. She wanted to tell them, *You will never use this; it will sit in your breakfront thirty years and you'll be lucky if you use it even three times,* but she knew it was a lesson they would have to learn for themselves. Funny the chasm between the life you envision for yourself and the life you get. When she and Nishit married, Reshma, a particularly wealthy college friend and roommate her first two years, had given them table settings for twenty (twenty!)—plates, bowls, cups, everything, even flatware—all one of a kind, black and white, very modern, designed by a famous Indian artist. Shanti fantasized about elaborate dinner parties, guests in gold jewelry and expensive silks. In fourteen years of marriage, Shanti and Nishit had not once used the place settings. They sat in the hutch in the dining room they also rarely used, and when they did have friends for dinner, they used the same plates and bowls they used every day—Corelle in the Snowflake Blue design Shanti had selected, thinking it seemed appropriate for their new lives in snowy Western New York.

Shanti had arrived early at the food court, thinking she'd have enough time to wolf down some Mr. Wok before Chris arrived, or at least she thought she was early; giving Kiran her watch had hampered her ability to keep close tabs on time. She had chosen one of the tiny round tables against the railing, not conscious of the fact that what stood between herself and Chris—first a bank counter; then a rectangular table wedged into a diner booth; now a metallic-finished pedestal table with a top not more than eighteen inches across—was, over time, shrinking. The table was so small there was only room for her food; she slung her purse over the back of the chair and set on the floor the shopping bag containing the crystal bowl, already wrapped, miniature gold wedding bells affixed to the bow.

Their meeting was ostensibly so that Chris could bring her specific questions from the boys going on mission. But Shanti, watching him cross the vast open space toward her, could see no notebook or leather portfolio in his hands; instead, he was cradling in one arm a large black trash bag. He pulled up a third chair and set the plastic bag on it upright, as if it were a third guest.

"Sorry," Shanti said, slurping noodles, then covering her mouth with one hand. "I was hungry."

"We *are* in a food court."

"Then you'll eat, too?"

Chris smiled and shook his head.

The sun was strong and streamed through the skylights, making the food court gleam. At a nearby table, a sparrow that had somehow gotten inside pecked at a bit of pizza crust some-one had left there.

"So," Shanti said, "what questions do the boys have for me?"

Chris held up his empty palms and shrugged. "When I asked them, they looked at me blankly, like I was speaking another language or something. Honestly, Shanti, it's all so foreign to them. I don't think they even know where to begin."

He had said her first name, Shanti noted, for the first time. He had pronounced it well, not perfectly, but the best she could have hoped for. She did not know that he had practiced it for weeks in front of his bathroom mirror and while driving in his truck; that he heard her name over and over in his head, soft like a lullaby, like the prayer that it was: *Shanti . . . Shanti . . . Shanti . . . Peace . . . Peace . . . Peace . . .*

"So, yeah, sorry," he said, "I didn't bring any questions for you."

"Then why are we here, Chris?" As soon as she asked, she knew she did not want him to speak. She did not want to hear the answer.

"Well, I had to give you this," he said, pointing to the black garbage bag sharing their table. "Actually, it's for Kiran."

"What is it?"

Chris opened the bag, revealing just the head of the roaring tiger.

"For Kiran?"

"He'll understand. Just give it to him, OK?"

Shanti looked down at her Styrofoam container and lifted a forkful of noodles into her mouth. Just as she did this, Chris leaned over and kissed her, his tongue all of a sudden in her mouth, probing the half-chewed food, the grease, the garlic; this, his first taste of her: Mr. Wok. Later, it would shame Shanti that this was what he tasted. But Chris by contrast was intoxicated. For years afterward he craved MSG, sesame oil, soy sauce, pouring more and more on whatever food was put in front of him.

Kiran didn't go to the arcade, not immediately anyway. In-stead, he found the camera store in one of the forgotten wings of the complex. He'd been there before, and it was the reason he wanted to come to the mall with his mother in the first place. He loved everything about the shop: the gray industrial carpet and fluorescent lights; the intricate, expensive cameras of all shapes and sizes in the glass display cases; the accessories, straps and flashes, zoom lenses and leather cases; the huge posters on the wall, examples of photographs one could take—flowers, mountains, a family posed in front of the Grand Canyon, Caribbean waters nudging a white sand beach. As an adult, Kiran would become a professional photographer, not an art photographer as he had hoped, or a fashion photographer, his second choice, but an events photographer—weddings, bat and bar mitzvahs, the odd quinceañera. He liked being able to slip in and out of other people's lives during key milestones, an observer, not a participant. Even in his own life, he'd often have a camera with him, something to hold between himself and the world. Now, despite having never taken a photograph, he found himself drawn to the cameras and the possibilities they promised. He hovered over the glass, gazing at the small sleek machines his allowance could never afford, until the sales clerk shooed him away.

Shanti wiped her lips with the back of her hand, trying to wipe away Mr. Wok and Mr. Bell, though the latter proved impossible to erase. In the moment he kissed her, Shanti had forgotten everything about her life. All her narratives about who she was in the world fell away. She was not wife, daughter, mother, friend, not house cleaner or bank teller or immigrant. She was only her naked, thumping heart, not even fully human, or perhaps, conversely, the most fully human she had ever been. And the only other human in the world was Chris. That was the moment he kissed her. The moment after he kissed her was entirely different. After the kiss, just after, truly seconds after, Shanti saw in the corner of her eye, peeking from behind a fat, white pillar, her blinking son. She had forgotten he was at the mall at all, just as she had forgotten she herself was there.

Kiran looked so small, standing on the far end of the gleaming food court. Shanti thought she had never seen him so small. Even when she held him for the very first time, when he was technically at his smallest, he had not seemed that way to her. In her arms, his tiny face just inches from hers, he had seemed huge; in fact, he was all she could see. She had pledged then—perhaps not consciously, but implicitly; the pledge was inseparable from the swelling of her heart, so large she worried it would literally split her body open—to protect him, just as she had made the same pledge with Preeti four years earlier. Now he was a brown speck in a sea of white, looking utterly lost. As small as he was, Shanti's maternal superpowers allowed her to zoom in and see clearly her son's bewilderment. The world he thought he knew—this shopping mall he'd visited a dozen times or more, this food court in which he'd eaten tacos and corn dogs and drunk Orange Julius—had transformed into something else: an upside-down world where his mother was kissing a man who was not his father.

Chris followed Shanti's gaze and saw the boy. Seeing the boy's distress—Was that the right word? Was that what he was seeing on the boy's face, in the boy's body? Is this what he was responsible for?—Chris instinctively moved toward him. Kiran turned and, lizard-like, darted away, searching for the nearest rock to wedge himself beneath.

Shanti looked in the hobby and toy store. She looked in the boys' section of JCPenney where they bought most of Kiran's clothes, even though she knew he hated clothes shopping and it didn't make any sense that he would be there. She didn't know about Kiran's affinity for the camera store, but she knew how he gobbled free toothpick-skewered samples at Hickory Farms and how he liked having his feet measured at the shoe store,

quantifiable confirmation that he was still changing, still growing. She checked all of those places before finally finding him
exactly where he was supposed to have been in the first place:
standing outside the arcade, statue-still, the chaotic cavern of
blinking lights and roaring race car engines and intergalactic
laser guns behind him.

"There you are," she said, smiling. She was holding the black
trash bag she had been dragging back and forth across the mall.
Her heart was racing, but she tried to sound calm. "You ready
to head home?"

Kiran said nothing but started walking in the direction of
the car. Shanti followed.

She shoved the trash bag into the trunk and slid into the
driver's seat. The car was very hot. It had been sitting in the sun
for hours. Kiran in the passenger seat rolled down his window
immediately, but Shanti kept hers up. She sat for a minute in the
hot car before starting the engine, allowing her face to flush, allowing sweat to stream down her face and a few hot tears to fall.

A few times, during the drive home, she tried to speak. She
had no intention of trying to explain the kiss (she had no explanation) or of asking Kiran not to tell his father (she didn't have
that right). She only wanted to know that he was OK. But the
air howled too loud past the open windows and the radio continued its schizophrenic skip through country-pop-oldies land
and Shanti found her voice too weak to make itself heard.

They were halfway home before Shanti realized she had
forgotten the shopping bag with the crystal bowl on the food
court floor. Never mind, she thought. She'd give instead the
customary gift at Indian weddings: cash. The crystal bowl now
crossed off the registry, no one would buy it. The couple would
not be saddled with a gift they only thought they wanted. They
would be spared at least this mistake.

She watched the Southern Tier landscape unscroll before her, the same landscape she'd just driven through, that she'd been driving through for years and would likely continue to drive through for decades: lazy streams skirting lazy hills, old farmhouses with wide porches, wood fences. The same cows she had driven past that morning—who neither knew nor cared what had happened to her in the food court of the Elmira mall—were still in the same place in the same roadside field, still chewing their cud.

As she approached their town, spotting the familiar green sign announcing four more miles to the exit, Shanti thought of something. She had once heard that the Indians—those *other* Indians—had never settled in the part of the valley where Shanti and Nishit now lived because they believed it to be cursed. She was told this by a woman who would sometimes come into the bank. "White folks can't read landscape," she'd said. "Leave it to us to be stupid enough to stay." But Shanti wasn't included in that "us," she thought. She wasn't white. Eventually the woman stopped coming to the bank and Shanti heard that she'd moved to California. Shanti heard that the woman didn't even bother cleaning out or closing up the house that had been in her family for three generations, which she inherited and inhabited alone. She loaded what she wanted (and what would fit) into the back of her Subaru and drove west.

At home, Kiran slammed the car door (had he meant to slam it?) and scurried off to his room. It was only much later, removing her rings and bangles and placing them in the jewelry box in the top drawer of the bureau, massaging night cream into her hands and elbows, and climbing into bed with Nishit, that Shanti realized she had not asked Kiran to return her wristwatch, and that now, not wanting to remind him of that day, she would never get it back.

* * *

"I've got to make this right with the boy," Chris said. "You've got to let me try."

Shanti twirled the cord from the canary-yellow kitchen phone around her finger. She wasn't sure whether to be alarmed that Chris had called her at home. Before the kiss, it wouldn't have mattered. But now . . .

"I'll take you both out to the lake. I'll bet the boy has never been fishing, has he? A boy growing up out here? He should know how to fish."

That Chris never referred to Kiran by name, only as "the boy," struck Shanti as strange. Was he afraid he wouldn't pronounce his name properly? Or was he trying to reinforce something? And what did he mean that Kiran "should" know how to fish? Was this a subtle (or not-so-subtle) criticism of Nishit?

Shanti had no intention of agreeing to such an outing. It was one thing for her to be walking the dangerous edge of murky waters, quite another for her to drag one of her children into the mire. But when the moment came for her to say no, her lips—remembering, on some cellular level, the touch of his lips—betrayed her, and the word they formed was *When?*

It happened toward the end of their day together, after they had driven up to the lake, Chris's pickup rocking along the potholed dirt road, tossing the trio about like a carnival scrambler; after Shanti had unfurled on the grass the Rajasthani block print bedspread, not the one that was currently on her and Nishit's bed, but the one that had been on their bed before it faded and frayed and they replaced it with another almost identical one; it happened after Shanti had cracked open the stainless steel dabbas, one with potato parathas flecked with cilantro, one with turmeric-yellow cauliflower sautéed with ground cumin and mustard seeds, one with pickle homemade with mangoes imported by the Indian grocer in Rochester; after Chris had said, "This is delicious," and Shanti had breathed a sigh of relief, hoping that he, having never had Indian food, would love it once he tried it; after Kiran had cracked open the tackle box, lifting the lid slowly like the lid of a treasure chest, after he'd been wowed by the vast array, bait in all shapes and sizes, bait that sunk and bait that bobbed, each piece asleep in its own small bed, the colors (neon, iridescent), the feathers that looked like earrings worn by certain teenage girls he saw (those earrings, bait of a different sort, Kiran supposed), after Chris had instructed Kiran how to select the right kind of bait for the right kind of fish; after Chris had knelt next to Kiran on the rocking dock, his hands guiding Kiran's as he threaded the bait and cast the line in a graceful arc (more graceful than Kiran thought himself capable of) over and into the water; it happened after Kiran had excitedly pulled the small brown fish from the muddy water and Chris had helped him remove the hook and release the fish back into the pond, and Shanti thought, What a strange fate, to spend one's life swimming in this tiny pond, nowhere to go, just around and around, to be caught and released, caught and released, and then she wondered, Does it hurt less? Each time, does the flesh toughen, does the hook sting a little less?

It happened after all of this. It happened so fast. One minute Kiran was on the rocking dock, the next he was in the water, *under* the water, flailing. Shanti didn't even have time to scream, "He doesn't know how to swim!" There was a moment she thought she had lost him, *she* had lost him, it was her fault, but so quickly Chris dove in. And then there Kiran was, in his arms, being pulled ashore.

It didn't occur to Shanti or Kiran that had it not been for Chris, they would not have been there in the first place; Kiran never would have fallen in. It didn't occur to them when Shanti coaxed Chris and Kiran out of their wet clothes and she wrung them out forcefully, with strong hands, thinking of her family's dhobi squatting on the hot cement on the roof in Pune, wringing out washed clothes over a storm drain. It didn't occur to them when Shanti hung the clothes on a tree bough, hoping they'd dry at least a little before they had to leave, watching Chris and Kiran sitting on a log in their wet underwear, thumb wrestling. It didn't occur to them when, as they cruised down the hill, down past the clearing in the woods, the farm, Ray of Light Ministries, down past Chris's house and toward Shanti's, Chris slung his arm across the back of the truck seat, the still-damp flannel of his shirt sleeve steaming behind Kiran's head, smelling of lake water and sunlight. It didn't occur to them when Kiran gazed up at his mother and she was smiling and humming a sentimental Bollywood song Kiran didn't recognize but was by Kishore Kumar, and her hair, pulled back in a long black braid, danced on her back as the truck bounced along. At the time, they only thought of Chris as their savior. It only occurred to them some years later, and separately: Kiran, age twelve, standing in the tall grass across from Chris's house, looking in; and Shanti, decades after that, holding Nishit's hand in the hospital after his heart surgery, thinking, Chris may have been Kiran's savior, but—even if she could only see it now, after a long life together, highs and lows, peaks and cursed valleys, and more days and months and years of stumbling around in dark caverns than she'd like to admit—Nishit had been hers. Just as she had been his.

Now, returning from the lake, Kiran dug out from the Tercel's trunk the black trash-bagged tiger he knew had been there since the day at the Elmira mall. That night he slept with it, and dreamed of being dragged deeper and deeper into dark water,

water filling his lungs. Then: Chris's arms around him, pulling him toward the surface, toward the light. Kiran pulled the tiger close.

Kiran loved the tiger, and loved—in a way he didn't quite understand—the man his mother loved, the man who had won it for him. He continued to feel this way, despite what happened later that fall—what happened in the woods, and the four-armed monster in silhouette stumbling out after—and the role Kiran thought Chris, however indirectly, played. It was as though the tiger had cast a spell.

In seventh grade, he would loan it to a shy, awkward girl in his pre-algebra class, who was going into the hospital for a surgery she hadn't explained to anyone, but which seemed to Kiran serious. Kiran would say, "He'll keep you safe," and he wouldn't understand that this gesture would make her fall in love with him, a love he had no interest in reciprocating, and that she would continue to pine for him until graduation and beyond.

And then there would be a third incident, a third spell cast, but that was on another continent, and still many years away.

Shanti said, her back turned to Nishit, "I can't live this way anymore." She stood in the kitchen, rubber-gloved, wiping the narrow pathway between backsplash and dish drainer, collecting mouse turds, shaking out scouring powder, scrubbing. Nishit said, "We'll catch it. It takes time." He watched her from behind. Her hair was long. Soon she would cut it and would wear it short from then onward, but now she still had the hair she'd had when she married him. Nishit watched her scrub, then he saw her stop, saw her shoulders suddenly round and convulse.

Tears came fast. She allowed herself to cry, allowed herself to knock over—not quite by accident—a break- and chip-resistant Corelle cereal bowl that, hitting the hard tiled floor, worse than broke or chipped, worse than shattered, *slivered* into shimmering shards the size and shape of nail clippings. Nishit rushed to her, trash can in hand, and they knelt a minute together before Nishit said, "Go. I'll take care of it." But Shanti, still crying, wouldn't budge, even when Nishit held her wrists, tried hoisting her up off the floor. Was it that she didn't want Nishit to have to clean up the mess she had made? Or was it that this was *her* kitchen, and she wasn't sure she trusted him to inspect the space beneath the refrigerator door or the floor under the butcher-block-topped cart, to find every splinter?

Afterward, she would know it was neither of these. She had stayed because she had wanted Nishit to witness her ugly tears. She had wanted him to see her broke open.

Shanti in a rose-colored salwar standing back against the altar, facing the congregation at Ray of Light Ministries, couldn't help remembering her own youth, Father Torres, how different his view would have been—little faces framed by pigtails, white-frocked brown bodies swallowed by God-size Victorian pews—compared to hers now—red-faced farm families firmly planted on plain pine. She noticed in particular the four young men, broad-shouldered, sitting ramrod straight right up front, and knew these must be the ones going on mission. Chris had said they were all eighteen, but Shanti could see clearly they were still just boys.

Chris had told her to keep her remarks short, that mostly she was there to field questions. She did not tell them that she had never been to Calcutta, that one of the only people she knew from that region of India was a Bengali man who was employed by her family for some years, a driver with long lashes and faraway eyes whom her father had fired for twice showing up late. Instead, she told the audience that Indians were among the most welcoming, accepting, and hospitable people in the world. "Your boys will have absolutely nothing to worry about," she said. "An Indian will invite anyone into his house. That guest, even if there only for ten minutes, will leave with a full belly and having drunk at least two cups of tea."

The woman who raised her hand first was a large woman holding a white handkerchief the detail of which Shanti could not have seen but which was stitched with red strawberries. Timidly, she asked, "Is it as bad as what all you hear? People"— she hesitated and then dropped her voice even lower—"starving, dying in the streets. Open sewage. Filth everywhere."

Another man, without raising his hand, popped up and addressed Shanti. "I saw something on TV about the caste system. There are people who aren't allowed to walk on the sidewalk or make eye contact with anyone or hold any jobs other than cleaning toilets, which aren't even toilets like we know them. They're just holes in the ground, right? And it's all because of what their religion says? About what family they were born into? And there's no escape?"

There was a murmur in the audience, but before Shanti could answer, the first woman spoke again. "I mean, when you hear about all that, it's clear how desperately our boys are needed over there, the world of good they'll be doing." Someone in back started applauding slowly, and then it caught, rolled in waves up and down the pews. Someone sitting near the four boys in the front row motioned for them to stand. They faced the audience, and the applause roared.

Shanti had told Nishit not to come, citing as her excuse that he would make her nervous (though of course she had other reasons for not wanting him there), but now, gazing across the sea of white faces, she wished for someone familiar, someone who understood. And then she saw Chris, and he saw her and he smiled. She wasn't sure what all was contained in that smile. Was it sympathetic, conspiratorial? Did he understand that she'd felt like an animal on display, that she'd never felt more than at this moment so far from home: a zebra in the Bronx, a lioness in Cincinnati? It didn't matter what the smile meant. It was a beautiful smile, big and warm, and for a brief moment it made Shanti smile, made the molecules in her body stand on their chairs and jump up and down.

Of course no one could have known that day that one of the boys, an especially beloved native son, would fall ill in Calcutta and die of a particularly virulent strain of malaria. The young man himself, so used to flexing his muscles, so used to the role of small-town hero, could never have imagined that he could be felled by something so minuscule as a mosquito, and in the course of doing God's work no less. Though no one from the community ever said anything, Shanti did sometimes wonder if they blamed her. Was there something more she could have said? Had she mentioned mosquito net? Had she stressed insect repellent? Afterward, she couldn't remember. She wondered if people were secretly bitter that, in trying to help one of *her* people, they had sacrificed one of their own. No one would appreciate the way the boy's untimely death had martyred him and made him immortal. He would never grow old, never disappoint, never fall short, the way so many would, the way Shanti's own children sometimes would (though Shanti would never admit it). This boy would be forever golden.

Amy witnessed the electricity that passed that afternoon between Shanti and Chris, saw in Chris's eyes the fire she'd seen so many years ago when he spoke to the man at the Gladiators for Christ show. Now, as then, she didn't blame him. She knew the seduction of those alternate lives—bending steel on stage, taking a dark-haired lover from the other side of the world. She had fantasies of alternate lives of her own. But she also knew about fire. She knew the way it would, if left unchecked, burn.

"If your hand is bigger than your face it means you'll die of cancer," Kiran said, barely looking away from the television set as he let Greg in, using one hand to pull open the sliding glass door and the other hand to balance a cereal bowl with a slice of store-bought apple pie smothered in a full half pint of heavy whipping cream. Greg had pressed himself up against the glass, peering in, before pummeling the door with two fat fists.

If Kiran had been paying attention—if he had seen how Greg was covered in sweat, how his mouth was formed in the shape of an enormous O—he would have known right away that something was wrong. And yet, in the years to come this particular if would be the least of the ifs that would haunt him. If his parents had been home. If his father had not been spending Saturday in surgery. If his mother, working a half day at the bank, had returned after noon as she was supposed to. If he had noticed the house seemed particularly quiet that morning. And the one that haunted him most: If he had said something to someone earlier.

Kiran spread his hand mask-like over his own face. "See, *I'm* not going to get cancer."

Greg, panting, put his open palm against his face, and just as he did this Kiran shoved Greg's hand hard. "Gotcha!"

"That hurt."

"Wuss."

"What?"

"Wuss!"

"Well, maybe I won't tell you what I came to tell you," Greg said, crossing his arms.

"I don't care."

"You'd care if you knew what it was."

"Doubtful."

"It's about your sister."

"Oh, then I definitely don't care," Kiran said, making a show of turning his attention back to the television set, though he was beginning to feel the first bubbles of worry in his chest and the back of his throat.

"Kiran, this is serious." Kiran looked at Greg. Greg looked scared. "You need to come with me."

"Just tell me."

"I can't. I don't know how."

So Kiran and Greg set off, stormed up the hill, up Sherman Road, past the Satterfields' house and the Parkers' and the Bells' and the Jaspers'—Mrs. Jasper out front fussing with something or other on the front porch, stopping to wave and call, "Where you boys going in such a hurry?" a question that went unanswered—past the dairy farm and the two barking dogs tied to doghouses on opposite sides of the road, past the frog pond, past Ray of Light Ministries, to the steepest part of the hill, Greg huffing and puffing, pushing his glasses up on his face, past the Ellmanns' house, which had the best view in all of the town, then through the maple grove, deep into the woods to the spot all the neighborhood kids knew so well, the spot, surrounded by pines, called the Cathedral.

When they arrived, the first thing Kiran noticed were the dozen or so neighborhood kids milling about, faces grave with amazement. Later, Greg would explain they'd been coming all morning into the afternoon, first in trickles, then in waves— Kevin Brachfield, Melissa Dennison, Kristin Pringle; Ronnett Chapman, who the previous year had fought Gretchen Crookshank behind Peter Logan's house after school; Timothy Meyers, whose birthday party Kiran and Greg had attended just last week, who had a Popeye-themed birthday cake the inside of which was dyed spinach green; Kelly Bell, Cheryl Higgins; both Yamamotos, Eric and Henry; Sherman Barry; Janice Baldassari, who in eleventh grade would become the subject of a persistent rumor about a three-way with Zach Miller and Jeff Burston; Caleb Cranbrook, who, eight years after high school graduation, Kiran would see behind the counter of a local video store and who would respond, when asked what he'd been up to, "Mostly working on my metaphysical drawings." Later, Greg would say that they'd all agreed someone had to tell Kiran but no one wanted to do it, and in the end Greg volunteered "on account of Shawn's my brother and you're my best friend."

Spotting Preeti, Kiran found there was nowhere safe for his eyes to rest, each detail more distressing than the last. She was tied to the trunk of a sapling, her wrists bound with a jump rope. Her hair was styled in a way he'd never seen before, tight braids on either side of her face, and she wore a fake leather headband with a plastic feather Kiran recognized from Greg's toy chest. Her jeans were dirty, her shoes were missing, her pink-and-yellow-striped socks, her favorites, were soiled. Her torso was completely bare, covered in goose bumps from the autumn chill: her small breasts evidence of her twelve-year-old body transforming. She said nothing and did not look up from her downward gaze at the pine-needle-covered ground beneath her.

Shawn stood nearby, clutching discreetly—though visibly—a bowie knife. "Pocahontas is mine." He was wearing the baseball shirt that had been crumpled next to Kiran when he crouched under Shawn's bedroom desk: the number thirty-eight in shiny red vinyl. Images of that afternoon flashed through Kiran's mind: the threadbare, too-tight brown towel around Shawn's waist, water drops freckling his shoulders. He thought too of another afternoon, watching Preeti through the wood slats of her closet door, her head thrown back as she wailed Pat Benatar lyrics: "Never again, isn't that what you said?"

Now, Shawn looked directly at Kiran. He smiled his crooked, snaggletoothed smile and winked. "Run along, slugger."

"Sorry," he said, kissing her cheek, her neck, the delicate edge of her collarbone. He repeated it, "Sorry," and with each utterance, "Sorry," his lips found another part of her body, another scar, another wound, offering each a kiss to make it better: "Sorry" her hair, "Sorry" her arm, "Sorry" her fingers, her wrists, her breasts. Under the bleachers at the high school field, Shanti melted beneath Chris's touch. It was their first time seeing one another since she'd spoken at his ministry. "Sorry I put you through that," he said.

"I felt like I'd been shot through with arrows."

That afternoon was chilly, but Chris felt warm against her. Heat radiated from his body, even though he was wearing only jeans and a T-shirt. It seemed to Shanti that in America she and Nishit were always cold. They'd never quite gotten used to the climate of Western New York, bundling themselves in sweaters when everyone else was in shirtsleeves. But Chris, he had spent his whole life here as had generations before him, and all that genetic material was inside him, instructing his body to generate warmth. At that moment what his body radiated was exactly what Shanti needed. When his mouth found hers, Shanti was surprised by his hunger, and frightened by her own.

It had been Chris's idea to meet there that Saturday, after Shanti's half day at the bank. And even though the cliché of kissing beneath bleachers was not one with which Shanti was familiar from her own youth, when Chris kissed her she understood right away that in his high school days he had kissed countless girls beneath these bleachers, had surely kissed his own future wife here. She knew in the years to come her own children would likely have their own experiences in this very spot.

Sunlight filtered through, creating alternating bars of shadow and light. A lone girl ran the track. As she passed by, Shanti imagined she could hear, in the girl, an echo of her own heavy breath, her own racing heart.

Back home, Kiran paced the subterranean family room, shuffling across the thin green carpet covering the concrete floor. What he'd seen in the woods was like being in the upside-down world again, Planet Narik. Earlier Preeti had been pining for Shawn, and now she was with him, they were together again, just as she had wanted. But everything about the scene was wrong. This wasn't how she wanted to be with him.

He didn't know what to do. His father was at the hospital. His mother should have been home by now. Prabhu Kaka was in his room—the guest room—as he always was, the door shut. Kiran didn't know Prabhu Kaka, didn't trust Prabhu Kaka, and his mother had instructed him not to bother his uncle except in an emergency. But wasn't this an emergency?

Kiran wished his mother were here. But what exactly would he tell her? How would he explain what he saw? Is that even what Preeti would want? But the question that was foremost in Kiran's mind was: What if then Shawn told what the two of them had done together? Kiran remembered the feel of Shawn's hard cock in his hands, the smooth, taut skin, the way Shawn shuddered when he came. It terrified Kiran. But he had felt something else too. There was power in being able to do this to Shawn, an older boy, a baseball star. Power and pleasure.

Kiran wondered what his mother or father would say if they knew what had happened, if they had seen Kiran's hand coated in Shawn's mess, if they had heard Shawn's sticky, rank laugh. What would they think of their son?

Eventually, Kiran abandoned his pacing and flopped down on the couch. It was scratchy and plaid; his parents had bought it a year ago secondhand from a family who did not have much money but who had been fortunate enough to inherit from a relative a beautiful sofa with shimmering beige floral fabric. Kiran had accompanied his parents to the house. The satiny sofa and the scratchy couch were jammed up right next to each other in the wood-paneled room with the dirty brown carpet. Kiran remembered thinking, when his parents sat on the plaid couch, testing it out, hadn't they made a mistake? Shouldn't they be bouncing up and down on the other one? Behind the satiny sofa crouched a young boy with elf ears and a pallid complexion. Kiran recognized him from school: an unpopular, bullied kid. Lobbed insults always gravitated toward him, circled him in permanent orbit. Inevitably, and at least weekly, someone would fart in his face. Not long after Kiran's parents bought the couch, one such incident occurred—during science class, while the teacher was in the hallway—and at the exact moment of the boy's humiliation, he looked at Kiran sitting in the next desk and his eyes said not so much *Help!* as, *Lucky: It could be you. It* should *be you. One day it will.* Kiran imagined him, after school that day, lying on the satiny beige sofa, licking his wounds, Kiran stuck with his scratchy castoff.

But he wasn't thinking of the boy now. Even as he gazed at the television—which he'd switched on almost by habit, his regular Saturday ritual of watching *Happy Days*, a small cassette recorder propped against the TV speaker—even as he watched Fonzie snap his fingers, summoning two women, "chicks" he called them, one on either side, or watched Ralph Malph trying to squirm his way out of whatever trouble he'd gotten himself into that week, Kiran thought only of his sister up in the woods with Shawn.

In the coming days, sequestered in whatever small, dark space he could find, he would listen back to the episode, again and again. He had memorized every line of dialogue, every joke and punch line, every word of Mr. Cunningham's inevitable dispensation of his midwestern, midcentury version of wisdom. Kiran was comforted that he knew exactly what would happen and how everything would end.

"Take me to her. *Immediately!*" Prabhu boomed in a tone Kiran had never before heard from him. Kiran had waited until almost five to pull himself from the couch cushion, red marks on his face where he had rubbed his cheek raw. Prabhu didn't change from the white kurta pajama he'd been wearing while lounging in his room. He threw on only a ratty brown sweater that had once belonged to Nishit, and in the foyer slid his feet into plastic chappals that slapped against the asphalt as he and Kiran raced up the hill.

When they reached the edge of the woods, Prabhu asked Kiran to explain where the spot was, and then he told Kiran to wait. Kiran watched Prabhu disappear into the woods, his loose pajamas ballooning in the wind.

Minutes passed; too many, Kiran thought. He fiddled nervously with the rakhi on his wrist, almost two months old, now just a ratty, faded piece of string. A pickup truck rumbled by; someone in the driver's seat he wasn't sure he recognized waved. He waved back. He coughed, choked by exhaust and dust. Geese honked overhead, bound south. Light waned. Where were they?

After what seemed to Kiran like a very long time but may have been only minutes, something finally emerged from the woods. At first it looked to Kiran like a monster. He couldn't decipher the shape. He saw it only in silhouette, and it seemed so tall, with four arms. As it approached he realized what it was: Prabhu carrying Preeti—still shoeless and wearing Prabhu's sweater—on his back. Looking at his uncle, Kiran never would have guessed he had the strength or energy to carry her this way down the hill all the way back to their house, but that's exactly what he did.

Preeti wouldn't meet his gaze, but Kiran stole glances and tried to piece together what he could of what had elapsed in the hours since he'd last seen her. Physically she looked fine. There were no obvious wounds, no visible scars. Her body slumped against her uncle's, her head rested on his shoulder. It bobbed and bounced as Prabhu, in kurta pajamas and plastic chappals, hustled down the hill, wanting to beat his brother and sister-in-law home, which he did, if only by a few minutes. When they reached the house, standing in the split-level foyer, he released Preeti from her perch. He kneeled down and held her head with both of his hands, one on each side. He held her there a minute, gently kissing her forehead and whispering, "Beti, beti," and then he let her go and she disappeared up the stairs.

"Why?" Prabhu asked, turning his attention to Kiran. "You sat here all day long, knowing your sister was out there. Why?" He was still on his knees, and his face, inches from Kiran's, was huge. Like the moon, that face would follow Kiran his whole life, emerging at night, ever present even when Kiran could see only a sliver or but a blur through clouds.

Just then, they both heard a key being inserted into the lock of the front door, the bolt being turned. Shanti swung open the door, jangling a ring heavy with keys. "Hi, darling," she said to Kiran. Her hair was mussed. The crisp creases from her careful ironing were dulled. "Your father isn't home yet, is he?" she asked, though she would have noticed that his car was not there. Kiran didn't know how he knew it—maybe it was the look on her face, the same one he had seen when he gazed at her in Chris's truck, Chris's damp arm behind them, or maybe it was something in her voice, some singsong glee he recognized from their day at the lake—but somehow he knew she had not been home that afternoon because she had been with Chris.

Kiran looked at his uncle. For now he would be spared from having to respond to his question, spared from the out-loud uttering, but not spared from the repercussions of what he knew to be the answer. For years these twin weights—shame and regret—would threaten to pull him under.

Preeti and Kiran had individually both begged Prabhu to say nothing about the events at the Cathedral to their parents, and yet, the next afternoon, sitting with his brother on the scratchy plaid couch, Prabhu knew that he must. They were watching golf, a sport with which Prabhu had no familiarity and in which he felt no interest. It was Nishit's game, not his. Nishit spent long weekend afternoons out on the green with colleagues. It was something he'd learned in America. In India, Prabhu knew no one who golfed. He remembered when they were growing up how passionate Nishit had been about cricket. Back then, could Nishit have imagined, Prabhu wondered, a future self who would find it impossible to name even one member of the current India cricket team?

"Brother," Prabhu said. Nishit turned to him.

Nishit had difficult words of his own for his brother, and he'd been waiting for the right moment. Shanti had helped him practice. *We are only saying this because we love you so much. Yes, life has dealt you a hard hand. Losing Neela Bhabhi wasn't fair. But you cannot continue this way. You've got to find your way back. If nothing else, think about your son. Think about Bharat's future.* But turning now to his brother, looking at his face, looking in his eyes, Nishit was distracted by Prabhu's eyeglasses, frames Nishit had bought for him at Sears when he first arrived. His glasses from India were outdated, the frames heavy, cracking plastic, the lenses thick and scratched. At Sears, Nishit had asked Prabhu to pick and Prabhu said he didn't care, so Nishit had chosen for him a smart gold wire-rim with tortoiseshell details. Nishit had paid extra for thinner lenses, and this was what distracted him now: the greasy smudges on the glass. Why had Prabhu not cleaned them? How could he be so careless? How could he see properly through all that grease?

"Give them to me," Nishit said, holding out his hand, speaking in a voice he usually reserved for his children. "Your glasses, give them to me."

Confused, Prabhu removed them, folded them, handed them to his brother. Prabhu's pupils struggled to refocus—his vision had always been quite bad—and then he looked down, finally closing his eyes. Because his eyes were not open, he did not see the anger and frustration in his brother's face, or that frustration melt into something else as Nishit untucked his shirt and used his shirttails to clean the lenses. Prabhu didn't see how carefully Nishit completed this task, holding the lenses up to the light, examining his work two, then three times. But he did feel his brother gently replace the glasses on his face. When he opened his eyes, Nishit was already getting up to leave.

Having been lurking on the stairs, though not close enough to hear their conversation or to know if Prabhu Kaka had betrayed their trust, Kiran saw his father now squeeze distractedly by him, not stopping to tussle his hair or even to say hello. When he went downstairs, he saw Prabhu Kaka on the couch, his head down, staring vacantly at his lap.

Kiran had sequestered himself in the kitchen pantry—holding the cassette recorder to his ear, listening back to *Happy Days*—when he saw something moving out of the corner of his eyes. He howled. Within seconds, as if by magic, Preeti was there. "Are you OK?" These were the first words she had spoken to Kiran since the incident with Shawn in the woods more than a week before. Kiran pointed. A creature, half alive, was wriggling helplessly, its neck pinned beneath the crossbar of a snap trap, blood dripping from its mouth. For the children, this was the mouse known as Mickey, formerly known as Minnie, the mouse their parents had promised to catch, not kill. They knew neither about the half dozen rodents Nishit had already disposed of in the preceding weeks, nor about the fifteen infants Shanti had shoved in a public receptacle outside the bank. It didn't occur to them that there had been mice before this one and that there would be still more mice to come.

Preeti acted swiftly, fetching thick gardening gloves from the garage. She scooped up the mouse with one hand, wielding a brick with the other, and headed out to the driveway. "Look away," she instructed Kiran, and then more loudly, when he didn't comply, "Look away!" Kiran, head turned, heard the brick *thwap* once, twice, three times, imagined he heard Mickey squeal and cry, then stop. When he opened his eyes and turned to his sister, she was breathing heavily, still clutching the brick, the weapon frozen midair.

Chris had not introduced Amy to Shanti that day at Ray of Light Ministries, although, standing before the congregation, Shanti had felt the intensity of Amy's eyes on her, as she did again now. It was unusual for Amy to come inside the bank. Previously, when she had bank business, she had pulled up to the drive-through. These were how Shanti's previous interactions with her had been. The women exchanged pleasantries through the crackling intercom and completed transactions via capsules sucked through pneumatic tubes: checks and deposit slips in one direction; cash, receipts, and lollipops in the other. This time, Amy parked the car and came inside with two blond children, one in her arm, the other waddling beside her, still not steady on her feet, holding her mother's hand.

Amy was wearing a gold cross on a delicate gold necklace. Shanti herself had never been religious. So much in Hinduism—at least the way those she knew practiced it—seemed to Shanti less about spirituality and more about superstition, about asking for things. If I do this, I will get that. If I make the right offerings to the right gods at the right times, I will get protection for my beloved brother, good grades on an exam, a new car, blessings for my marriage, the birth of a son. Shanti remembered visiting her friend Meena in Chicago. The morning of Shanti's departure, Meena, who was driving her to the airport, was running late. Meena's children had been ornery that morning, and she had barely managed to get them out of the house and onto the school bus. And Meena didn't want to leave morning dishes in the sink. Just when Shanti thought they could finally leave, Meena said she had to do the morning puja. She *always* did it, and especially on a day when Shanti was traveling, it was her duty to procure the proper blessings to ensure her guest's safe passage. So Shanti waited another fifteen minutes, sitting quietly with Meena in front of the mandir while Meena mumbled her prayers. Afterward they were so late they had had to race through the snow to the airport, and Shanti felt grateful that the children weren't with her, that they were back in Western New York safe with Nishit, because she felt sure the car was going to crash and that they were going to die and that it would be all because Meena had had to say her prayers.

Looking at Amy's cross, Shanti wondered what exactly it meant to her. A month earlier, during a weekend of free HBO-Showtime-Cinemax, Shanti found the children in the basement, a vampire movie flickering in the dark. She should have made them stop watching, but in the minute or two it took her to realize what was on-screen, she got hooked and sat down with them. Besides, she could tell the movie was ending soon; the action was in its final stages. During a climactic struggle, the heroine of the movie presses a cross into the forehead of a vampire, and it sears the vampire's flesh. He bares his teeth, shrinks back, cowers. Kiran jumped into Shanti's arms, and she stroked his beautiful hair, still brown though it would turn coal black over time. Even in that moment Shanti felt more for the vampire than she did for the woman. He couldn't help who he was, couldn't control his need. That night, awake in bed as Nishit snored beside her, she heard with every intake of his breath the sizzle of the vampire's flesh.

"Gorgeous children," Shanti said to Amy. "Tell me their names again." *Again*, though Shanti wasn't sure she had ever known their names to begin with.

"Jane," Amy said, slightly raising the infant in her arms, and then "Sarah," nodding toward the girl holding her hand. "Jim and Kelly are in school."

Jim, Jane, Kelly, Sarah. Yes, those *would* be their names, Shanti thought. Easy names. American names. Names that could go anywhere and do anything. When he first started school, Kiran came home from the first day grumbling, "Why'd you give me such a dumb name? Everyone calls me Karen." And Nishit had said, "Count your blessings, son. I have 'shit' in my name," and Kiran was so shocked to hear his father say "shit," he didn't know if it was OK to laugh. She might have expected Preeti to have had it easy: Preeti, pretty. But of course pretty was a lot to live up to, even if you *were* pretty, which Preeti was. As time went on, Shanti worried that in choosing her name, they had unwittingly influenced the course of her life; that pretty was all Preeti would want to be.

"You have children," Amy said. It wasn't a question; it was a statement.

"Two," Shanti said.

"I know."

"How can I help you today?"

"I need to get into our safe deposit box."

"One minute then," Shanti said. She closed up her station

and came around from behind the counter. She kneeled and offered a lollipop to Jane, and Jane looked at her mother before taking it.

"What do you say?"

"Thank you."

"Thank you, *Mrs. Shah.*"

"Thank you, Mrs. Shah."

Shanti handed three more lollipops to Amy. She had counted them out behind the counter. Sarah, the baby, was too young for lollipops, but Shanti thought four children, four lollipops. Maybe Amy would eat it herself. Or she would give it to Chris, "From Mrs. Shah." Shanti thought of the lollipop she had slid Chris two months earlier.

She led Amy and the children into a back room, passing an automated shoe shiner Kiran loved to play with when he visited. "Wait here," she said as she disappeared into another room and fetched the box. "And you have the key?" she asked, and Amy replied, "Yes."

"I'll leave you then. Just press the buzzer when you're ready for me."

As she waited, Shanti couldn't help wondering what Amy was doing, what she was adding or subtracting or double-checking in the box. Shanti didn't know what was in there, but she could imagine: titles, wills, certificates of insurance, items needed should your home be ravaged by the unexpected: a fire, a twister, a thief.

When Amy finished and pressed the buzzer, Shanti felt the weight of being summoned. She remembered her weeks cleaning houses before she got the bank job. She thought of what Mrs. Sharp had left her in the toilet.

In the room, Amy had left the locked metal box on the wood table, and she was already stepping away from it. "It was good of you to speak at our congregation, Mrs. Shah. You are welcome there anytime." She looked Shanti up and down. "Next time, you'll be sure to bring your husband." Amy exited. Shanti slid the box back into the wall of identical containers.

It was an October day, and when Shanti left the bank late that afternoon, instead of going straight to her car in the parking lot out back she took a walk, starting on Market Street and then turning down one of the tree-lined side streets with the grand old houses. Fall was one of the few things about America Shanti truly loved. There hadn't been fall in Pune, not in the same way. There the variation from season to season was less dramatic; the seasons blended into one another. There was less of a sense of time moving forward and circling back. She loved the turning of the leaves, the colors, the way they fell and covered the sidewalks. She loved back-to-school: cellophane-wrapped twenty-packs of pencils, Elmer's glue, spiral-bound notebooks, wide-ruled for Kiran, college-ruled for Preeti, new clothes, new shoes, first days. In India, school had been year-round, and while Shanti agreed that such a system was probably better for education, she also felt there was something to be said for long summer vacations, the idea that there was a time for everything. Summer was about running free. Fall was about reining it back in.

There was a nip in the air, and as Shanti continued to walk farther down a street she'd never been on, she flipped the collar on her coat and pulled it close to her neck. It was a new jacket. A couple weeks earlier, when Shanti was standing at the hall closet in front of the jumble of coats—light coats, heavy coats, all different sizes—Nishit had said, "Something is wrong. I can tell." And because she couldn't tell him, didn't quite know herself, wouldn't have been able to put words to the emptiness she felt, she said, "Nothing. I'm just thinking about Reshma."

Nishit, remembering Shanti's spectacularly wealthy college friend, reflected on the reality of the life his wife was living versus what she might have dreamed of. He knew she and Reshma had been inseparable in college, roommates talking together late into the night. He knew Reshma had given Shanti a glimpse into a lifestyle very different from her own practical, middle-class background, her unassuming bungalow—shared by three brothers' families—in a respectable neighborhood, bland furnishings, a jointly owned white Hindustan Ambassador parked on the street. By contrast, Reshma's father when visiting would have arrived in a silver Mercedes with black leather seats or some equally exotic machine. Reshma herself married—quite young—a boy from an equally wealthy family. Is this what Shanti was trying to tell him? Whatever wealth Nishit was to accrue as a doctor was still many years away. Now there were still debts to be paid, dollars to be sent to relatives in India, money to be saved for Preeti and Kiran for college. Was Shanti trying to tell him that the life she expected, the life she deserved, was not the one he had given her?

That evening, Nishit had taken Shanti to JCPenney and insisted she buy something new, something nice, something not on sale. "Full price," he had said, and Shanti found a plum-colored Liz Claiborne coat, plucked it from the rack, hastily tried it on, barely looking at herself in the skinny mirror on the end of the aisle, not even bothering to look in the three-way mirror by the dressing rooms. She had not wanted to see her reflection.

She hadn't lied when she'd told Nishit she was thinking about Reshma. Perhaps she wasn't thinking about Reshma in that exact moment, standing in front of the hall closet, but she had been thinking about her quite a bit lately. Late one night in the darkness in their dorm room, Reshma had told her about her betrothed: "I don't love him. I barely *know* him. Maybe I will grow to love him, maybe I won't. It doesn't really matter." Shanti had heard her shift in the darkness, had seen her shadowy figure roll away. Reshma lay on her back, looking at the ceiling. "He is the man I belong with," she said. "It is my destiny." At the time, Shanti had wanted to ask Reshma what she meant, but that was not the nature of their relationship. Shanti did not ask Reshma questions.

Shanti's own engagement and marriage was six years away, but she would remember that conversation with Reshma when Nishit was first brought to meet her in the bungalow in Pune— all of her uncles and aunts hovering. Nishit was handsome enough. Smart enough. Ambitious enough. Were sparks supposed to fly? Shanti wasn't sure. No one had prepared her for this moment.

Now, many years later, Shanti was wondering about Reshma and Ketan. That's what she had been thinking about that day when Nishit asked her what was wrong. Had Reshma and Ketan's marriage been happy, had Reshma made the right decision? Shanti hadn't seen them since her own wedding fourteen years ago, and she hadn't been in regular contact, never knowing where to send letters or which phone numbers were still operational. Reshma and Ketan moved so much; he was always checking in on this family business in Kenya or monitoring that investment in Singapore, or Reshma and the children were spending the summer months in Mussorie or, one year, in Switzerland.

Every now and then Shanti would receive a hastily written letter from Reshma with a recent photograph tucked inside— the family on vacation posing in front of the Louvre or the children sitting on a plaid blanket in the grass by a river. In college they had spent countless hours together dreaming about their future lives. Now they both had children—each a girl and a boy—the other had never met. A few days earlier, Shanti had opened the shallow top drawer in her dresser, where she kept Reshma's letters and photos. She searched for clues, anything that might tell her what Reshma and Ketan's married life had been like. She noticed, in her short letters, how little Reshma mentioned herself. She noticed, in one photo, how far Reshma and Ketan seemed to be standing from one another—the children between them—how their bodies seemed to be turned away from one another. But then there was another photo with their arms around each other and bright, eager eyes.

Shanti was walking in circles now, in the unfamiliar neighborhood adjacent to the bank. She was deliberate about not straying too much, worried that if she walked too far in any one direction she might get lost. Nishit would have laughed at her, the girl from Pune, not a huge metropolis but not a small village either, afraid of being lost in this tiny town.

At the bank, when Shanti and Amy were together in the back room, Shanti thought Amy smelled like Prell shampoo, not that Shanti knew what Prell smelled like. She had never bought it. She only knew it from the commercials with the beautiful spokesmodel with the blue eyes and the teeth like pearls (though in three years she would know the scent well; Prell would become Preeti's brand of shampoo). Yet even not knowing the smell, it is what she thought: *Amy smells like Prell.* And something about it triggered a realization for Shanti that wasn't so much logical as it was cellular. She felt it in her body. Chris was drawn to her because—like the boys going on mission to Calcutta—he had never been anywhere; just as she was drawn to him because—despite having lived in this town fourteen years—she had never been here.

* * *

From the daytime soaps Shanti spent hours watching when she first arrived in America—*Another World*, *All My Children*, *One Life to Live*—("So I can learn the American idiom," she assured Nishit [and herself]), and from movies (American, not Hindi), Shanti was familiar with what was said when one spouse finally comes clean to the other, sometimes in the kitchen, late at night, the kids asleep, one spouse standing back to the sink, arms crossed, the other seated, bent over the kitchen table, one lone pendulum light hanging above: *I've found myself stuck living a life I don't want.*

Shanti would not have one of those late-night kitchen scenes with her husband; she would not stand at the sink, he would not be slumped at the table. By the time she circled back to her car parked in the bank lot, she felt sure of this. This town was no Llanview or Bay City or Pine Valley, and she was no Erica Kane. She was Shanti Shah. Her very name meant peace. She would not leave Nishit. And she had no intention of seeing Chris again. In the years to come, she and Nishit would have other late-night kitchen conversations: there would be Preeti's brief period of rebelliousness, the sneaking out at night, the short skirts, and then, unexpectedly, Preeti's conversion to Christianity, her joining the very church Chris attended, her fiery Bible-thumping. There would be Kiran's coming out, after college but before he went to India, the letter he mailed them, handwritten on lined paper ripped from a spiral-bound notebook and sealed in a plain white business envelope, and which Shanti read first and then Nishit later that evening, seated at the kitchen table, Shanti sitting diagonal from him, her hand resting on top of his.

Just as Reshma had said so many years ago about herself and her own husband, Shanti and Nishit were meant to be together.

It was their destiny, and who was she to question destiny? Their names were near anagrams: Shanti, Nishit; an "a" for an "i." One letter was all that separated one from the other.

At the airport, Prabhu wore a blue Buffalo Bills toboggan pulled low on his head and a heavy sweater beneath a plaid flannel jacket lined in quilted synthetic fabric, articles of clothing discarded by Nishit or bought cheap at a discount store, clothes Prabhu would surely shed immediately upon landing in India if not before. Nishit watched him wandering down the long wing, clutching a cheap duffel with a prescription drug logo, a pharmaceutical freebie. Moments earlier they had embraced in the airport lobby, and in a moment of sentimentality, Nishit had bent down and touched his older brother's feet. Nishit felt silly almost immediately and popped back up and looked around to make sure no one he knew had seen.

Back home, the children had said their own shy good-byes. As far as Nishit could tell, and despite his fervent hopes, the children hadn't bonded with their uncle. It wasn't their fault. They were from different worlds.

Now he watched his brother, unrecognizable all bundled up, bumbling down the corridor. He couldn't help but think of a character from what had been one of the children's favorite bedtime stories: Paddington, in his hat and oversize overcoat and brown suitcase and paper tag imploring, "Please look after this bear." Lost: looking for a hand to grab hold of. Please look after this Prabhu.

Nishit flashed on a childhood memory. He didn't so much see it as feel it: the afternoon sun on his face, a warm breeze. He was five, his brother eleven. Their mother had instructed Prabhu to trim his brother's fingernails. Nishit leaned out the second floor window, his brother's hand holding his, the snip snip snip of the nail scissors. Nishit tried to follow the tiny clippings to the ground, to see where they landed, but Prabhu warned, "Be careful, you'll fall," his grip on Nishit both tender and firm. Though Nishit hadn't said it then, he thought it now as he watched Prabhu disappearing: *Don't let go of me. Never let go.*

WESTERN NEW YORK, 1985

Chris pushed his grocery cart into the line behind Shanti's. He hadn't noticed her at first, and when he did—when he recognized the pixie haircut she'd been sporting the last few years and the slender back of her neck—he considered trying to pull into another lane. It was solely for her benefit so she wouldn't feel awkward, he told himself; he was not the type of man to avoid something or to hide. Still, it proved too late. Another cart had parked itself behind his.

It had been three weeks since he'd taken Nishit to the roadside barbecue, an encounter Nishit had never told Shanti about. She knew nothing of the weeks her son had been standing across the street, peering into the Bells' house.

Shanti, glimpsing Chris, tried to feign like she hadn't. She pulled her shopping list from her coat pocket and pretended to scrutinize it.

"Got everything?" she heard Chris's voice ask. It vibrated through her, and for a second Shanti felt a surge of panic that she had forgotten something essential, and she found herself glancing quickly over the products crowding the checkout aisle: chocolate bars, packs of gum, batteries, nail clippers, lint brushes.

Looking up, she said brightly, "Mr. Bell, how have you been?"

"Mrs. Shah: Can't complain."

Two days earlier, Chris, at twilight, had crossed the street to Kiran. "You do know this can't go on?" he had asked. Kiran nodded. His cheeks were wet. Chris wiped them, one at a time, with his thumb.

"And you?" he said.

Shanti smiled.

How Chris missed that smile! Seeing it now lifted him, and made him ache.

"Ma'am?" the cashier said. Shanti spun back around. The customer who had been in front of her was already disappearing out the automatic doors. The empty checkout belt whirred, its thick seam disappearing with a *thwump* beneath the metal guard.

Chris started helping her unload her items onto the belt, their arms, their hands, so close to one another as they reached into the cart. Shanti distracted herself by taking silent inventory: Pepperidge Farm thin-sliced bread, two percent milk, Kraft singles, spaghetti; potato chips, cucumbers, iceberg lettuce; Yoplait yoghurt for Preeti, protein powder for Kiran, Lorna Doones for Nishit, because he liked to have just one, on a plate, in the evening as he sat in his swivel chair in the family room next to the yellow lamp. Her cart was piled high with groceries for the entire week; the days, the meals, stretched out in front of her.

When the last of her purchases had been placed on the conveyor, Shanti nodded to Chris. "You're very kind."

"Nice seeing you, Mrs. Shah," he said, but she had already turned toward the cashier and was fumbling in her purse for a checkbook.

Out in the parking lot, Shanti turned the ignition, the car rumbling to life, and sat for a moment listening to the engine throb. She drove four blocks before turning around and heading back to the supermarket. She didn't even lock the car door as she dashed inside, down the starkly lit aisle, the loudspeaker humming easy listening, and toward the hot bar, where she picked out six Buffalo wings and dropped them into a wax-paper bag.

She'd bought them for herself—Nishit was, of course, a vegetarian, and the kids, in the past year, had followed suit—and she'd intended to eat them at home, a snack, a private indulgence, before preparing dinner for the family. But halfway home she turned down the potholed dirt road toward the lake, where she sat cross-legged on the rocking dock and devoured her wings.

Satiated, she gazed across the water. The leaves were starting to turn; a fiery orange had already engulfed a group of maples. Soon the geese, who came every spring to mate and to hatch and raise their young, slickening the grasses with guano, would be heading south.

Shanti told herself she had been hungry, that was all; that was the reason she stopped at the lake. The smell from the backseat was too tempting. She wasn't trying to hide anything; after all, her family knew she ate meat.

She dumped the wax-paper bag full of bones into the trash can by the parked car, and then returned to the water's edge to wash her hands clean in the cold water. She found a container of moist towelettes in the car and wiped her hands again, rubbed at her mouth and her lips, doing a check in the mirror. Still, she knew that there would always be something—her poor appetite at dinner, her breath, a small piece of chicken caught between her teeth—that would give her away. There was no hiding. One way or another, they'd know.

Part
Two

WESTERN NEW YORK, 1991

At first Bharat thought it might be America itself that he was allergic to. In his twenty-five years, he'd never had this reaction in India: hives that bloomed suddenly in itchy thickets all over his arms, his legs, his torso, forming whole landscapes, peaks and valleys, ridges and ravines—a topical map of his suffering. It was unbearable, burning his skin, sometimes lasting just minutes, but sometimes for an hour or more. Often it happened in public, at some dinner party his aunt and uncle had dragged him to, or while he was in class, Introduction to Accounting at the local community college, which his uncle had insisted he attend, even though he'd already earned a college degree in accounting in India. He'd have to try his best to keep his composure, to keep making small talk with his uncle's colleague or to answer the instructor's question about gross versus net earnings, when all he wanted to do was collapse on the floor and curl up and wait for the pain to pass.

He wondered if it was something in the air, some gas or foreign molecule peculiar to this country, or something in the soil, some chemical—a pesticide maybe?—that was entering his body through the food.

Eventually he realized it had something to do with his body temperature, that when it rose unexpectedly—for any reason, like stepping from the cold into a warm building, or walking briskly, or feeling angry or embarrassed or anxious—that's when he broke out in hives. Still, he longed for a classification, a medical term to tag the condition. He understood the comfort that comes from knowing the name of your pain. Denied official diagnosis, he devised his own taxonomy. Taking lexical cues from urticaria, the medical term for hives, he dubbed his suffering Americaria.

When Bharat was young, there was a boy in school no one liked. His name was Aziz, but everyone called him Asleaze or Disease or Oh, Please. Aziz was always off alone, and when he explained that he couldn't play cricket, or anything else for that matter, because he was allergic to his own sweat, one of the boys said, "Naturally, even *you* can't stand yourself." Bharat hadn't been the one to start the teasing, but years later he would be ashamed of the extent to which he went along with it. At the time he hadn't wanted to see that the teasing was connected to the fact that Aziz was the only Muslim boy among them, but deep down he always knew.

Shanti had set Bharat up in Kiran's room, which had been recently vacated, Kiran now a freshman in college. It didn't seem appropriate to put him in Preeti's room—funny Shanti still thought of it that way; Preeti hadn't lived at home in more than four years—and the guest room of late had become overgrown with unfiled papers, forgotten junk mail, bills, and receipts, sprouting from carpet, from chair, from bed, spreading like weeds. It seemed to Shanti that their lives were always in a state of transition; they were always sorting through this, filing that, trying to put things right. Kiran's room was the option that made the most sense.

Bharat had never met his American cousins. He had pried a few stories from his father, Prabhu, but Kiran and Preeti had been so young then, and his father, even when pressed, revealed very little about those months here. Bharat really had very little to go on. So he tried to piece together what he could from what he saw.

As he lay in Kiran's bed, he noted the Marilyn Monroe poster on the bit of wall between the closet and the door, a life-size still from *The Seven Year Itch*, the famous scene of her standing over the street grate, struggling to hold down her skirt. Another poster was for the Cure, the heavily made-up lead singer with his thick mascara, red lipstick, wild eyes, and wild hair. From the wall shelves peered a yellow ceramic Ganesh, a visible crack in the arm where it had been broken and repaired, and a poorly constructed cat-shaped wooden doorstop with "Kiran '87" carved crudely on the underside. A large stuffed Bengal tiger sat guard at the foot of the bed.

On the dresser was a triptych of framed photos: Kiran in a formal portrait wearing a suit jacket and a tie; another more casual photo of him in a sweater, perched in the opening of an enormous circle cut into a wall; a third of him standing with one foot on a fake boulder, the suit jacket slung over his shoulder, dangling from a hooked finger. Kiran's hair was thick and long, falling almost to his shoulders, a length that must have displeased his parents. Bharat had received a print of the formal portrait in the mail last May, accompanied by a note from his aunt identifying it as "Kiran's Senior Photo." Bharat was not familiar with the tradition of senior photos and thought it strange that graduating from high school to go to college was considered a transition worthy of commemoration, as if this by itself were an accomplishment rather than just one small step, no more significant than any other, toward a destination that was still a long way away. The mailed parcel had also included a photo labeled "Prom," though that picture was not displayed here. Back in India, the comments had been polite. "He's a nice-looking boy," Kamala, Bharat's stepmother, had said flaccidly, but what everyone was really thinking was *How strange he is*, and *Who is this dumpy girl he is holding?*

Examining the triptych, Bharat was thinking something else, too. He was remembering his father's visit a decade earlier. He had understood even then that part of the reason for his father's visit was to see if another life was possible, not just for himself but for the whole family. Fifteen at the time, Bharat had not been sure what to hope for—to stay, or to go. Over the years, Bharat sometimes wondered what his life might have looked like had they immigrated. Now, in Kiran's room, he was collecting clues not only about his American cousin but about his own alternate American self.

Bharat was in America because of what the astrologer had said. It had been a cool spring morning, mist hanging like rags snagged in trees, when he and his parents headed out, their butts wedged into the narrow backseat of the auto rickshaw like toes into too-tight shoes. Armed with star charts for Ameera—Bharat's intended—Kamala had so many questions for the jyotishi. Was it a harmonious match? What was the most auspicious date for the wedding? How many children would they have, and what sex? Would the couple be happy? Would they prosper?

Ten minutes into their journey, Kamala already knew she would be miserable for the rest of the day, and she had no choice but to brace herself. She had worn new sandals, aiming to impress, and hadn't anticipated how badly they'd pinch her feet. She had no idea of the true misery that would be revealed by the end of the day, and that that misery would stretch on for months.

As the auto rickshaw puttered through a maze of uneven alleyways, Kamala recalled her own marriage to Prabhu after the death of his first wife. She had known full well no one would consider her a catch. She was short and extremely thin-framed—no hips, no breasts—her neck, torso, appendages, nothing more than twigs. Her complexion was smooth, but three shades darker than most of her would-be suitors (and their mothers!) would prefer. Her face was pinched, and all of her features were pulled forward and distorted like stretched putty. Still, she knew that it was her father's actions more than a decade earlier that had truly cursed her. Kamala's mother, until the day she died, always referred to the incident as a fall—"he fell"—though everyone knew that he jumped. Kamala's mother looked at that window in their sixth-floor flat for a full year before finally having it bricked over, a sacrifice in an already dark and stuffy sitting room. If Kamala's mother had had money, she would have moved. Even after the entire wall had been replastered and repainted, Kamala felt sure she could see the faint outline of where the window had been. Kamala's mother might have thought she was filling a hole, but for Kamala she was creating one: a constant reminder of what was once there (even if what had been there was itself a hole to begin with).

So, given her looks and her sad personal history ("very inauspicious," any matchmaker would have proclaimed), Kamala knew she'd have few prospects, but sometimes she wondered, if she had known the full extent of Prabhu's troubles (as his parents certainly must have), would she have married him? Sometimes she blamed his parents for not having been completely forthright. And yet was there anything a mother and father wouldn't do for their son if they thought it might bring him happiness, even if it brought someone else suffering? Now she was marrying off her own son, and wouldn't she do the same? *Step*son, to be precise, but she had never once thought of Bharat that way. Prabhu had made it clear even before they married that he did not want another child. He didn't want to risk a repeat of what had happened to his first wife, Neela. "Besides," he said, in a rare instance of being clearheaded and practical, "there isn't money to raise more than one." This was fine with Kamala. When she first held Bharat, not even a year old, his perfect, tiny body curling instinctively against hers, she felt immediately that it was a blessing greater than any she had right to expect.

So when the astrologer, upon completing Bharat's own star chart, answered none of Kamala's questions and instead said, directing her comments to the parents, not to Bharat, "Your son must quit India," Kamala felt her heart pound and her chest tighten. "September through December. That's the danger period. His life is at risk if he stays here." When pressed for details, the jyotishi revealed few, saying over and over, "It is written," adding only that this was a *critical* period in his life, a *dangerous* one. The actual word she used was something like *slippery*, and Kamala seized on this in the weeks afterward, her panic building. "What will he slip *on*? Or slip *from*? Or slip *into*? Why are we sending him away? If he's in danger, who better to protect him than his mother and father? What if we keep him in the house? We won't let him out. Just for four months. We won't even wash the floors; nothing to slip on." But she heard, in the jyotishi's words, chilling echoes of the past—*He fell*—and she knew they had to act.

When Prabhu spoke to his brother in America, following

Kamala's instructions, he glossed over the threat of danger. Yes, the astrologer had mentioned something, but who really believed in that stuff anymore? he said to Nishit. The main reason they were sending Bharat to America, Prabhu claimed, was because it might be his last chance, at least for some years. Soon he would be marrying Ameera, and then there would be a baby and then another. Who knew when he would get a chance to see America, and shouldn't every young man see a little of the world before he settled down? Of course Prabhu wasn't quite so articulate in explaining all of this—he stammered and grunted and filled the spaces with *um*s and *uh*s and *um*s in his usual way—but Nishit understood. And without making his brother suffer the indignity of asking (although Nishit *had* hesitated a moment, *had* allowed the briefest moment of silence, hoping his brother for once, just *once*, might admit that he needed his help and might ask for it), he said he'd purchase the plane tickets, make all the arrangements, and organize some activities to keep Bharat occupied in America, including a tour: the Grand Canyon, Las Vegas, Niagara Falls, the whole bit. "You have nothing to worry about, brother. Just send him."

ousin-brother. Kiran had grown up hearing this term. Always "brother" because—sad for Preeti—there were no female cousins (sad, but also not; how all the aunties and uncles doted on her! what beautiful dresses and diamonds and bangles they heaped on her!). As far as Kiran's parents were concerned, first cousins were the same as siblings, and Kiran grew up with a troop of lanky, troublemaking "minkeys" (his father's term of endearment). He spent almost every summer with some cousin or the other, all of them close in age, the children of Shanti's three brothers. Kiran rarely went to their houses; they would almost always come to Western New York, their parents oohing and ahhing over the bucolic setting and extolling (jealousy in their voices) the safety of small towns. The cousins crawled like ants over every inch of the neighborhood, the woods, the creek. They caught crawdads, collected quartz. They spent hours weaving daisy chains, stretched them across Sherman Road, and cheered when a pickup truck came crashing through. They built backyard forts from kitchen chairs and wool blankets, hiding so long underneath that once, during a particularly potent heat wave, Mrs. Yamamoto made a rare appearance at the Shahs' front door, having donned a large straw hat and sunglasses just to cross the side yard and ring the doorbell; she gesticulated wildly, saying nothing more than "Chickens are dying!" over and over, and it was only several minutes later, after Mrs. Yamamoto had returned home, that Shanti understood what the neighbor was concerned about. They picked fights with neighborhood kids, the cousins a tag team, tube socks pulled up to their knees. They played Marco Polo in the shallow end of the town pool (after Kiran finally learned to swim) and Smear the Queer in the lot for sale next to the Dickinsons' Tudor and marathon games of air hockey in the chlorine-scented concrete rec room at the Y and Castle Wolfenstein on the Apple II Plus on a metal desk in the corner of the subterranean family room. They raced bikes down the big hill past the woods, past Ray of Light Ministries, the dairy farm, the two barking dogs tied to doghouses on opposite sides of the road, often wiping out in one of the fields or in the tall grass along the side of the road. The cousins left their mark on the land, their blood in the dirt, their sweat slicking the trunks and branches and boughs of climbed trees. Their histories were inscribed here, the double helixes of their DNA vining up, across, around every bit of land, indelible reminders for Kiran of the glorious World of Cousins in which he'd spent his youth.

As for Shanti, if she had hoped for something from her brothers' visits, a closeness, a late-night sibling heart-to-heart, she was disappointed. She should have known better. They had not been close as children; why would they be in adulthood, even if they now had the shared experience of being newly American, adrift in a world not quite theirs? Her brothers came only to drop and collect their children, Shanti's house a summer camp. They barely stayed one night. For dinner, they requested and then praised dishes their mother had made, their own wives looking askance. They remarked how wonderful it was their children were growing up together, tying tight bonds, unable to see the ways in which Shanti needed them, in which they needed each other. Her brothers were blind to the signals: Shanti lingering alone in the kitchen late at night, herself not quite knowing that what she was waiting for was her brother, whichever one was visiting, to need a glass of water, to see her in the breakfast nook holding a cup of ginger tea with both hands, to slide in next her: "How have you been, sister?" She hoped that as her own children became adults they would have a different relationship than she had with her brothers, that they would know how to read the signs.

The cousins as children had all been mischievous boys, but at some point in their teens they all transformed into responsible, accomplished young men—valedictorians and National Merit Scholars, Ivy Leaguers studying to become doctors and scientists and investment bankers—all, that is, except Kiran. Though not a terrible student, Kiran had not excelled, and he considered himself lucky to manage admission to an upstate branch of the State University of New York. Kiran marveled at how his cousins had shed old selves as easily as they shed old clothes, or so it seemed to him. He didn't know the way each of them in his own quiet way struggled: one cousin who worried that no matter what he did, he would never be successful enough to please his demanding parents; another who would always regret swapping his college girlfriend, the love of his life—an African American woman from South Carolina—for the parent-approved Gujarati girl from Edison, New Jersey; a third whose anxiety and panic attacks he'd manage to keep secret until one Christmas break when his father-in-law found him doubled over on the cold tiles of the guest bathroom, unable to move. And just as the cousins themselves transformed, the World of Cousins—which for so much of Kiran's life, whether he was completely conscious of it or not, was a safety net—was changing into a different kind of net, a fishing net, and he was thrashing around, trying to escape it.

Bharat—being Kiran's lone Indian cousin and from his father's side, not his mother's—had not been part of this World of Cousins. Having never met him, Kiran had no idea what to expect.

When Kiran returned home for four days for fall break, Bharat had been living in the house barely two months, but Kiran could see plainly—everything in Bharat's demeanor told him this—that Bharat was miserable. Bharat had accompanied Kiran's father to fetch him from the train station an hour away. Kiran's first glimpse of Bharat was of him on the platform, slumped in such a way that it seemed to Kiran that it was just a matter of time before gravity had its way and made Bharat fully and forever part of the pavement. But when Kiran approached, Bharat's whole body transformed. He rushed toward Kiran, smiling an enormous smile, and took Kiran's hand, took his whole arm, shaking it firmly, almost maniacally. Kiran recognized in Bharat's huge eyes a state Kiran himself knew well: desperation.

Bharat remembered the first time, upon his arrival to America, that he had hugged his uncle. Nishit Kaka wore a crisp dress shirt, not like the damp shirt his own father had worn the day Bharat hugged him good-bye in India. And the smell! Later, he would learn this was the smell of laundry-detergent-plus-fabric-softener. (Fabric softener! First his kaki used softener to soften the fabric, then she sprayed starch on his uncle's dress shirts to stiffen them!) Later Bharat would come to smell this way too: his dress shirts would be softened and then starched. But at the time of hugging his uncle (after touching his feet, of course), he thought, *This is it. This is the smell of America.*

But Kiran did not smell like this. Not that he hugged Kiran the way he had hugged his uncle; everything in Kiran's body language signaled to Bharat that this would not be welcomed. And even though he hadn't expected it (he *certainly* hadn't expected it), it *had* crossed Bharat's mind that Kiran might touch his feet (he was, after all, his elder) or might call him Bharat Bhai as a sign of respect. But none of this happened, and in the end all he got from Kiran was a limp handshake. But even from that distance it was clear to Bharat that Kiran did not smell like laundry-detergent-plus-fabric-softener. He smelled stale. He had traveled by day by train, a short trip really, just a few hours from his college in upstate New York, but the smell was of overnight bus.

Kiran could imagine that Bharat had been anxiously awaiting his arrival, had been counting on Kiran to rescue him from the boredom and isolation he must have felt. Yet in the car during the drive home, Kiran found himself pulling away from both his father and his cousin, especially his cousin. Sitting in the passenger seat, Kiran had an invisible force field around him. His father couldn't see it. Bharat couldn't see it. But if they tried to penetrate it, they'd know—they'd smack hard into the wall, and the harder they tried, the more it would hurt them.

Two months earlier, when Kiran's father had brought him to college, he had stayed two nights at a nearby hotel in order to help Kiran settle in. Spotting the Indian boy moving in down the hall, Nishit had been solicitous, had asked the boy where he was from ("Bangalore"), had asked if he had any family here to help him set up ("No"), and then had insisted the boy come with them on excursions to Kmart, to the grocery store, to dinner at Applebee's. The morning he left, Nishit had told his son, "You should be friends with him. He is exactly the type of person you should be friends with." Seeing Kiran's face, Nishit said, "I know you think he is uncool. That's all you care about now: cool. In ten years, cool will mean nothing in your life. But by then it will be too late to correct the mistakes you made when you were busy trying to be someone you are not."

As soon as his father left, Kiran continued to do everything he could to avoid all Indians. Whether they were new immigrants ("fobs," Kiran called them, "Fresh Off the Boat," like the boy on his hall, like Kiran's own father had been thirty years earlier) or second-generation Indian Americans (like Kiran himself), Kiran wanted nothing to do with any of them.

To someone else, someone like Kiran's father, Kiran's actions might have seemed harsh and exclusionary, evidence even of some internalized racism, and they might have been right, though that's not how Kiran saw it. For him, his actions were self-preservationist, preemptive. The reason Kiran wanted nothing to do with these Indians was because he believed—and he believed this in the deepest place of his heart—that if they knew him, really *knew* him, they would want nothing to do with him.

Though it had only been two months, this was the longest Shanti—in eighteen years—had been apart from her son. She knew what it was to have a child go off to college, but with Kiran . . . well . . . it had been different. Preeti had left for college four years earlier, but in a way she had already been gone for years. A part of her had hardened, and Shanti couldn't break through. She'd turned away from them and toward Ray of Light. Seeing Kiran now, watching him from the kitchen window making his way up the walkway (was it her imagination? were his steps getting bigger, faster? was he racing toward her?) duffel bag in hand, wearing the Kenneth Cole leather jacket he had picked out in Rochester, the one they had bought him just before he went away, his father asking, "Are you sure you want this?" because it looked so unlike the Kiran they thought they knew, seeing all of this, seeing how confident he was, and tall (had he grown?), Shanti thought, He is a man now, a young man, but a man. Then he flung open the front door, hard, so that it banged against the beadboard wall, dropped his duffel bag onto the slate floor of the split-level foyer, shrugged off the leather jacket—that beautiful, buttery leather jacket—and, without hesitation, tossed it on the floor next to his bag, and Shanti thought, No, he is still a boy, and she threw her arms around him. In that embrace, she imagined she could feel half of Kiran melting into her and the other half trying to squirm away.

"So why exactly are you here?" Kiran asked Bharat over the dinner table. It was all of Kiran's favorite foods: chana masala, bindhi, chapatti, dhokla, and for dessert keer. But Shanti noticed he was mostly just pushing things around.

Why was he asking Bharat this question? Shanti wondered. She herself had explained it to him over the phone.

"I wanted to meet my American cousin, of course."

"Now you've met me," Kiran said.

"Oh, I'm sorry. Did you think I meant *you*? I meant Preeti."

Nishit laughed so suddenly he spit out a bit of food.

"Preeti's not here. So clearly you've failed. Speaking of which, how is your accounting class going?" Kiran stole a glance at his father, who had confided over the phone how puzzled he was that Bharat was doing so poorly. "I heard you're tearing that shit up."

Bharat's Americaria raged. He could feel hot lava slowly rising, ready to ooze from his pores, run in rivulets down his arms, his legs, his neck, his torso. He stifled the urge to claw at his skin. These hives, he decided, were a test. He took a deep breath. He was not going to fail.

"My life is not so interesting," Bharat said. "After all, you are the one who has just come home. How are your classes? Tell us everything."

Under the table, Kiran petted the cat his parents had gotten that May to combat their impending empty-nest syndrome. Though she wasn't his, Kiran had wanted to name her, and Shanti agreed, imagining when she called for her she might (even if fleetingly) feel a piece of her son still home. Grace Jones, Kiran called her, even though she had none of the diva's fierceness or sharp angles; this Grace Jones would have been better named Marshmallow. Kiran insisted his parents always use her full name and was distressed upon returning home to hear "Grace" or (gasp) "Gracie." Worse, in his absence, his parents had declawed her (surprising to Kiran, given his mother's refusal years earlier to clip their birds' wings). It was a sad scene, even cruel, Kiran thought: Gracie swatting insistently at a satin ribbon she had no hope of ever holding.

"I'd love to tell you about college," Kiran said, "but there isn't time. I'm meeting friends in half an hour. I still have to shower."

Kiran pushed his chair away from the table and stood up, his plate still half full. Shanti looked from the plate to Bharat to Nishit. Wouldn't Nishit say something to his son? Was it always her job?

"Kiran," she said, a pleading in her voice.

"Mom, I can't stay in tonight. I already promised Tina. Besides, I *never* get to see my friends anymore. And no, I can't invite Bharat." He turned to Bharat. "Sorry, dude, it's a private party."

"Kiran!" Nishit said sharply.

Kiran threw up his arms, spun, and bolted up the stairs into the bathroom.

Twenty minutes later, when Kiran was rooting around in the hall closet for his leather jacket, he felt a hand at his back.

"One thing," he heard a soft voice say, and he looked over his shoulder and saw Bharat. "Just one thing I ask you." Bharat held out a hand grasping some folded bills. "A packet of Marlboros. Reds, not Lights. Please. I'm almost out."

Kiran turned back to the closet, found his jacket. "I'm not your servant," he almost said, but said instead, "Cigarettes will kill you, dude. I don't want any part in it. My conscience won't allow it. Besides, do you know what evil imperialists cigarette companies are? Is that really where you want your money going?"

"Please," Bharat said. "You know I have no car, no way of going anywhere on my own."

"Sorry." Kiran pulled on the leather jacket and wondered if Bharat caught the stale smell of cigarettes that had permeated the grain, the fabric lining. He'd become a fiend, spending hours in the dorm lounge with Michaela and Jeffrey, sometimes not even waiting until one cigarette was done before lighting up a new one. They were there every evening, often very late into the night. Increasingly, they were there in the afternoons, too, and even mornings. Kiran knew that almost any time of day he could go to the fourth-floor lounge and Michaela would be there, or Jeffrey, or both. The three had become such fixtures on the ratty couches—the TV always blaring, at least one cigarette always lit—that the other residents on their floor had all but abandoned the lounge to them.

Kiran opened the front door and, seeing Bharat standing frozen on the slate floor of the foyer, said, "You'll thank me later."

Bharat shook his pack of cigarettes, though he hardly needed to. He remembered from earlier in the day that there was only one left. In India, when he finished a pack of cigarettes, he would carefully dismantle it and save the shiny foil lining. He wasn't sure why. He had no use for it. He supposed he was a magpie that way, drawn to that which sparkled. He liked everything about these foil papers: the way they caught light, the sound they made in his hands, the smell, part tobacco, part something else. He smoothed them on the dresser with the heel of his palm and stacked them in a shoe box in the top drawer. He loved smoking, loved especially the quiet moments alone, in a park, or by the stream, or outside the temple, or on the porch of his house sitting on the jhoola swing. Each shiny sheet represented twenty such moments, not that he thought of it exactly this way. But he did feel a certain calm pleasure when he'd open the box to add another sheet and see the stack. In America, he hadn't bothered saving them.

Bharat stood on the patio. The way the yard sloped made the house look bigger from behind than from the front: a giant in the dark. Lights blazed in the living room; the TV was loud enough that he could hear it from outside. The other windows were dark, but he could just see in the kitchen window a flash of Gracie's glowing eyes.

In spite of the clear night, the glorious moon, the pale stars, in spite of it all, the sky felt oppressive to Bharat. Its hugeness pressed down on him, and he felt crushed beneath the weight. The stars, after all, were to blame for his exile in America. He wasn't even sure he believed in stars or fate or astrologers. He'd come to America because his parents had told him to and he was a good son; he did what his parents said. From early on he'd been keenly aware of the ways in which his parents suffered. He'd seen how his father struggled to make his way in a world he simply didn't seem fit for. Bharat didn't want to add to their trouble.

He shook the cigarette from the pack, held it between his lips. He wouldn't light it, not now. He wanted to save it. He knew he would need it later.

They weren't supposed to be there. On top of the water tower. It was Rick's idea.

Kiran had met Tina, as planned, and they had gone to Carla's house and Carla's dad was there, smelling, Kiran noted, like whatever hard-labor, low-wage job it was he did. Slumped in the brown recliner, Carla's dad wore a stained shirt, his eyes already glazed over, and no matter how many times Carla asked him, he would not go watch TV in his bedroom, as Carla assured them he usually did. "This is my house," he kept saying. "*My* house." So finally Rick suggested they go to the water tower. They took two cars.

There were seven of them: Kiran and Tina; three girls Tina knew from the dance studio she'd been studying at since she was six, girls Kiran only knew peripherally; Rick Fitter, who had gone to Kiran's high school but who Kiran didn't know at all, wasn't even sure *who* knew him or *why* he was there; and Rick's older cousin Matt, who no one had met, who was a senior at Penn State and had a silver Ford Probe with a power sunroof and ID to buy beer.

There was a lot to carry up the ladder, what with all the beer and the boom box and the blankets, and Val, who was just fifteen (and talented enough to have a real shot at being a professional ballerina, the girls concurred) was wearing such a stupidly tight skirt, when all the other girls were wearing jeans, that eventually the struggle was so much she gave up. She giggled—"Nobody look"—pulled her skirt all the way up, bunching it around her waist, and scampered chipmunk-like the rest of the way up the ladder.

Once they were on top of the tower, it wasn't long before Matt and Val paired off. Kiran was partly surprised by this and partly not: on one hand, they were the two best-looking people up there; perhaps it was natural that they should gravitate toward each other. And yet there were at least six, maybe seven, years separating them. Still, Kiran had known as soon as he met Rick and Matt at Carla's house that they were on a mission. He could tell by the overpowering smell of cologne. He could tell by the impatience in their eyes and their voices, the way they kept looking at one another, the way they looked *through* everyone else because they were focused on something in the distance, some future time they'd already planned out when they'd all be drunk and in the dark and there would be music playing and the boys would be paired off with girls and there would be enough of a chill in the air that the girls would slide beneath the blankets with the boys without even quite realizing that this is what they'd done.

Kiran watched as Rick tried his luck with the remaining three girls: Carla, Tina, Sissy. Rick didn't seem to care which one he ended up with. He wanted to fast-forward to being beneath the blanket. But unlike his cousin, who had the advantage of being new and exotic and older, Rick was known, even if none of them really knew him. Kiran vaguely remembered him from the halls. The kids had called Rick's crew Jean Jackets because that's what they wore: spring, summer, fall, even winter when it was ten below. Sometimes, instead of Jean Jackets, they'd call them Dirts, as in "I can't believe Mrs. Patterson is making me do my project with a Dirt" or "Don't hang out at that sub shop; it's strictly for Dirts." And yet someone had agreed to meet up with Rick and his cousin tonight. And when Kiran saw Tina throw back a beer and scoot a little closer to Rick, he understood.

He'd never been up here, had never even noticed the tower on the hill with the town name painted on it. Was this what teenagers did, what they had been doing all along, coming up here to drink? Or was it just a Dirt thing? Either way, how was it that he'd never known? What else did he not know?

Maybe it was the newness of it all. Maybe it was the long day traveling, the train ride, Bharat at the station, or maybe it was because it was his first time home since college. Maybe it was the height, the perspective of being above, looking down on the tiny town, barely a town. Maybe it was because it was dark or because, other than Tina, he didn't know these people; they were background, minor characters in a life he believed he'd already moved beyond. Maybe it was the music (Van Halen), or the beer ("Beast"), or the fact that he'd barely eaten. Whatever it was, Kiran felt disoriented, lost, and despite the chatter, strangely alone. He lit a cigarette and thought of Michaela and Jeffrey and the ratty couches in the fourth-floor lounge. He thought, too, of Bharat. What was he doing now? Watching TV with Kiran's parents: some terrible mindless sitcom? Or smoking? Had he figured out how to remove the screen from the window in the bedroom and climb out onto the roof, the way Kiran always had?

In his peripheral vision, Kiran noticed Matt removing his flannel shirt and holding it as Val slid her small arms into the sleeves. It was true, Kiran thought, turning to watch the two of them: Matt was undeniably good-looking. Kiran admired— even in the night shadows, even from this distance—the way his arms and shoulders and chest filled his gray T-shirt. He could still smell his cologne.

Carla, who was lying on her back, probably feeling a little dizzy in the same way Kiran was feeling a little dizzy, said, "Whoa, look at the moon. It's huge!"

"And rising," Matt said, and then to Val, in a stage whisper audible to everyone, "like my dick." Val giggled.

Kiran ached. How easy this was for them. How natural. How smoothly they slid now beneath the blanket Matt had brought (a "tailgating blanket," he had said proudly, as if Penn State tailgating were an accomplishment akin to graduating Harvard summa cum laude). Kiran ached for this ease. He ached for the boys in their tees and flannel shirts and cloying cologne. He ached for a dumb guy with a hard dick and a terrible pickup line to try to pick him up. Val's giggle? To have one chance to giggle like that, Kiran would give everything.

He stood up too suddenly and felt the effects of the four beers he'd drunk on a mostly empty stomach. He wished he'd eaten more of his mom's food earlier. He tottered across the tower, in the darkness not quite sure where the edge was.

Shanti removed the bedspread, a traditional Rajasthani block print in reds and beige and black, folded it neatly, and stacked it in the closet, from where she retrieved the blue comforter she'd bought at Macy's at an after-Christmas sale a few years back. Nishit was downstairs, sorting through bills, CNN on the tele- vision. He had become obsessed with the collapse and dissolution of the Soviet Union, following every twist and turn since the decisive events of August, muttering excitedly—his voice equal parts exultation and apprehension—"It's a new world."

Kiran still hadn't returned from his night out. Shanti hadn't recognized him that evening, hadn't known the son who spoke to his cousin that way. She should have said something at the dinner table. At the very least she should have spoken to Bharat afterward, apologized on Kiran's behalf, reminding him that he was welcome there, more than welcome. She was glad he was there.

One evening just a few nights after Bharat first arrived, they ordered pizza delivery, cheese with mushrooms and onions and capsicum. Bharat took two slices. As he was shaking crushed red pepper over them, the cap came off and all of the pepper flakes fell at once. Nishit helped him scoop most of the excess flakes back into the jar and screw the cap back on, but there was still way too much red pepper on the pizza. It was impossible to pick it all off.

"Throw those out," Nishit said. "Just take two new slices."

"No," Bharat said, "I like spicy."

"That's way too spicy," Nishit said.

Understanding that Bharat did not want to waste, Shanti said, "Look, beta, there is so much pizza. How can we eat all these slices on our own? Just throw those out and take new slices."

Bharat shook his head. He bit into the slice. Shanti flinched as she watched his eyes water and his face turn red. She knew, despite the pain, despite the fact that it was searing his mouth, that he was not going to throw out these slices, that he was going to eat every last bite, not even drinking water because he didn't want them to know that he was suffering.

Another time he accompanied her to the grocery store.

When she asked him to get a pound of green beans, she noticed how he carefully selected each one instead of grabbing handfuls the way Kiran always did. She watched him pinch each one, turn it over, inspect it from all angles, before dropping it into the clear plastic bag. Then he walked over to the scale, checking the weight more than once. He wanted to get it exactly right.

It happened so fast. Val only half in Matt's car, the passenger door still open, and no one else having even gotten in yet. The sudden squeal of tires, the car bolting halfway down the block, then stopping abruptly—brake lights bloodying the blue street—Matt leaning over Val to pull the door shut. The seven of them were supposed to distribute themselves among the two cars and head back to Carla's house to continue the party, but Matt seemed to have other plans. The five remaining watched his car disappear around the corner.

"What the fuck!" Sissy said. She stormed five steps in one direction, spun around, stormed back. It took a moment for what had happened to sink in for everyone.

"Let's wait a few minutes," Tina finally said. "Maybe Matt's just joyriding around the block."

"Is Val a virgin?" Kiran heard one girl whisper to another, but he didn't catch the answer. Kiran, not quite sure where to look, glanced at his shoes. A breeze blew down the tree-lined street, leaves like cards being shuffled in a deck.

"I would've gone," Carla muttered to no one in particular. "He didn't have to take her. I would have gone gladly."

Kiran looked at her: her round wire-rimmed John Lennon glasses, her frizzy hair pulled back in a loose braid, an extra-large T-shirt that read "Lilac Festival 1988."

"They probably went back to the house," Sissy said after several minutes, sounding uncertain.

They piled into Carla's subcompact. Tina had to sit in the front, otherwise she got carsick. In the backseat, Sissy, having claimed a window, wasn't budging, so Kiran squeezed into the middle, Rick on his right. In the small seat, Kiran's and Rick's thighs pressed against each other, and when the car turned, their bodies collided, fused, until they straightened themselves. Their thighs might not have been touching the whole time had Rick sat with his knees together, like Kiran did, but Rick didn't, or wouldn't, or couldn't. Some men couldn't. They must sit with their legs wide open always, as if to announce, *My boy down there, he needs all the space he can get.*

"Probed in the Probe." Rick chuckled.

"She's fifteen," Carla said.

Kiran was aware of the heat of Rick's thigh against his own. Was Matt touching Val's thigh at that very moment? It was so difficult to know what had happened back on the street. Hadn't Val wanted to go with Matt? Or had she been taken, as Carla seemed to suggest? Kiran couldn't help thinking of his sister so many years ago in the woods, her naked torso covered in goose bumps.

At the house, there was no sign of Matt and Val. Inside, Carla's father had not retired to his bedroom as they had hoped. He'd passed out in the brown recliner. Carla couldn't rouse him. They distributed themselves between the couch and the love seat on either side of the recliner. Tina and Rick claimed the love seat, Tina curling catlike against him. Carla switched on cable: *The Lost Boys.* Her father wheezed like a woolly mammoth, and Carla kept upping the volume.

The girls—perhaps to distract themselves from thinking about what might be happening to Val—debated which of the teenage vampires was the hottest. "What do you think?" Carla asked Rick.

"I'm no faggot."

Kiran looked at Rick. Something about the way his face hardened when he said "faggot" seemed so familiar to Kiran. In fact, all night he'd thought he recognized Rick, and it was only now that he realized he was the elf-eared boy from the scratchy plaid couch his family had bought secondhand when he was a child, the boy who was teased and farted on in school.

"No," Carla said, "but, like, if someone was holding a gun to your head, and you had to say?"

"I'd take the bullet."

"You'd rather be shot in the head than say which guy is hotter?"

"I told you: I'm not a fag."

"How about you, Kiran?"

"Huh?"

"Which one?"

He hesitated a moment. Rick, when farted on, had looked at Kiran as if to say, *It should be you.* "I'm with Rick."

From the love seat, Tina frowned. Kiran worried. What did she think she knew? He held her gaze for several seconds before looking back to the screen.

The scene was this: The Lost Boys are hanging from a high bridge, a train rumbling overhead. One by one they let go, disappearing into the darkness below. The newest vampire is the only one left. He doesn't yet know he is immortal, that he can fly. He doesn't believe. He clings to the bridge. But eventually he can't hold on any longer. He closes his eyes and lets go.

They didn't ring or knock, just stumbled in: Val, limp, was wrapped toga-style around Matt, chest-puffed, chin forward, shit-eating grin tattooed on his face: "She's maybe had a little too much." The girls all popped up and extracted Val from

Matt, then collapsed, all four of them, onto the couch, kittens in a litter, purring, petting, licking each other. On the love seat, Matt and Rick snickered, elbowing each other. Kiran sat knees-to-chest on the floor by the couch. Carla's father huffed, belly heaving. The TV flickered, though no one was watching anymore. Fifteen minutes passed this way.

"Better head," Matt finally said. "Long drive to State College tomorrow."

In the car, driving Tina back to her house, Kiran asked, "What happened?"

"What do you mean?"

"With Matt and Val. When he took her." Unsure of the wording, Kiran revised. "When she went with him."

"She wouldn't say."

"She seemed fine. Didn't you think? She didn't seem"—he searched for the word—"hurt." Kiran remembered sidelong glances at his own sister, atop Prabhu Kaka's shoulders, surveying her for signs of injury as they all huffed down the hill.

"No," Tina agreed. They pulled up in front of her house. The porch light glowed yellow. Her parents had left lights on for her in the living room, too. Tina unbuckled her seat belt. "Sometimes it comes later."

When he reached home, Kiran didn't go inside. He sneaked around the side yard, walking the property line like a tightrope, six-pack left from the water tower swinging in his hand. On the back patio, he cracked open a can of Beast, chugged then crunched it. He opened another. With one hand he popped the tab, with the other he fumbled in his leather jacket for his cigarette pack, dropping it twice on the concrete. He lit a cigarette, took a drag, took a sip of his beer, looked up at the sky, at the moon. *It's huge . . . and rising.* But it wasn't rising, not anymore. Midnight was long gone; the moon was in descent.

Back at college, there was a game Kiran and Jeffrey and Michaela played. When not sullying the fourth-floor lounge, they liked to sit outside the dining hall, rating students passing by. They'd imagine that a giant anvil was falling from the sky, about to crush Person X and Person Y. You only had time to push one out of the way. Who did you choose? Recently, Michaela had introduced a twist. It was *you* under the falling anvil; you and Person X. Who would you save? It was a dumb game, Kiran thought. Wouldn't you always save yourself?

Kiran glanced at his bedroom window. He saw Bharat watching, his face in shadows and moonlight. Kiran took a long, exaggerated drag from his cigarette and exhaled luxuriously. He raised his beer to Bharat, and then looked away to take a swig. When he looked back, the face he saw was not Bharat's but Prabhu's. It was ten years earlier. They were standing on the slate of the split-level foyer. Prabhu had asked Kiran a question. The key in the lock of the front door was turning.

I just want to sleep in my own bed," Kiran had said, but Shanti insisted it was too disruptive to shift Bharat just for four days; besides, where would she put him? "It's OK for you to sleep in your sister's room, but not Bharat."

"Why not?"

"It's not . . . pukka . . . what do you say? *Kosher.*"

Kiran harrumphed. Since when had his meat-eating mother cared about kosher?

That conversation had played out over the phone a couple of days earlier, and now Kiran, drunk, tripped into Preeti's room. The clothes he'd worn on the train, which he had strewn on the floor, had been folded neatly and stacked on his duffel bag. His bedcovers had been turned down.

It had been four years since Preeti occupied this room with any regularity, but it was exactly the same (as far as Kiran could tell; admittedly, he was most used to viewing her room and its contents through the slats of her closet door). Yellow daisies on the wall. A cheerleading trophy on the dresser. On a high

shelf, a dollhouse. An enormous corkboard with small memen-
tos from every party, every outing, every date: a ticket stub,
an invitation, a silver streamer, a cocktail napkin, a tiny slip
of paper with a Chinese fortune. Kiran had not been invited
to parties when he was a teenager, and the parties he did go to
did not have invitations or napkins or streamers. Over Preeti's
bed hung a white cross edged in gold paint. On the bedside
table, next to the alarm clock, was a page from a Verse-A-Day
calendar dated January 14, 1983, and preserved in a gold frame:
"I call on the Lord in my distress, and He answers me. Psalm
120:1." Kiran shed his pants and shirt and slid under the covers
in his boxer shorts.

He last saw Preeti over the summer during a family vacation at Myrtle Beach. It was meant to be a gift for graduation
(Kiran from high school, Preeti from Ole Miss), though a week
of forced merriment with family hardly seemed celebratory to
either sibling.

Preeti had a job in a greenhouse and was aiming to apply for
nursing school come fall, a plan she announced over dinner at
Fiesta Cantina their second night there.

"Why would you want to do that?" Nishit asked.

"I want to help people," she drawled in a southern accent
she'd perfected within weeks of arriving in Mississippi. She
fluttered blue-shadowed eyelids.

"Then be a doctor," he said just as the food was arriving.
There was a flurry of flautas and tostadas and chimichangas.
Orders were mixed up. Kiran slid Preeti's enchiladas down the
wooden table after having accidentally taken a bite. "Ew" flickered across Preeti's face as though they were children and she
thought he had cooties. Once the plates were finally settled,
Nishit said, as if to himself, but loud enough for everyone to
hear, "I raised my children to be doctors, not nurses."

It took a moment for Preeti to absorb the blow; it rippled through her body before settling. "Doctors treat diseases," she said, finally. "Nurses treat people. In the end, we are the ones left holding the patients' hands."

Preeti was quiet the rest of the meal, prim in her chair, taking tiny bites she politely chewed. She was wearing full makeup, everything about her trimmed and tamed, polished and coiffed, nails painted, pulse points perfumed. Her armor, Kiran thought. Still, it was a step up from the kabuki whiteface of her high school days: foundation five shades too light layered like cake icing. Many years from now, seeing a Christmas card on Kiran's fridge—Preeti and her family posing in their best red and white, gold crosses around the necks of mother and daughter—a drag queen friend would say, "Your sister's serving Grand Ol' Party Anita Bryant *realness*," though of course there was nothing real about it. It was a mask like any other. Or armor: that was the right reference point. At Fiesta Cantina, every inch of Preeti was shellacked, her body made waterproof, impermeable: nothing getting in, nothing getting out. Perfect protection. But from what? Or from whom? It was only them there.

In Preeti's bed, Kiran tugged at her pink comforter, tucking it under his chin. The pattern was roses, but the flower he was thinking of now was lilac: the lilacs from Carla's shirt that night, the lilacs that bloomed in their own yard in May. Not *their* yard, technically; the bush probably was more accurately in the Yamamoto's yard, just on the edge of the property line, but the branches spilled over onto their side, and Shanti insisted that those blossoms were fair game. The week they bloomed she clipped them, arranging them in vases around the house: one in the kitchen, one in the family room, one on the small table in the split-level foyer. The thick smell thrummed through the house, settling into every corner, every crack. Shanti kept them too long, and their sweetness turned rank. Or was it that their sweetness faded, revealing the rankness that was always there underneath? Kiran wondered. It was like Rick's and Matt's cologne, he thought, like Rick and Matt themselves.

Before Kiran knew it, he had pulled Preeti's comforter fully over his head.

When Kiran, as a child, visited his friends and played in their rooms, he was surprised to realize that they made their beds by merely pulling their comforters over their mattresses and smoothing them out. It was so simple. In his house, it was different. He had to remove the comforter, fold it, put it in the closet, remove the night pillows, fluff them, put *them* in the closet. In the closet was the bedspread; that's what got unfolded, what he laid on the mattress, tucking it tightly, just like his mom had shown him, all four corners, all four sides, even the long side pushed up against the wall, *Just because you can't see that side doesn't mean it doesn't have to be tucked tight.* There were the day pillows, the ones covered in the same fabric as the bedspread, plus a round pillow, plus a bolster. He was to do all of this before anything else. He was thirteen when he stopped. By then he was old enough to shut his bedroom door and bold enough to say "Stay the hell out," and even then his parents had bigger worries about Kiran than whether he was making his bed. And in college, well, in college he hadn't even washed his sheets this semester, let alone made the bed.

Kiran, still half asleep, more than half asleep, ninety percent still asleep (it was nine A.M.; it would be another five hours before he left the room and started his day), stumbling down the hall returning from the bathroom, stopped to watch, through the crack in his bedroom door, Bharat making his bed, Kiran's bed, in just the way Kiran's mother had instructed Kiran so many years ago.

But adult Bharat, unlike child Kiran, had not needed instructions. He was observant, compliant. He had noticed, his first day there, exactly how the bed was made, and each morning he replicated it meticulously, the design on the bedspread perfectly centered, the pillows arranged, ordered, tilted in precise angles. He passed hours alone in this house every day. He knew every corner, every inch: the faded spot on the living room carpet, the slightly crooked picture frame, the creaking step, the stray glass bead on the dining room windowsill. Day after day he had heard the house whisper, had listened to it breathe. He knew its secrets.

The door groaned open. Kiran cleared his throat but said nothing.

Bharat swung around and greeted his cousin standing in the doorway: "Good morning."

"Morning." Kiran coughed. "Slept well?"

"It's your room. You should be sleeping here. I told your mother."

"I know. Don't worry about it."

"How did you sleep?"

"Still sleeping," Kiran said, rubbing his eyes. "Hey, what did your father tell you about his time here?"

"That was a long time ago."

"I know. I was just wondering."

"Papa doesn't talk much. You know that."

"Yeah, but he must have told you some stories."

"He told me some stories." Bharat placed the last pillow, fluffing it first. "You should go back to sleep. You had a long night."

* * *

Bharat found that the photograph often caught him off guard, though why should it? It was always there, just as it was in his own house in India: the slightly blurry, stern-looking portrait of the mother he had never known. He was certainly used to being in houses where his mother loomed day and night like sun and moon. Still, he found himself forgetting. He'd return from community college, climb the stairs, feeling lost, and there she'd be, at the top in the alcove, looking back at him, and he'd wonder—as he did about his own self—What is she doing here?

It was the only photograph of her as an adult (other than a few wedding photos, which were too painful a reminder for Prabhu to permit anyone to see), and so the expression on her face was the only one Bharat knew. He was told this representation was not representative. By all accounts (though there were not many; his father barely spoke of her, and his grandparents weren't much better) she was a joking, joyful woman; girlish; eighteen; still just a girl. The photo, taken for an application for a passport she didn't live long enough to receive, showed none of this.

Bharat was now seven years older than she was when she died. She was the same age as Kiran. Would she have been proud of her son? *Was* she? Was she watching over him the way her picture was?

Bharat wanted to believe. There were moments he sensed her beside him. Then he'd think it was only an air current from an open window, and he'd go to close it. He wanted to believe and didn't want to believe, the prospect of being constantly watched both comforting and terrifying. Like everyone else, he had selves that shone bright, and selves he knew were best left unseen.

* * *

Nishit had delivered his pain-is-inevitable-even-beneficial discourse many times. It was not a coach's pat no-pain-no-gain chant, but rather the philosophy of a surgeon who was accustomed to seeing bodies over time deteriorate and fail. Medically speaking, according to Nishit, everything after a certain age—say twentyish—was downhill. Our bodies never again would be so resilient, so pliant. Our brain synapses would never fire so fast. Our heart would never be so strong. Breakdowns were inevitable, Nishit said. A car could only run so long. Pain, too, was a warning, a light on the dashboard; it told us when we needed service, when we needed fuel, and when it was time to stop. Nishit was referring to physical pain, but if asked, he would insist that the same applied to other kinds. Emotional pain, like physical pain, was a fundamental truth of being alive.

It was dinner, Kiran's last night at home before returning to college. Shanti noticed him and Bharat at the table not talking, not even looking at one another, alone behind whatever walls they had erected. She wished—despite Nishit's insistence about pain—that she could take theirs away. Would Nishit say she was robbing them of something essential, a part of the very thing that made them human?

She had watched them these last days: Kiran, waking late, staying holed up in Preeti's room, then emerging ears encased in headphones; Bharat, sleepwalking, counting days, hours, until his exile would end. She watched them slide silently past each other in the hallway, strangers; worse than strangers. For reasons she didn't understand (and that even Kiran didn't fully understand), they were foes. This same sliding past would play out the next morning at the train station, cousin-brothers slipping in and then back out of each other's lives, a hard rock now wedged between them. She felt Kiran's pain especially acutely, and knew—the way mothers know, the way Kiran did not—the pain that lay ahead for him.

Pain management. Nishit spoke of this, too. It was an essential part of treatment postoperation. On a scale of one to ten—one being just a tingle, ten being unbearable—what is your pain? With children, Nishit would show them a chart of cartoon faces depicting a spectrum from elation to agony. Which one are you today? Point. As doctors, Nishit would say, their job was to guide their patients to describe their pain accurately. Then the doctors could see what they could do about managing it.

Seeing the boys with their walls up, Shanti knew they had devised their own defenses. What choice did they have? Still, she wished for them something else. She knew—from observing Prabhu so long ago, from watching Preeti these past few years, from struggling herself—what went into managing one's pain, and what, in the process, was lost.

Without realizing it, Shanti did end up contributing to an element of Bharat's pain management—not a cure, but a treatment for the Americaria Shanti didn't even know existed. It was discovered by Bharat by accident one day when Shanti, feeling chilly herself and fully aware that Bharat, unaccustomed to such cold, must be feeling even more so, had suggested he might enjoy a soak in a hot bath. She knew it would seem strange to him—no one in India took such baths, and lowering one's self into a tub of stagnant water and expecting to somehow emerge clean would seem to him preposterous—but she assured him he'd feel better afterward.

As a child in India, Shanti had taken bucket baths. Mornings and evenings she was given a plastic pail of hot water with which to wash her body. She was careful with the water, meting it out sparingly with a plastic tumbler, only half a tumbler for her face and hair; another half for her hands, arms, legs, feet; a quarter for her private areas. Her aim was to save as much water as possible, so that at the very end she could dump the bucket over her body.

She loved the feeling, the sudden rush of water on her skin: a mountain waterfall, a monsoon rain, a cloudburst. It was intoxicating. She challenged herself, each subsequent bath, to save more and more water so that the bucket, at the end, would be fuller. She loved it just as now she loved rainstorms, rushing out onto the screened-in deck whenever storm clouds gathered. Were it not for what she knew would be harsh judgment from Mrs. Yamamoto, her other neighbors, and certainly her own husband, she would have stood in the yard, her arms open, her face skyward.

Shanti had drawn the bath for Bharat—in the tub in her and Nishit's master bedroom, since the common bathroom had only a shower stall—adding a generous pour of her expensive coconut spa oil and unscrewing three of the four sconce bulbs to create more relaxing lighting. As the tub filled, she found herself thinking of Preeti's baptism eight years earlier. Ray of Light had not required a full-immersion baptism, not for adults, but Preeti had wanted one, so Chris himself built the water tank into which she was lowered.

Born again. That's what they called it, and Shanti could see it was true. Born fresh, born anew. Someone new. Shanti was surprised her daughter hadn't traded *Preeti* for some bland Christian name. Mary. Or Ruth. Preeti had worn, of course, white: in the west, the color of innocence; in India, the color of death. Corpses wore white. So did widows. Brides, embarking on new lives, wore red.

Preeti's transformation had already started, but the baptism made it complete; Shanti could see this clearly. When Preeti was lifted from the water—Chris supporting her on one side, the pastor, Chris's brother, on the other—her face displayed a joy (or was it a relief?) Shanti hadn't seen in many years, if ever. Watching Chris hold her daughter, Shanti remembered the feel of his strong hand on her own back.

Bharat's submersion in water provided a relief as well, if not quite on the same scale as for Preeti. Normally his hives arrived unexpectedly, sometimes taking—from the first prickly tingle to full-on angry red rash—an hour or more to develop, during which time he'd be progressively more and more miserable. But the hot water sped up the process: two or three minutes of intense discomfort, and then it was over. Not only that, he found that he was often, though not always, free from another outbreak for the rest of the day.

He told his aunt that the bath had worked. Not in soothing his Americaria (he had told no one about this affliction), but in warming his chill. She said, "Good; it's there when you need it." On days he had class there was no opportunity. In the morning, Shanti or Nishit would drop him, and then after his class he'd wait an hour or two until his ride was ready, a neighborhood kid named Greg who Bharat had been told was best friends with Kiran when they were very young, though they'd eventually drifted apart. But on days he was able to bathe, it was a tremendous relief. He found that when the process was sped up like that, whatever chemicals or hormones his body produced to deal with the hives also had a mild euphoric effect. He came to even, at times, in a strange way, appreciate his ailment. Bharat had grown up with a father who was numb. To feel intense pain followed by euphoria? This, Bharat decided, was preferable.

Increasingly, Michaela was missing. In her absence, Kiran and Jeffrey grew closer. Jokes shared by three were now shared by two.

She'd taken up with a warlock named Walter, a dwarflike twenty-four-year-old, already balding, who worked at a gluten-free bakery. Together, they were always trekking out to the remote farmland where Walter's pagan community observed their celebrations and ceremonies. It was an annoyance for Jeffrey and Kiran for any number of reasons, not the least of which was that Michaela was the only one among them with a car. Now they had no choice but to dawdle on campus. Not that they had any serious intentions of vacating the fourth-floor lounge any more than absolutely necessary; still, it was nice to know there were options.

Michaela convinced them to join her for a full moon festival. She picked them up in her whale of an Oldsmobile, she and Walter both wearing wool capes, and together they drove out past the edges of town, the bare branches of late autumn trees reaching toward them like gnarled hands. "Be open," Michaela said more than once in the car. Walter rested his head on her shoulder as she drove. Kiran glanced at Jeffrey sitting next to him in the backseat, allowing his gaze to linger a moment on Jeffrey's shoulder.

About twenty or thirty had gathered in the dry grasses of the open field, mostly middle-aged white folks, women with glasses, pear-shaped men with beards, though there was the stray twentysomething here or there as well as some very young children. A man with wispy hair hanging halfway down his back greeted Jeffrey and Kiran warmly. "Michaela speaks so highly of you both. You are very welcome here." The wood from a bonfire whistled and cracked.

After invocations to the north, east, south, and west, they all formed a circle around the bonfire. Each was given a white candle inside a waxy paper cup. The wispy-haired man, gesturing toward the moon, said, "The Goddess knows your darkness, and loves you anyway." They were instructed to visualize their deepest regrets, their most profound sources of shame, and to allow the flame of the candle, once lit, to consume them. Almost against his will, an image did pop into Kiran's head, one that visited him often. But he was able to dismiss it quickly, distracted by Jeffrey in stitches beside him.

The giggles started with Jeffrey, but Kiran quickly caught them. The boys tried their best to hide them. Side by side, they quietly convulsed. Kiran glanced over at Michaela, who looked so earnest, her eyes squeezed shut, holding her paper-cup candle, arms extended toward the moon. That only exacerbated the situation.

Afterward, in the fourth-floor lounge, Kiran and Jeffrey chain-smoked and snickered. Were they serious? That ritual? Those spells? Jeffrey laughed, stubbing out a cigarette, his eyes sparkling: pyrite in clear water. Kiran felt it ripple through him. Earlier, when they'd formed a circle, Kiran had held Jeffrey's hand, and it sent electricity surging through him. When he let go, his body was still tingling. Had Jeffrey felt what he felt?

"And Walter? What a putz!" Kiran said, appropriating one of Michaela's favorite insults. In the anvil game, they agreed, Walter would always end up a splat on the concrete. Though even as Kiran said this, he was thinking something else; thinking, instead, of the end of the ceremony, when they had danced around the bonfire. Kiran had not wanted to look like a dork. He hadn't so much danced as marched, trudged. Jeffrey, on the other hand, had whooped it up, but he was only being ironic. Yet Michaela and Walter: how happy they looked together. Their movements were uninhibited, utterly unself-conscious, their capes swirling around them. Kiran envied their ecstasy and abandon, but mostly he envied that they had each other. In another semester, Michaela would drop out of college and marry Walter, and not long after they would have a baby and, living above the gluten-free bakery, struggle under the weight of responsibility and parenthood. But now, dancing, they looked as if, given the right wind—and in the pull of the full moon, strong enough to swell tides—they could lift off and take flight.

Not that he was deliberately plotting against him exactly, but bearded, ponytailed Dick Phalen, adjunct instructor of accounting, did find a certain pleasure in watching Bharat squirm. After all, the questions Dick posed in class were not difficult, especially given Bharat's prior education. But Bharat never answered, not even when called on. He'd shake his head, looking tiredly at the desk in front him. He never turned in homework, didn't hand back quizzes or exams.

Three generations of Dick Phalen's family were spread across this town. He had not appreciated the way Dr. Shah—who'd been here what? barely twenty years?—had telephoned him at home and requested Dick make space in his already overenrolled intro class for his nephew visiting from India. He'd bristled when Dr. Shah, before making his request, had asked after his son, Timothy, whose femur Dr. Shah had set after a skiing accident the previous year. He had allowed them to pay the part not covered by their insurance over time, in monthly installments, announcing this concession not in private in his office and not in a discreet letter sent to their home but rather, hurriedly, in his crowded waiting room, where Dick's friends and neighbors and acquaintances might (and surely did) overhear.

So it was with some relish that Dick, after another of Bharat's in-class nonresponses, said, "Mr. Shah, it seems once again you are unprepared," adding, as he perched on the edge of his desk, "One wonders what they're teaching over there." And it was with even greater delight that, days later, he encountered Nishit at the gas station, waiting at the register, and was able to say, "It's a bit delicate, but I'm wondering, Dr. Shah, if there's something, how should I say it? *wrong* with your nephew, a learning disability perhaps? Because he seems entirely incapable of answering even the most basic questions regarding accounting. I'm sorry to report this, Dr. Shah. I know he is not taking the class for credit. Even so, I thought you'd want to know."

"He's an asshole."

Bharat had made a beeline from the classroom to the first exit he could find leading outside, the frigid air a salve for his angry Americaria. He lit a cigarette.

"Seriously, the name Dick could not be more appropriate."

Bharat looked at the young woman speaking to him. How could he be both dick *and* asshole? he wanted to ask. It didn't even make sense. Of course, Bharat had understood what she meant and knew she was just trying to be kind.

His class was not large; still, surveying her acid-washed jeans and hooded sweatshirt with enormous Greek letters, her sandy brown hair pulled back in a purple scrunchy, her full cheeks that first reddened and then whitened in the cold, he wasn't sure he recognized her. Maybe she sat somewhere behind him in the tiered auditorium. Or maybe she just looked like too many of the other students for him to distinguish her.

Later he would learn that she was a local daughter returned from one year at the University of Rochester in order to complete her core requirements at community college, where they'd be cheaper. She was planning to go back, though. She would tell him all of this when they were in her basement one evening watching *Dirty Dancing*, eating popcorn. Bharat would hear from upstairs the popping, then the ping of the microwave door clicking open and shut. He would anticipate that she'd bring down two separate portions of popcorn, one for each of them, but instead she'd pour all of the popped kernels into one large plastic bowl they would share.

"Don't let him get to you," she said now. "Maria, by the way."

"Bharat."

"I know."

Bharat was not used to kindness from classmates. Not that they were mean, but they had not been what Bharat would call warm. He wondered if it was the weather. The season's first snow had fallen a week earlier. Bharat had watched from the window until his aunt, seeing him, said, "Come." They walked together through the neighborhood, up the hill, past farm and woods. The snowflakes were enormous, like lacy cutouts made by schoolchildren. Bharat felt like he was in a movie. "It's nice now," Shanti had said, "but it becomes oppressive, and you think it will never end. Fortunate for you, you'll miss the worst of it. Come New Year's, this valley will be devoid of color, even more so than it already is." She chuckled, and Bharat understood she was making a joke about the racial demographics. Shanti sighed. "All we'll see is white and gray for three months. *If* we're lucky. Could easily be four." Bharat had already noticed his classmates starting to cocoon: layers of coats and sweaters, knit caps and gloves, thick scarves wrapped twice around necks and noses and mouths.

Standing on the sidewalk, neither he nor Maria was quite dressed for the cold. Behind them, the bland concrete structure built in the sixties sulked. "Are you going back in?" Maria asked, her teeth beginning to chatter.

"Yes. I have another hour before my ride." Still trying to tamp down his hives, he added, "But I'll stay out here for a few more minutes." He held up his cigarette. "I'm not quite done."

"I can give you a ride. I have to grab something inside, and then I'm ready to go. I'm happy to take you."

"You're so very kind, but I shouldn't. My ride is expecting me. He's in class now. He won't know what's happened to me."

Bharat offered the explanation, but it wasn't the whole reason. When Maria smiled at him, he had felt heat rise in his body. Sitting in her car next to her, he'd be risking another painful outbreak. His body was clearly trying to tell him something.

Kiran had begun seeing cranes. On the staircase in his dorm, balanced on the banister; on the counter in the bathroom at the end of the hallway; at the base of statues on the quad where Kiran smoked; on the desk he always sat at in his Cold War Rhetoric class; in the fourth-floor lounge on side tables and the arms of chairs: tiny silver origami cranes. It was weeks before Kiran even noticed the cranes, and still more weeks before it occurred to him that their placement was hardly random, that perhaps they were being left—could it be possible?—for him. But no, believing himself undeserving not just of the objects themselves but of all that the cranes represented—happiness, fortune, and in this case, though he couldn't have known this, love—Kiran couldn't accept that they were meant for him. Still, with some reluctance, he started collecting them, swiping them quickly like a thief from their perches. The shimmering creatures, made from the foil lining of cigarette packets, smelled of tobacco. And just as Bharat had kept foil papers in his drawer in India, Kiran too allowed these cranes to populate a dresser drawer in his dorm room.

Kiran couldn't imagine that they were meant for him, just as he couldn't imagine that someone had closely observed him, had memorized his schedule, first his Tuesday-Thursday schedule, then his Monday-Wednesday-Friday schedule, eventually even his weekend schedule, for Kiran was predictable and had only Jeffrey and Michaela; Kiran couldn't imagine that a shy boy in a trench coat who mumbled when he spoke (which wasn't often) was now shadowing Kiran in reverse, always just steps ahead of Kiran, leaving tokens of love where Kiran was about to pass. He couldn't know that the shy boy, as he shaped the sheets into avian kisses—the folding itself a sort of magic, nothing added, nothing taken away, the ordinary becoming extraordinary through nimble fingers, flicks of the wrist—thought of Kiran, imagined, with each fold, touching Kiran's skin, feeling Kiran's soft lips brush his neck, waking in a dorm room filled with Kiran's breath.

When the boy sat next to Kiran at a party and, unable to speak his love, and of course knowing that Kiran smoked, offered Kiran a cigarette, Kiran didn't notice that the boy had written along the length of the cigarette, in tiny meticulous blue letters, "You're fucking beautiful." Instead, Kiran immediately lit the cigarette, and the boy watched his declaration, with each of Kiran's puffs, slowly disappear into smoke.

But Kiran couldn't see the boy, couldn't see what he had written or recognize the cranes for what they were, because all he could see was Jeffrey: Jeffrey sprawled on the filthy couches in the fourth-floor lounge, the bottom of his T-shirt riding up, exposing wisps of hair disappearing into his waistband; Jeffrey in the quad, copying class notes from days skipped, his hair afire in the sunlight; Jeffrey stopping to tie his sneaker, looking up at Kiran and smiling.

There was a time, not long ago, Bharat couldn't have imagined himself in this position. These weeks in America, sitting in the community college classroom in the introductory accounting class in that auditorium with those tiny flip-up desks, not enough space to do any real work, barely big enough to open a textbook let alone take notes. The instructor in his ponytail and tie loose at the collar and ripped jeans and the students in their shapeless hoodies and unwashed hair. He'd done none of the work, not willing to waste time on material so many levels below him. He was a good son. He would come to America when told. He would make the bed perfectly. He would inspect the green beans one by one and weigh them to a fraction of an ounce. He would even smile through insults heaped by his American cousin. But one insult he would not accept: he would *not* be forced into proving his worth in an introductory-level class whose material he had mastered by age sixteen.

He knew Nishit Kaka must think he was stupid.

"Your instructor said he's offered his help again and again. You don't go to his office?"

"I don't need help."

"How could that be? You're failing. If you don't understand the material . . ."

"I understand the material. I got As in India."

"This isn't India."

No, Bharat thought. This is a third-rate community college in a fourth-rate town. But he didn't say that. He also didn't say, I attended all the same schools in India you did.

His body was a desert being dive-bombed, hives exploding on every hill and every valley. He thought how strange it was that this war could be waged in his body, *on* his body, and yet his uncle, sitting next to him on the couch, could be oblivious. His uncle's idea of what was happening as they were sitting together was so very different from what was really happening, at least for Bharat. It made Bharat wonder how often this happened in life, how little we really knew about what the person next to us was experiencing, how that person could be feeling intense pain invisible to everyone else.

"Why are you here if you're not even going to try?" Nishit asked. They were sitting in the subterranean family room, looking at each other, but in that moment neither of them was thinking about Bharat's grades or community college. They were both thinking of Prabhu.

Nishit was remembering his brother sitting there a decade earlier, how helpless he looked in the smudged eyeglasses Nishit had bought him, how Nishit had had to remove them and wipe the lenses for him.

Bharat was also thinking of his father, how Bharat and his stepmother afterward had been so hopeful when Prabhu first returned from America, how they had prayed that the visit would have energized him, shaken up old patterns, provided new perspective. But if anything, America had had the opposite effect. Prabhu had sunk even deeper into whatever darkness it was he dwelled in. Bharat could see it even as his father descended the stairs from the plane onto the tarmac, and as much as he'd hoped it was weariness from travel that dragged him down, Bharat knew it was not. Though Bharat recognized it wasn't reasonable or logical, it was hard not to blame America at least a little, hard not to include his uncle a little in that blame.

Bharat sat blinking at Nishit. There was no answer to his question, at least none that Bharat was willing to give, or that Nishit would be willing to hear.

"There's no reason not to go," Shanti said. She had just come home, and Bharat was helping her put away groceries. Plastic bags rustled on the counter and floor. Shanti shelved a packet of dinner napkins in an oak cabinet, new from a recent remodeling, and she admired the soft, smooth way the door tapped shut. It was a silly thing to care about, she realized, but she had always hated how much noise the old cabinets made.

Bharat was explaining that Maria had asked him to be her date to a semiformal at her sorority in Rochester. Maria was on leave, but knowing she'd eventually return, her sisters had invited her anyway.

"It doesn't mean anything," Shanti said. "It's very common to go to these kinds of things as friends. Both Preeti and Kiran went to their proms with classmates who were just friends."

But were they "just friends"? Bharat wasn't sure. He hadn't told Shanti about how close he and Maria had sat on the couch in her basement, their thighs practically touching, or how their hands brushed against each other's when they reached into the shared bowl of popcorn, or the way Bharat had felt himself blushing when Patrick Swayze and Jennifer Grey danced on-screen, or how Maria, during one of those moments, had flashed him a smile he could only characterize as mischievous.

Shanti, assuming Bharat was worried about Ameera, his intended, awaiting his return, said, "I assure you, there is absolutely nothing improper about it. In India, maybe. Here: no. It is all very innocent." Shanti handed Bharat two boxes of Lorna Doones and asked him to put them in the pantry, though she didn't need to tell him; he had learned so quickly where everything belonged. She tossed him a carton of Marlboro Reds. "Don't get the wrong idea," she said. "I don't approve." Bharat was touched. He hadn't even asked.

"Are you sure it's the right thing to do?"

"Listen, you're only here a few more weeks. Might as well do everything you can. You came to experience America, didn't you?" But he hadn't come to America for the experience. He'd come because his stepmother, having traumatic flashbacks of losing her own father in an accident that wasn't an accident, had given in to superstition, to fear of losing, yet again, someone she loved more than her own life. Superstition and fear—that's why he'd come, those were the reasons.

Shanti was sensing what Bharat was thinking, but she was

remembering something else: the kiss she'd shared with Chris beneath the bleachers. Despite the complications it had created in her life, she had never regretted that moment, not once. She loved Nishit—truly she did—but the passion she felt with Chris beneath the bleachers was something she had never experienced before or since. In the years to come, the memory of that afternoon would carry her through some difficult times, reminding her that for a few moments she had lived not for her children or for her husband, and not in accordance with what was expected of her by her culture or by her extended family back in India, but gloriously and selfishly and intoxicatingly just for herself.

"You're here now," she said to Bharat. "Be here. Stop being there."

No matter the years that go by, the apartments Kiran lives in, cities he moves to then flees, the men he loves, the ones he fucks, the ones who love him, the jobs he drifts in and out of, the identities he dons and sheds, the lives he survives; no matter the distance he travels, the time zones he crosses, the hair on his head that grows and grays and thins, the following is always in the present tense.

They are drunk.

They are drunk and high.

They are drunk and high, having spent the better part of the day smoking pot and drinking Jack and playing Risk on Jeffrey's PC.

The lights are all out.

The lights are all out but one, a side lamp, not standard dorm-issued, but rather something some past student, long graduated, dragged from home and left, a family castoff, a brass floor lamp with a shell-shaped shade.

The lights are all out but one, and the television, on mute, is flickering *Baywatch*. The long couches are arranged in an L-shape. Kiran is on one, lying ramrod straight, everything in a line, arms at his side, legs together. Jeffrey's lank frame is splayed on the other, appendages fanned out like tools of a Swiss Army knife: bottle opener, corkscrew, long blade, file. The heating vent groans. Jeffrey sighs. David Hasselhoff dashes across the sand and dives into a wave.

Their sofas are lifeboats, the carpet the sea.

"Hot lava," Kiran says.

"That doesn't make sense," Jeffrey says. "Hot lava would melt our boats. It's a sea."

"A sea of hot lava," Kiran says.

Their eyes closed, their boats spin.

"Don't tip over," Jeffrey says.

Kiran feels waves. They crest and crash. He closes his eyes tight, trying not to hurl. Time passes. His mind wanders. He is adrift.

Moments later, he has climbed across the coffee table aboard Jeffrey's lifeboat. If asked he'd say, "Mine sprung a leak," but Jeffrey doesn't ask. Jeffrey is passed out, mumbling something under his breath. Kiran slides under Jeffrey's arm, his face to Jeffrey's chest: plaid polyester and plastic buttons. Kiran breathes against him, smelling his own breath mixed with Jeffrey's body, his sour shirt. His mouth closes around a button. He sucks as though it is a hard candy, a Life Saver.

Jeffrey pops up. He is a mummy rising from the tomb, a monster reawakening. "Whoa!" He shoves Kiran hard. Kiran goes tumbling into the sea.

He doesn't know which is worse: the unbearable burn of the hot lava or the sense that he is drowning.

* * *

It had been years since she looked at any of the letters. It was because Kiran was now in college and she, consequently, had been thinking about her own college days and about Reshma that Shanti was revisiting them, or so she told herself. She found them where she had left them, tucked in the back of the top dresser drawer, tied with blue string. She removed the string and scattered the letters and accompanying photographs on the taut Rajasthani block print spread of the bed she and Nishit shared. She hadn't heard from Reshma in more than a decade; the phone calls, which had never been frequent to begin with, had stopped not long after the letters. Recently, a mutual friend mentioned that Reshma and Ketan had split some years ago. They'd waited until the children were teenagers and off in boarding school in Switzerland, and then they did it quietly and without much fuss.

Shanti picked up a letter at random, skimmed it, put it down, then picked up another. She glanced from photo to photo, the smiling family on safari in Kenya, at the Colosseum in Rome.

They'd been so close in college. Shanti had been there when Reshma and Ketan were matched, had whispered with Reshma at night in their dorm room. *Maybe I will grow to love him, maybe I won't. It doesn't really matter.* Now she and Reshma were strangers. Divorce, even if amicable, couldn't have been easy on Reshma, yet she hadn't written or called.

From the mutual friend, Shanti heard Reshma was living now in London. Remembering Reshma's affinity for modern design—the place settings she'd commissioned for Shanti and Nishit and which they'd never used—Shanti imagined her in the penthouse of a glass tower, all windows floor to ceiling, 360-degree views. White leather couches and sculptural lamps.

Many years ago, Shanti searched these photos for clues about Reshma and Ketan—their love, their life—but what had she thought she'd find? Could the external, frozen in a photograph, ever reveal what was going on inside? What relation did a body or a face have to the inner contents of a human heart?

When she'd first entered the bedroom, Shanti hadn't noticed that the door to the master bathroom was shut, so she was surprised when Bharat emerged, damp but fully dressed, steam rising from his skin. Bharat was surprised, too. He was surprised to find his aunt lying like that on her perfectly made bed, surrounded by old envelopes, wrinkled letters, greeting cards, fading photographs—artifacts from someone else's life.

"Oops, sorry."

Shanti quickly wiped the back of her hand across her eyes, trying to conceal that she'd been crying. She looked up at him. "It's fine, beta."

Noticing his aunt's tears, Bharat stammered, "Is there something I can do?"

"Really, it's nothing. I'm just reading old letters from a friend I once loved, but somehow we drifted apart. Don't mind your sentimental aunt."

As Bharat was leaving, he heard his aunt's voice. "Even if you love your life, it's hard not to wish sometimes that it had turned out differently." But Shanti was no longer thinking of Reshma. She was thinking of seeing Chris in line at the grocery store six years earlier, the question he had asked her—"Got everything?"—the pain of knowing that the answer would never be yes.

Maria arrived at the Shahs' front door in strappy gold sandals and a magenta sari, a sharp contrast to the gray snow on the lawn behind her. "Surprise!" she said. She hadn't told Bharat she'd be wearing a sari. She'd borrowed it from an international student at the U of R. The girl had shown her how to wrap it, but alone that afternoon, trying to replicate the technique, she'd done something wrong. Bharat could see this clearly; something was not quite right, though he couldn't place what it was. Everything seemed slightly askew.

Bharat was wearing his own trousers and dress shirt and a suit jacket his aunt had borrowed from Kiran's closet, a jacket Bharat recognized from Kiran's senior photos. There had been a flurry of activity just before Maria arrived. Days earlier, when Bharat tried on Kiran's jacket, Shanti had admitted it probably hadn't been dry-cleaned, but they both agreed it seemed OK. But wearing it this afternoon, Bharat was dogged by a musty smell he couldn't shake. He'd tried spritzing the jacket with the dregs of an all-but-empty Polo by Ralph Lauren bottle he found in the medicine cabinet, but it only seemed to make things worse. His uncle and aunt had assured him he smelled fine, but he suspected otherwise.

Shanti wanted a photo and asked them to stand in the living room in front of an arrangement of large potted plants. Bharat was familiar with this backdrop from so many of the photos Nishit and Shanti had mailed to India over the years. He'd tracked Preeti and Kiran growing up before these very plants. There had even been a photograph of his own father in this spot—Nishit and Shanti flanking him, Preeti and Kiran in front. As Shanti called, "Say cheese!" Bharat wondered and worried where this photo might travel. He didn't want anyone in India seeing it.

"You look beautiful," Shanti said to Maria. "Yes," Bharat said, "you do: beautiful." But even if the statement was true, it wasn't quite what he was thinking.

"It'll be a blast, I promise," Maria said as she started the engine of her hatchback. But Bharat knew better. He could already feel dark clouds moving in.

* * *

It was something students sometimes said in Kiran's fiction writing workshop, a class he didn't much like, but for which he had reluctantly allowed his adviser to register him because it fit his schedule and fulfilled a requirement. It wasn't uncommon for a student to stutter, when criticized for a particular scene being unbelievable or for a detail ringing false, "But . . . but . . . but . . . it really happened that way," as if, in fiction, truth mattered. While Jeffrey wasn't exactly questioning the believability of Kiran's story, he certainly was accusing Kiran of something.

It had been a week since Jeffrey had pushed Kiran into the sea of hot lava. They hadn't spoken of the incident, not even in the moments immediately afterward. Kiran had lain on the filthy carpet of the dorm lounge, pretending to be passed out, until he heard the couch springs squeak and the door to the lounge creak open and shut. The past few days, when Kiran poked his head into the lounge, Jeffrey had been nowhere to be found. A new group—taking advantage of the original trio having loosened their grip on the common room—had set up camp, staked their claim: two goth girls and boy with a leg brace. They'd draped sheer black fabric over the shell shade of the brass lamp.

Then, one afternoon, Jeffrey was there again, leaning on the arm of the couch, a textbook open in front of him, a highlighter in one hand, a cigarette in the other. Kiran had just come from the computer lab, where he'd printed a story for his fiction class.

"Will you help me proofread this?" Kiran asked, tossing the stapled pages into Jeffrey's lap. He had not intended to ask Jeffrey to read the story, but, seeing him, he'd panicked. There was so much else he couldn't say or ask. But this he could. "It's due tomorrow." (Much later Kiran would wonder: conscious or not, hadn't he wanted, in some buried part of him, Jeffrey to read it?)

Jeffrey sighed. It was easier not to argue. He shoved his textbook aside and went to work on the story.

"This is disgusting," he said when he finished, tossing the pages aside, his nose wrinkling as if he'd stepped in dog shit. "Why would you write this?"

"Because it happened."

They were both silent. Kiran searched Jeffrey's face for clues. Jeffrey, collecting his textbook, his highlighter, his half-empty pack of cigarettes, said only one word to Kiran as he exited the lounge. It would be the last word he ever said to Kiran. Winter break was just around the corner, and the chill that had entered their relationship in the last week would crystallize and freeze solid. At the start of the new semester, Jeffrey would have all but disappeared, and Kiran would know better than to seek him out. The dorm lounge would be fully appropriated by the goth girls and the boy in the brace, their black fabrics now covering couches, side tables, windows.

The word: "Dude."

Afterward Kiran would interrogate this utterance, unpacking layers of sorrow and censure, pity and disgust. He would marvel at the worlds contained within this monosyllable. It would pinball around his head.

The story: An eight-year-old boy is molested by a fourteen-year-old boy. But in the story it's not an assault, it's a seduction. The eight-year-old is complicit, willing. In the story, he wants it. After the initial incident, he pursues the older boy, he goes to him again and again, stealing moments to slink into the older boy's bedroom when he is over playing with the older boy's younger brother. They meet in the bathroom, the basement, the part of the woods called the Cathedral, lying naked together among pine needles, the older boy's baseball jersey their blanket.

That Jeffrey responded the way that he did, Kiran considered his own failing, not a moral failing or a failing of personal character, but rather a failing of literary ability (to which Kiran had never made any claim to begin with; he was a photographer, not a writer). Kiran believed that if he'd had the words to describe, in his short story, the situation properly—if he knew the words to describe the constellation of water drops on Shawn's chest, broad and wondrous as the night sky, proof of other worlds, other galaxies; or the taste of his lips, sweet like salted caramel; or his hands, the hands of a baseball star, All-American, hands that knew how to pitch and bat and catch; if Kiran knew the words for the pleasure (not pleasure, more than pleasure: ecstasy) he felt when he traced his finger along the vinyl number eight on Shawn's baseball jersey, its own infinity loop, Kiran's finger circling round and round and round; or when he laid his ear on Shawn's chest, thinking of what his father had once told him about the sound inside a seashell ("It's the sound of the ocean; the whole ocean is inside"), wondering at the ocean inside Shawn; if he knew the words to capture the tender way Shawn would brush the hair out of Kiran's eyes, the feel of Shawn's fingers on his forehead; the wisps of hair on Shawn's neck and jaw, and more hair down below, soft curls that suddenly turned coarse against Kiran's hand and cheek; a sour smell, of hormones, of adolescence, a smell that intoxicated Kiran, the scent of a body in transformation—if he had known how to do this, then surely Jeffrey, and anyone else who might ask, would understand.

Kiran believed this just as—a decade earlier—Shanti believed it about her own transgressions with Chris. Not that anyone had criticized her, not openly, but on rare occasions when she received a certain nasty look in the drugstore and she wondered, just wondered, if perhaps Pearly Franklin or Sarah Bradshaw or whoever it was somehow knew about her and Chris (although they had been so careful), she thought if only these women had felt what she felt—his large, hot palm under her blouse on the small of her back, stubble on his cheek, his hardness through his jeans (jeans Amy had picked out for the way she knew he would look in them)—they'd be shooting her other looks, looks of jealousy, not judgment.

Of course, as is often the case with the stories we tell ourselves, eighteen-year-old Kiran's recollection of those afternoons were at odds with how eight-year-old Kiran had experienced them. The memory had lived in his body all these years, transforming as his body transformed. It was like looking at multiple photographs of the same scene taken from different angles. In the photograph his eighteen-year-old self was seeing, all of the fear and confusion felt by his eight-year-old self disappeared into the background; front-and-center, in crisp focus, was desire. But which photograph was true? Were all the photographs true? Were any of them? Was his experience of those afternoons now any less true than his experience then? In some sense, wasn't his memory of it now more true, in that it continued to influence how he saw his past, present, and future?

After the Wicca ceremony, on the couches in the fourth-floor lounge, Jeffrey had not asked Kiran what he thought of when told to visualize his deepest regret, and if Jeffrey *had* asked Kiran, Kiran would not have told him, but this is the image he saw: the four-armed monster in silhouette stumbling out of the woods. But the regret itself was more specific than that. Kiran worried about the reason he had waited so long to report what was happening to Preeti. He hadn't wanted anyone to find out about what he and Shawn had been doing together. But was it really because of the shame, as he had continued to tell himself? Kiran worried it wasn't. He worried it was really because then they would have had to stop.

* * *

Bharat had begged Maria to leave the semiformal early, and now they were driving home. The snow came down faster than Bharat thought possible. Maria's wipers swiped at the snow, but it was futile: declawed Gracie swatting at a ribbon. The highway was completely covered. Shallow tire tracks, barely visible, were their only guide; that and the occasional guardrail reflector winking in the light of their headlamps.

"If I've done something wrong, just tell me," Maria said. She'd layered a shearling coat over her sari and swapped her strappy sandals for snow boots stashed in the trunk. Bharat looked at her as she concentrated on the road. Her teardrop bindi had slid sideways.

At the semiformal Maria had buzzed and bubbled. She'd been giddy, effervescent, winding her way through crowds, introducing Bharat, touching his arm lightly, bangles on her wrists. He had done his best but had little to say. It wasn't just that he was worried about his smell. When she wanted to dance, he demurred. Then he asked to leave.

"Why did you dress this way tonight?"

"Is *that* what's been bugging you?" she said, craning her neck, trying to decipher the faint outline where road became bank became ditch. "Back at the house you said I looked beautiful."

"You do. It's just, I wish you'd dressed . . . you know . . . normal."

"Why? What's wrong with this?"

Bharat found himself unable to say. Did he feel exoticized? Or did seeing a young woman in a sari make him miss India? Was her earnestness making him feel guilty for not telling her about Ameera? Or had the juxtaposition of the silk sari and shearling coat brought into focus how much he did not belong here? He didn't know the answer. It was like his hives, a pain he didn't understand and could not name.

"Americaria," he said.

"What?"

"I'm suffering from Americaria." He'd never said the word out loud—never even imagined doing it—and once he did, he heard how silly it sounded. "It's just a name I made up for my condition."

Maria shifted, sighed. "These months have been really hard for you, haven't they?"

"Yes," he said softly, a quiet admission to himself as much as to her.

The snow kept falling. The car crawled south, switching from highway to country road, burrowing deeper and deeper into the foothills of the mountains. By the time they reached it, the familiar green sign announcing four more miles had disappeared.

At the end of his four months in America, Bharat made the requisite trip to New York City. From there he'd be joining a tour group that would make its way across the United States, ending up in Los Angeles, where Bharat would catch a flight back to India. When he first arrived in America, he'd been excited about seeing the Big Apple. The thought helped get him through the lonely weeks in the small town. But now that the time was here, he hardly cared anymore. He just wanted to go home. But he knew in India he'd be asked to show his photos, and if he didn't have one of himself standing at the top of the Empire State Building or on the Liberty Island Ferry, the green statue behind him, people would wonder. He remembered seeing a photo album, a couple of years earlier, from someone else's trip: a neighbor girl about his age. She had been fitted for contact lenses especially for the trip. She was going to meet relatives. It was her first time in America. She had shown Bharat her puffy album with tulips on the cover. The photos were all in plastic sleeves. There must have been four hundred.

Shanti and Nishit drove him. They stayed overnight at Nishit's cousin Rohit's apartment in Fort Lee, New Jersey, and the next morning, they all drove into the city—Rohit's family of four and the three of them all crammed into Rohit's Mercedes station wagon. Bharat sat in the way back. Rohit's girls should have sat there, but they cried and clung to their mother and in the end it was Bharat who was put back there. Like luggage, he thought, and in some ways he understood that this was a fair comparison. For both his uncle and for Kiran, he must have seemed like baggage from the past.

After their sightseeing, Kiran was to take the train from his college upstate and meet them at Rockefeller Center for dinner. Bharat hadn't seen him since his visit home during fall break. Kiran had bowed out of Christmas. There was a skiing trip with some friends from college and something else, Bharat couldn't remember; even Nishit Kaka had seemed unclear when he explained it all to Bharat.

Waiting, Nishit kept saying, "Ten more minutes." He and Bharat stood outside the Metropolitan Museum of Art Store, where they had agreed to meet, while the others popped in and out of surrounding establishments, partly to browse, but mostly to keep warm. The girls were cranky and tired, and everyone was hungry. From outside the store Bharat had a good view of the enormous tree towering above the sunken skating rink. It was beautiful, it was all beautiful, but Bharat thought there was also something a little sad about the decorations, the elaborate shop windows, now that Christmas had passed. It was like seeing the ripped streamers and confetti the morning after the party. Finally Rohit said, "It's been an hour and a half. Kiran is not coming."

"Something must have happened," Nishit said.

Twenty minutes earlier Shanti had used a pay phone inside to call Kiran's dorm room. The machine had clicked on and beeped and Shanti had held the receiver for several seconds, trying to think of what to say, what message to leave, but in the end all she left were thirty seconds of ambient noise from the bustling corridor in the cavernous building. Much later Kiran would listen to that message and hear in his mother's silence everything she had stopped herself from saying, everything he knew she wanted to say and that he knew he deserved. He would listen to it again and again over the course of the next few weeks, a kind of torture, listening, each time, with anticipation, for the final sigh, the final exhalation of disappointment and resignation before his mother hung up the phone, until finally Kiran erased the message.

"I just hope he's OK," Nishit said as they walked the three blocks to the parking garage where they'd left the car. They'd decided there was no point eating in the city now; everything in the area was so expensive. They'd just drive back to Fort Lee and eat in the apartment.

"I'm sure he's fine," Shanti said.

"But something must have happened. This isn't like him."

It was *exactly* like him, at least of late, but Shanti didn't contradict her husband.

Back at the car, everyone resumed the seating arrangements from the morning, though it would have made sense now for the girls to sit in the way back. They were tired now, they would fall asleep in the car; they could just lie down back there. But before anyone could suggest this, Rohit lifted the back gate and said to Bharat, "Hop in, my friend," and Bharat obeyed.

Bharat slumped down and craned his neck so he could see out the window: an uncomfortable position, a terrible way to see the city. His perspective was skewed, the angle was strange. It was dark now. Lights sliced through the car—traffic lights, streetlights, lights on the signs and in the windows of the stores, store after store after store. He was riding backward, looking back at the city he was leaving, the country he would soon be leaving, too, the four months that were coming to an end.

They'd only driven three or four blocks when Bharat saw (or thought he saw), on the sidewalk, Kiran eating a hot dog. Bharat repositioned himself, put his face right up to the window to get a better look, but the light changed and the car lurched and Bharat lost his balance. "Wait," Bharat said, and then more loudly than he'd intended, "Stop!"

Rohit slowed the car. "What is it?"

Bharat pressed his face to the window, but the young man eating the hot dog was gone. "Nothing," Bharat said. "Sorry." Bharat's hives flared. He wanted to rip his skin off.

Had he seen it correctly? Hadn't that been Kiran? Wasn't that his leather jacket? And, wrapped around his collar, one of the plaid scarves Shanti had bought? She had mailed him one, given a second to Nishit, a third to Bharat as a Christmas gift, apologizing the minute he opened it. "Oh, what was I thinking? You won't have any use for such a heavy wool scarf in India. We'll return it." But Bharat wanted to keep it. As much as he had struggled in America, some small part of him liked knowing that when he returned to India on the other side of the world, his uncle, and yes, even his rotten cousin, would be wearing the same scarf he was; that they were all still, despite all their differences, somehow connected.

Interlude

A few years later, on a different block in the same city, a different cousin, a minkey, cousin-brother from the World of Cousins, traveling home by car service late at night after a sixteen-hour day as a first-year analyst in an investment bank, would have a similar experience of looking out the window and thinking he sees Kiran but not quite believing his eyes. The figure he would see would be laughing with two men, one of whom would be wearing tight leather pants, and the figure he would believe was Kiran would be swathed in a gold sari—not *swathed*, because swathed means enveloped, swathed means cocooned, and this figure would be neither. His midriff would be bare and the sleeves of his blouse very short; there would be gold metal bands wrapped snakelike around his upper arms, and though it would be dark, the cousin would notice, as the figure passed beneath a streetlamp, that his skin was shimmering with body glitter.

A few weeks later, when the cousin was scheduled to meet Kiran for brunch, he would arrive first, and while he waited for

Kiran, standing on the sidewalk, not seated at a table because the restaurant would only seat full parties, he would wonder, would worry, what Kiran would be wearing. He would remember the gold high heels, perilously high, and how assured the figure had seemed, how he didn't teeter but stomped. Waiting, he would realize he didn't know Kiran, and he would remember how close they had been as children, the long summer visits, letters written to each other on birch bark, the lake, the way they would take turns swinging from the bough of a tree and then letting go, plunging into the water. He would both long for that closeness and worry in retrospect what that closeness meant. When Kiran finally did arrive, twenty minutes late ("The F train was a disaster"), Kiran would be wearing jeans and a crewneck sweater and the cousin wouldn't mention what he thought he saw and Kiran, without lying, would be careful what he revealed about his life. Without realizing it, sitting at the table, they would turn away from one another, and this pattern would continue for almost two decades until one day the cousin would invite Kiran to his apartment on the Upper East Side. The cousin would have made more money in twenty years than Kiran would make in twenty lifetimes, and the apartment would be enormous, an entire floor of a building, with an elevator that opened into the apartment itself, and there would be a Chinese vase the size of an eight-year-old child and an original painting by an up-and-coming artist ("Art is a great investment," the cousin would say) and three separate sitting rooms. As he walked through the apartment, Kiran would worry that his shoes weren't clean enough, the same way as a child sitting in his cousin's parents' car he would worry his pants weren't clean enough, his hands weren't clean enough, because the seats in that car were plush velvet, royal blue, and the seats in his parents' cars were only ever easy-to-clean vinyl. Something in the apartment would surprise Kiran: an air hockey table. The cousin would have just bought it; in fact, it was the reason he had invited Kiran. They had played as children in the chlorine-scented concrete rec room at the Y. They would play now, and after an hour, when Kiran started to make excuses to leave, the cousin would say, "One more." When the cousin made a particularly good shot he would say "Sorry," and Kiran would remember he did that as a child, too, said "Sorry," sorry for hitting a fabulous shot, sorry for winning, sorry because it meant someone else lost. And even though that had been the cousin's verbal tic, not Kiran's, Kiran would do it now, say "Sorry" every time the puck went careening into the goal slot. Back and forth: *sorry, sorry, sorry*. Four hours would pass, and although they wouldn't talk about their two decades of near silence, they would have said that day all that they needed.

By that point in his life, Kiran would recognize how *sorry* stretched like a slick slide over huge swaths of his past. He understood this, even if he couldn't always bring himself to ride that slide for fear of where in his past it might plop him. Still, during Kiran's time in India, he'd never said sorry to Bharat for how he'd treated him in America. He'd had opportunities, had even tried to form the word, but he never quite managed. If he had, would things have turned out differently? Would Bharat, blind with rage in the yard under the peepal tree, have stopped himself? And if he had, would it have mattered?

Part
Three

WESTERN INDIA, 1998

B ut the baby hasn't even been born yet," Bharat said, trying to sound calm from behind the iron fretwork of the front door's security gate. "Come back then."

"Come back?" Guru Ma asked. The half-day journey had been an exhausting one both for her and for Pooja. The distance was not very far, but the roads were pocked and broken and indirect, and the buses were slow. And of course there had been the bus driver who had refused them passage despite their tickets and had threatened them with a tire iron, calling them "disgusting." It was especially difficult for Guru Ma. Pooja was still young, fourteen or fifteen (even Pooja herself wasn't sure exactly). But Guru Ma, though not particularly old in years, felt ancient in body. Lifelong poverty had taken its toll. "You want me to come back?" she said again. "You are telling me no? You would dare risk being cursed by a hijra?"

"No, no, nothing like that. But you have to admit, the blessing is supposed to be given upon the birth of the baby. I will welcome you at that time. Besides, if I pay you now I'm sure some other hijra will show up when the baby is born and demand additional money for the blessing."

Guru Ma looked at the man before her: his meticulously trimmed mustache, his narrow shoulders, his belly just beginning to show the telltale swell of middle-class privilege. She could tell he wasn't going to budge. He had made up his mind, made his offer, and now—standing in *his* doorway, a crowd of *his* neighbors gathered on the street, watching—he considered it a matter of pride. But behind him, Guru Ma glimpsed someone else—another man, a younger man, hair to his shoulders, and a T-shirt and way of standing that marked him instantly as foreign. She could see it immediately: he did not belong here any more than she did.

Guru Ma stepped away from the door and spoke a minute or two quietly to Pooja. She turned back toward Bharat. "Brother, I am doing you a favor," she bellowed. Bharat was now standing outside the front door's iron security gate, brushing the top step with his foot, as if Guru Ma had left behind dirt. "I am not coming back, but I'm leaving behind my daughter. The second the baby is born, you pay her. You hear me? The *second*!"

This was not the outcome Bharat had wanted, but he could see he had no choice. Guru Ma had already started to walk away. As she made her way down the lane back to the main thoroughfare, Bharat and Kiran both could already feel her absence. It wasn't just that with her went the crowd that had been following her as soon as she and Pooja had stepped foot in town. No, Guru Ma's presence itself had been gigantic. She was a star. Not the twinkle-twinkle-little-star of lullabies, but the blistering, volatile ball of fire that, up close, all stars actually were. Her presence was incendiary, all-consuming. Now she was gone, leaving behind a hole. Pooja, a flickering ember, was trying not to become ash.

If Kiran had not known quite well that this was a desert town—brown, always thirsty (the opposite of rainy, snowy Western New York)—he could have easily believed Guru Ma was the one who had left this earth scorched. The yard in front of the three-story stone house looked, by all accounts, untended: dry, rocky dirt; a few scraggly bushes; a peepal tree only half alive, literally half, one side blooming, the other bare. It was under this tree that Pooja settled. Over the years she had become adept at simultaneously being absolutely anywhere and being nowhere. So much so that, almost immediately, it was as if she'd always been right there: another bush withering in the yard.

Later that day—after she had stayed under the tree for some hours and it was clear she wasn't going anywhere—someone finally explained to Kiran about Pooja. He'd asked Bharat earlier, not two minutes after he had shut the door on Pooja, but Bharat brushed at the air with his hand and said, "Nothing. No one." Two hours later, pointing out the open window to Pooja sitting beneath the tree and inspecting the frayed edge of her lehenga, Kiran asked again, and Bharat said—again brushing at the air—"She is no one. Just ignore her."

Kiran tried asking Ameera Bhabhi, but she was preoccupied—as she always was these days—chauffeuring her belly from sofa to chaise longue to daybed. She clearly relished her upgraded status—Queen of the House—however temporary (she knew it only lasted as long as the pregnancy). "Ameera, are you comfortable? Do you need a foot rub? Let me bring you a shawl." Bharat and his mother vied for the title of Chief Supplicant. Sometimes when Ameera wanted something she would simply sigh, as though it were too taxing to even form words, and then the person within earshot would have to scramble to divine what Ameera may have wanted—lime soda? biscuits? pakora? an extra fan? or the opposite, warmer socks? best to bring it all!—and would come bumbling back into the room, arms full.

Kiran didn't try asking Prabhu Kaka, who barely left his room these days. Kiran had seen him only once since arriving two weeks earlier, which was his first time seeing him in seventeen years. Standing in Prabhu's dark room had felt to Kiran like a haunting—Prabhu Kaka himself ghostlike, the past's specter hovering, twelve-year-old Preeti's voice calling out from some distant other place—and Kiran had no intention of going back in there.

Finally, as night was falling and they were getting ready to eat dinner, he went to the kitchen to ask Kamala Kaki, whom he'd kept as a last resort due to her poor English and his own so-so Hindi. She was sitting cross-legged on the floor, rolling puris. She put down her rolling pin and held up a single finger, shaking it back and forth. "Not girl," she said. "Not boy." Then with a flat hand she made a chopping motion into her lap. Three times. Three quick chops. "Understand?" she asked. Kiran thought he did. He remembered learning about hijras in college in a gender studies class. Some hijras were biological hermaphrodites, but most were castrated men. They were considered neither male nor female but were recognized as a third gender. They were religious beings, devotees of the goddess Bahuchara Mata. For centuries they had occupied a place of respect and power—many people believed hijras had the power to bless or to curse, especially when it came to fertility and childbirth—but were now mostly prostitutes and beggars.

Much later that night, as Kiran was trying to fall asleep, he remembered something else. He got up from his bed and looked out the window. It was a Hindi movie from his childhood, *Amar Akbar Anthony*: three brothers separated as infants, one raised Hindu, one Muslim, one Christian. As adults they reunite, but they don't know they're brothers. In those days, the India Association—which was really only a dozen or so families, scattered across fifty miles of rural Western New York State—would get a different Hindi film every two months, reels someone would fetch from Buffalo or Rochester, and they would screen the film in a different family's house each time, the projector and the portable screen both property of the association purchased with dues each family paid. Kiran would sit in his mother's lap, or when he was older sit next to her, and she would whisper into his ear English translations. There was a particular scene Kiran remembered, a comic scene, garish women dancing suggestively in the street, singing off-key in deep voices. Everyone in the room laughed. Even as a small child, Kiran had recognized that laugh not as a regular laugh, but something much meaner. Kiran looked up at his mother. "What is it? What is everyone laughing at?" "Nothing," his mother had said. Now, looking out the second-floor window of his room, Pooja lying in the dark beneath the tree, Kiran thought he understood.

The next morning Kiran awoke thinking of Pooja. Power cuts in the middle of the night had halted his overhead fan, and Kiran had left the curtains open. The morning sun barreled through the window of his east-facing room: a lion pouncing on him, laying its full weight upon his body, roaring the day into life.

The details were murky and half lost to that other world, but Kiran knew Pooja had visited him in his dream. He awoke with an image of a vast field of giant sunflowers, like the ones he'd grown up with in Western New York. He and Pooja were making their way among the five-foot-tall stalks, flower heads the size of humans'. Were they trying to find a way out? Or were they happy to be wandering, lost together?

The previous day, as they watched each other through the gated doorway, standing like children hiding behind their mothers' skirts—Kiran behind Bharat, Pooja behind Guru Ma—their eyes had locked and something passed between them. In that moment, Kiran had felt with Pooja a kinship he didn't feel with his own kin. He understood what it was to be standing outside the doorway.

Upon awakening, Kiran had the immediate impulse to rush to the window, but something stopped him. He worried that Pooja wouldn't be there. Could she actually camp beneath the peepal tree without pillow or bedroll or blanket? He was skeptical. How long could she possibly stay there? Until the baby was born? How long would that be? What would she eat? If she was gone, as Kiran suspected she would be, he wanted to delay his disappointment.

Besides, during his time in India, Kiran had grown mistrustful of the window in his room, as though it were deliberately trying to deceive him. Day and night, through the open window, he heard children playing. Not just during school hours, when one might expect it, or in the evening after the worst of the heat had passed and people started coming alive again, but during all hours of the day. He heard the crack of cricket bats, laughter, the happy squeals of girls being chased. But when he roamed outside, he was unable to identify where the sounds could possibly be coming from. He searched every direction but found no schools, no playgrounds, no open spaces where children might gather. He heard, too, morning and evening calls to prayer, yet saw no mosques, and the Muslim section, small as it was, was fully on the other side of town.

And then there were the shrieks—cries he heard for days on end, so primal and human he worried someone was being hurt. He hadn't believed Bharat when he'd told him what they were. But then he saw them: two peacocks, or rather one peacock and one peahen, picking their way among the trash and the ruins of a burned-down building in the nearby abandoned lot, which seemed to have been designated as the dumping ground for the neighborhood. The male had spread its tail, iridescent and proud and impossibly beautiful among all that had been discarded.

Kiran resisted the impulse that morning to search for Pooja from his window.

He went instead to the small sink in his bedroom, splashed cold water on his face, and did not wipe it off, it felt so good on his face and neck. He pulled his hair back into a ponytail, traded his pajamas for a pair of cargo shorts and a T-shirt, and went downstairs to find breakfast.

That evening, Kiran folded food into a large leaf he'd plucked from a potted palm, food he'd surreptitiously saved from his own dinner: a bit of rice moistened by a few spoonfuls of dhal. He brought it out into the yard and, crouching, wordlessly laid it before Pooja.

Pooja herself had no explanation for the phenomenon; it was as much a surprise to her as to anyone else. Still, she understood that it added to her authenticity in the eyes of the townsfolk, buoyed their belief that she possessed powers. That was a good thing, she supposed.

They arrived the same day as she did, blackening the sky in undulating waves. The flap flap flap of their wings rippled through the town, rushed down the jumble of narrow streets in the old section like water from a cloudburst too sudden for the ground to absorb. Notoriously clever, these crows were no one's friends. They seized food, ravaged farms and gardens, squawked menacingly at passersby, swiped shiny objects left unattended. Always alert, always watching, they were nonetheless easy to forget about, the way they settled in trees, black leaves hiding among the green. Then something would excite them and make them take flight: all of a sudden the rumbling above startling as thunder.

Bharat had always known he would have a baby. He took for granted that—as an only child, and a son, at that—it was his duty to do so. What was surprising, at least to Bharat, was how the desire—the genuine, deep, pit-of-your-stomach desire—had taken hold of him, palpably and viscerally, one evening a few years earlier.

At the time he and Ameera had already been married a year and had been trying to conceive, without much luck. Bharat didn't mind. He was enjoying those early days of marriage, the occasional opportunity here or there to linger in bed with Ameera in the morning, to sun himself in her incandescent laughter and smile. Even though childless, they still weren't alone, of course: his father and stepmother lived with them. But the ancestral house was large, and it was the closest they'd ever come to being alone, and they were, after all, still getting to know each other.

On that particular evening, Bharat had gone alone for a stroll. The neighborhood was beginning to quiet; dim yellow streetlamps lit the lanes. People were pleasantly tired, having had their evening meals, their warm bucket baths. Everyone was moving slowly, the hot, sweaty day finally behind them. Soap-scented, they lazed in loose-fitting nightclothes, kurta pajamas, the occasional lungi. It was at the milk stand that

Bharat saw them: a boy and his father. The father placed some coins in the boy's hand and then, beaming with pride, and with such exquisite tenderness, lifted the boy to the counter to pay. The counter clerk smiled at him, and he smiled back, and the light from the shop fell on the boy's face in such a way that Bharat couldn't help thinking—full well knowing it was a terribly sappy sentiment, a cliché if he'd ever heard one—that the boy with his enormous, bright eyes, his luminescent face, his crisp white kurta, looked like an angel. Knowing that the father must have moments like this every day, that for him this wasn't a particularly special moment, Bharat felt such a pang of jealousy. Not just jealousy of the father, but of the son as well. Bharat did not have such childhood memories of his own father. He'd always known his father loved him, but as for tiny shared moments of joy, he could remember none. His father was so serious, so quiet. Bharat would be a different kind of father. He would laugh and lift his child into the air every chance he could get. From that moment of seeing the father and son at the milk stand, Bharat knew he wanted this. Now, years later, he was about to have it.

Bharat had indicated to Guru Ma that he'd pay the offering once the baby was born, though in truth he wasn't sure he would. What exactly was he paying for? He didn't believe in curses and didn't want to submit again to the same sort of superstition that had sent him into exile (unnecessarily, he was convinced) in America seven years earlier. He didn't believe in any of that. After all, when he and Ameera were struggling to get pregnant, it wasn't the Hindu priest, the numerologist, or the vaiddh who helped, and certainly not a hijra (never mind their purported powers to bestow fertility); it was the ob-gyn. It wasn't ancient potions or prayers that did the trick; it was clomifene tablets and intrauterine insemination.

The economic liberalization of the 1990s meant a changing India. It wasn't the India that Bharat had grown up with. His country felt to him full of possibilities, on the brink of something new. The communal riots that would ignite in the nearby city were still four years away. They would rip through the city and across the state, leaving, by some accounts, two thousand dead, mostly Muslims. Afterward there would be allegations that the largely Hindu police force did nothing to stop the slaughter. Bharat would remember the boy from his school—Aziz, Asleaze, Disease, allergic to his own sweat—and the taunts from his classmates: *Of course, even* he *can't stand himself.* He would shake his head in profound disappointment, thinking, "Nothing has changed. This is like Partition. It is 1947 all over again." But that was still four years away. Now Bharat was full of hope.

He found it difficult to muster sympathy for the hijra beneath the tree. In his eyes she was only a beggar. Worse than a beggar, because she preyed on people's fears and superstitions, claiming powers bestowed by a goddess. No, that was the old India. He was bringing a new life into the world. Which world did he want for his baby? The old India? Or a new one?

"Nice shoes," Bharat said, though they were not particularly nice shoes. They were cheap skateboarding shoes, never mind that Kiran had not been on a skateboard since childhood. Bharat was holding one, turning it over in his hands. "Heavy," he said. "Solid. Not like Indian shoes." He handed it to Kiran. Seeing Kiran's confusion, he said, "Come on. We're going out."

Kiran searched for the tag. "These were made in Bangladesh," he mumbled to Bharat, but Bharat didn't seem to hear. Kiran pulled on the shoes, having tied the laces loose enough that he could slide them off or on without having to untie or retie. Bharat held out two baseball caps and Kiran selected the blue one with the Yankees insignia because it was cotton, not stiff synthetic material, and he thought it would be more comfortable.

"Shouldn't we be wearing helmets?" Kiran asked, standing in front of the Hero Honda motorbike, even as he realized it was a silly question. He hadn't seen anyone wearing helmets.

Bharat gave him a green bandana. "Tie this around your neck. If the dust or exhaust fumes get too much, cover your mouth."

"What about the car?"

"You want to go in the car?"

Kiran hesitated. "No."

"The bike will be faster, especially if there's traffic." Bharat smiled. "You're scared? You don't trust me?"

They'd only been riding for a couple of minutes, had made not more than three turns, and already the baseball cap had flown off Kiran's head twice and Bharat had had to stop the bike and pick it up and hand it back to Kiran to put back on. The second time Bharat put it on Kiran's head himself, first tightening the band very tight, then pulling the cap low onto Kiran's head, angling the bill down with a rough motion; Kiran felt like a child being reprimanded. He did not want to hold on to Bharat when they rode. At first he tried to clutch the bar on the back of the seat, and then he tried putting his hands lightly on Bharat's shoulders. But when they were out of traffic and hit a long stretch of empty road, Kiran had no choice but to encircle his arms around Bharat's waist, press his chest into his back, and hold on tight.

Kiran noticed the other people around him on cycles, sometimes whole families: a man in front; a woman behind him riding sidesaddle and clutching an infant; an older child holding on in back. He thought about how in America if the child's car seat were facing in the wrong direction you'd get a ticket and be branded a neglectful parent or get a visit from Child Services. As they picked up speed, Kiran had visions of Bharat stopping short, of himself flying forward, his head hitting the pavement. His skull suddenly seemed so fragile.

It was evening. The sun was setting and the markets were reopening after shutting down during the afternoon heat. Couples and families congregated in outdoor cafés. Vendors served tin plates piled high with fried snacks. Bharat switched on the headlight. He hadn't told Kiran where he was taking him, and Kiran hadn't asked. So much went unsaid between them that Kiran sometimes wondered if it was a language barrier, even though Bharat spoke perfect English and Kiran's Hindi had become, well, passable.

What Bharat hadn't told Kiran was that he didn't know where they were going either. Just that he had seen in the jumble of footwear by the door Kiran's huge sneakers looking out of place—bright and loud against the brown chappals and Bata slip-ons—and he'd had the urge to remove them. And just when he was holding them, Kiran happened by and saw, and Bharat, to save face, had to hand him the shoes and say they were going out.

On the bike, Bharat wondered what Kiran saw. He remembered his own first impressions of America, peering from the car window during the long drive from the Buffalo airport to his aunt and uncle's house. Green. Everything had seemed so green. It had been an unusually cool day in late August, early morning; he was exhausted from being in transit for almost two days, breathing only the stale air of planes and airports. In the car, he cracked the window. The air was cool and rich. And green. He felt like he had never in his life seen quite this color.

Brown must be what Kiran was seeing now in this desert landscape, Bharat thought. Dust and dirt from the roads: brown. The air from the heavy traffic: brown. Bodies and faces and skin: brown.

It had been a little over two weeks since Kiran arrived from America. Kiran's parents had given Bharat instructions: "Show him where he's from. Help him understand." Understand *what*, they had not said. Perhaps they were hoping that being in the house itself would shift something in Kiran, this his ancestral home, nothing like the split-level construction he grew up in, a brand-new house, a house with no history.

Bharat's aunt and uncle, without going into details, had described Kiran as "broken," his state as "fragile." Bharat could see for himself that this wasn't quite the same Kiran he'd encountered seven years earlier (just as Kiran could see the same thing about Bharat). Kiran's eyes had taken on a dullness Bharat recognized from his own father's eyes: chunks of coal wedged in half-open lids. Still, Bharat was cautious. He felt compassion but kept it within a container. He didn't trust Kiran. He'd never thought of his own father's sorrow as stemming from selfishness, but he couldn't help wondering if Kiran's problems weren't simply solipsism, a lingering, navel-gazing teenage angst in which his first-world privilege gave him the luxury of continuing to indulge long after his teenage years were over. Still, even if Bharat felt he couldn't quite trust Kiran, he wanted to do right by his uncle, and especially his aunt, who had been so kind to him. For her, he would try his best to help his cousin-brother.

As he drove, Bharat considered where they could stop. A Mughal ruin? Was it too dark for that? A temple? Evening Lakshmi Puja? Should he drive him by the grammar school Nishit Kaka had attended?

Before he knew it, forty minutes had passed. They had arrived in the nearby city. And somehow they had ended up in the place Bharat least expected: one of the trendy new western-style coffee bars cropping up around the region. In quiet corners in back, lovers sat, some of them teenagers, some older, holding hands across tables, hoping disapproving parents (or spouses!) wouldn't see. A fair-skinned family with a plump little girl eating a whipped-cream-topped tart commandeered the leatherette couch. The sound track was heavy silverware clinking against plates and, overhead, Celine Dion belting "My Heart Will Go On."

Kiran wanted a shot of espresso, but it wasn't on the menu. "I see the machine," Kiran said to the server, "and you clearly put shots in your mocha-frappé-latte-ccinos or whatever, right? So you can pull one shot for me, just serve it straight?"

"No sir. Sorry sir. We wouldn't know how to charge that, sir."

"Charge me for a cappuccino. But hold the milk."

In the end Kiran was served, in a huge glass mug, a frothy concoction the color of wheat. He sipped, making faces. Bharat slurped, making his own faces, thinking about how his passion fruit smoothie was quadruple the price and an eighth of the quality of the mango lassi available two blocks from his house. But of course, at places like these, you weren't paying for the drinks: you were paying for the experience.

It occurred to Kiran, looking at Bharat across the table, that if Bharat still harbored resentment toward him for his bad behavior seven years earlier, Kiran couldn't tell. Still, he wouldn't blame him. Kiran *had* been a shit. Not just for the four days he was home during fall break, but the evening he was supposed to meet Bharat and his family at Rockefeller Center. He had ridden the train into the city as promised, had spotted them across the plaza, waiting outside the Metropolitan Museum of Art Store. He watched them from a distance for several minutes. His mother had found a bench and was sharing a colossal cookie in a paper wrapper with Rohit's girls and their mother. Bharat and Kiran's father were standing together, fiddling with a camera. Bharat was trying to help him with something: loading or unloading film or adding a flash, it was unclear from Kiran's vantage. Rohit was nearby, worrying his watch. Kiran checked his own timepiece, his mother's slim wristwatch she'd given him at the Elmira mall. In another two years, in the flurry of moving from one apartment to another, he would lose it, but for now he still regularly carried it in pocket, imagining (impossible as it was) he could feel its *tick tick tick* against his thigh.

Kiran couldn't join them. He had known it as soon as he'd seen them in the shadow of the towering Christmas tree, laughing families all around them. He thought of Jeffrey shoving him from his lifeboat into the pool of hot lava, and the next time he saw him, the word that fell from his mouth and exploded like an atom bomb, the fallout still settling. *Dude.* Irradiated, toxic, Kiran had to keep his distance. He couldn't risk contaminating his family.

"So," Bharat asked between sips of his smoothie, "what are your plans?"

"For?"

"For the future."

"Ah, the *future*." Kiran balanced a sugar cube on the tip of his spoon and made like he was going to catapult it. "No future!" he snarled in his best Johnny Rotten, knowing full well Bharat wouldn't get the reference.

"Didn't your parents say you studied photography in college? What do you plan to do with that?"

Kiran didn't answer. He had no idea. In the three years since graduating, he'd managed only low-level positions in fields not even remotely related to photography.

"Kiran, it's time to grow up. How old are you? Shouldn't you be thinking of your future?"

"How old were you when you came to America? Flunking Accounting 101? Smoking cigarettes on the back patio? Playing dark and mysterious stranger to some unsuspecting local girl while back here you were practically engaged? Were *you* thinking about *your* future?"

Bharat's face tightened. "In the end I've done my duty. I've made my parents proud. Will you be able to say the same thing?" Bharat took Kiran's hand across the table, unconsciously mimicking the lovers. "I'm trying to help you."

Pooja was perhaps ten when she first came to live with Guru Ma. Officially she was still Prakash then, but she had never really been Prakash; she had always been Pooja. Even the name Pooja—meaning "prayer"—had come to her when she was very young. She could remember being three years old, falling on some rocks or being hit by her mother or being left alone all day, and telling herself: *It is Prakash who is suffering. Pooja is OK.*

She lived with her mother and younger sister in a one-room shack made from scavenged lumber and corrugated metal in a chaotic shantytown along the sloping bank of the river. Looming above them was the skeleton of a hotel being slowly built; it had been almost two years already, and while many of the shantytown residents had managed to find temporary employment on the construction site, they also knew that once the hotel was completed, they would have to leave. Never mind that the shantytown had been there long before the hotel; the hoteliers would not want such views for their guests. Prakash's mother found occasional work—when they needed her—carrying rocks from one part of the site to another, and Prakash found work fetching tea during the breaks.

The day Pooja left home, she hid nearby, camping out in a quiet part of the hotel where there was no active work. She had hoped her mother would call for her—"Where is that rotten boy of mine?"—and if she had, she would have gone back. But her mother said nothing. Pooja slept there that night, and the next day, from the shadows, she watched her mother carrying rocks on her head like it was any other day, like it was not the day her son had disappeared. Pooja watched her for an hour, maybe longer, watched her in a way she never had before, her mother trudging back and forth from one rock pile to another, sweat slicking every single part of her so that her whole body seemed to be liquid, like a dirty puddle. She had to stay straight-backed so the rocks wouldn't tumble from her head, and she wore worn-out chappals, but at least she *had* chappals; so many of the other women did not. At home, Pooja's mother had been a terrifying presence; here, she looked cowed.

That night, Pooja walked. She walked through the town to its dark edge and then along the road to the next town, where she knew there was a community of hijras. That morning Guru Ma was standing in her doorway, hair unkempt, slight stubble on her cheek, but standing in the doorway nonetheless, as if she'd been waiting for her.

For his first several years living in America, first on his own and then with his bride, when something went wrong or when there was an unexpected boulder in the road and he wasn't sure he could find his way over or around, Nishit would think, We can always go back. In fact, Shanti had held on to her Indian citizenship until 2001 for that very reason. (It was only in the wake of 9/11 and her own private grief over the death of Chris's daughter, Kelly Bell, and the some three thousand other souls like her, and the way that Chris—despite his previously un-wavering, God-works-in-mysterious-ways faith, his resolve and assuredness in every situation—became a zombie, it was only after all of that that Shanti realized she was never going back to India, that this was her only home.)

When the phone call came late one night, Kiran's flatmate Penny's voice on the other end—"I'm sorry, Dr. Shah, I wasn't sure what else to do, I've never seen him like this"—Nishit's first instinct was, *Let's send him back*; "back," even though Kiran had never even been to India. Actually, it wasn't his first instinct. His *first* instinct, his and Shanti's both, was to insist Kiran return to Western New York. They wanted to hold him as close and as tight and as long as they could, as though he were a toddler who'd tripped on the stairs and needed reassurance that he was OK, that whatever sharp pain he had felt when he fell was fleeting and would leave at most a scratch. But he and Shanti understood intuitively that home was part of his hurt and that coming there would not help him. That's when Nishit thought of India. It came to him in the image that so often replayed in his head: him and his brother sitting in the second-floor window, Prabhu clipping his nails, his grip on his wrist both tender and firm. *Don't let go of me.* Nishit knew that's where Kiran needed to go. The more he thought about it and the more he discussed it with Shanti, the more they agreed. Seeing India, seeing where he was from—yes, *from*, Nishit and Shanti stuck by that word, never mind where Kiran was born and raised, he was *from* India—and being in the very house where Nishit had grown up would give Kiran perspective on his own life.

The next day Nishit made his own late-night phone call, to his brother (late night for Nishit, late morning for Prabhu), his words an echo of another very different transcontinental conversation seventeen years earlier: "Brother, I need you."

Morning, battling a summer fever exacerbated by a heat wave and which he self-treated with a high-dose injection of paracetamol, Nishit drove straight through the six hours to New York City. He loaded what he could of Kiran's belongings into the minivan, struggling down the five flights of Kiran's sixth-floor walk-up with garbage bags full of clothes and toiletries and paperback books and piles and piles of unopened mail, Kiran barely able to help, stumbling up and down the stairs like a sleepwalker. For years to come, when Nishit and Shanti visited their son in whatever apartment or house he happened to be living in at the time, Shanti would always clean. No matter how meticulously Kiran thought he had scrubbed before his parents' visit, Shanti would find a shelf of books with a fine layer of dust on their upright edges or kitchen cabinets smudged with fingerprints and she would go to work. Now it was Nishit who was tidying up after his son, more than tidying. He'd swept and mopped the floor, scattered cobwebs from corners, wiped soot from the windowsill, and now he was on his hands and knees scrubbing at a stain on the grubby baseboard. Would Penny and her new roommate—Kiran's replacement—even notice how Nishit had cleaned? He sprayed more and more cleaning solution, applying more and more pressure to the stain, while Kiran, slumped against the wall, weakly protested, "Dad, that was there before I moved in. It was already like that." Even before Kiran said this, Nishit knew the futility of his actions. Apartments like these— old apartments with decades of tenants—could never be cleaned; they bled filth from every crack, every seam. Outside the window that faced a brick wall, the gray light blackened, and Nishit set down the scrub brush. He knew they needed to get on the road. They still had a long drive home.

Over the phone, Penny had told Nishit about the job Kiran had stopped going to, the days on end of not leaving the apartment, barely leaving his room, the nonpayment of rent ("I was happy to cover Kiran one month, Dr. Shah, but I can't afford any more"). Nishit heard in her voice a hesitation and knew there was more she didn't want to say, and, truth be told, Nishit wasn't sure he wanted to hear.

Three weeks later Kiran was on a flight to India.

Guru Ma had warned Pooja about dogs. Funny that this is what she warned her about, rather than the men like wolves. Not that all men were like this. Some were deer and some were doves and some were kittens. But most were wolves, Pooja thought.

Hanuman had come to her beneath the peepal tree in Bharat's yard. She hadn't invited him, but she hadn't either pushed him away or slapped at him with the flat bottoms of her chappals as so many did. Though she tried to feign indifference, by the third day she couldn't help scratching behind his ears, running a hand, a slender, bangled wrist, once or twice down the full length of his body, not absentmindedly the way she sometimes saw the ducan-walla sitting outside on a kerosene can stroking a stray. She did it deliberately, with a smooth, firm motion. She liked that—even before she had petted him, even before she had started fixing meals of scraps for him (scraps from scraps Kiran brought her)—he kept coming to her, kept coming back to her. When at night she returned from being with the men, there he was under the tree, waiting for her. And when she slept, he lay not against her, but near her, near enough that she could hear and feel his heavy breath and he—she felt sure—could feel hers.

Guru Ma had said dogs were dirty. She'd said this years ago, when Pooja first came to live with her. She said a hijra above all else must be clean, and dogs were the opposite of clean, particularly these dogs, stray dogs, *street* dogs, filthy beasts who came sniffing at her door, who lay on her steps all day as if the steps belonged to them, as if the dogs were the ones who swept them. But even then Pooja had felt a connection to the dogs. She had known what it meant to have nowhere to go, to sleep on a step that was not yours. She had known what it meant to stray. Surely Guru Ma had known these things, too.

Pooja initially named the dog Hanuman, Hanu for short, in honor of what she interpreted as his devotion. But later she wondered if this was correct. Was he truly devoted to her the way the monkey-god Hanuman was devoted to Sita; was that why the dog kept coming to her? Or was she mistaking devotion for something more simple, more basic: desire? Wasn't it something all animals felt: this desire to lie as close as possible to another beating heart?

"Are you sure you are a boy?" Chota Kaka teased, almost an hour after Kiran and Bharat had arrived. As he chortled and trumpeted, making huge, elephant-like sounds, the other men in the room began shifting uncomfortably. "I know Bharat says you are one boy, but you seem like one girl. Are you sure you are not really one girl?"

After their tense conversation at the coffee shop, Bharat had decided that, before heading home, he and Kiran might stop in at the house of some relatives, given that they were already in the city. He was following Nishit Kaka's instructions to show Kiran where he was from. Chota Kaka—Nishit's father's brother—was someone Nishit Kaka would want Kiran to meet.

Kiran had been able to see immediately upon their arrival that Chota Kaka was drunk. It amazed Kiran how many drunk men he had encountered since being in town. He'd see them at all hours of the day, in the shops or on the street. It was especially surprising considering alcohol was prohibited in this particular region and couldn't be purchased legally anywhere.

Chota Kaka's name seemed to Kiran a paradox: *chota* means small, but he was huge. With his swollen round body and his brightly colored kurta, Chota Kaka resembled a hot-air balloon, but without the lightness. He lay only half upright, beached on a rattan chaise in the center of the room.

Kiran turned to Bharat in hopes he might defend him, but for now Bharat remained silent. Kiran couldn't blame him.

"I know how we can find out," Chota Kaka snorted. "Drop your trousers."

He was looking straight at Kiran, wild-eyed, pointing. "No? Why so shy? The women are in the other room. Maybe that is where you should be."

"Aré, Chota Kaka, leave him alone," Bharat finally said. "Just because he has long hair?" He tried to play it off as a joke. No one wanted to cross Chota Kaka or hurt his feelings. They were family, after all.

"It's not just his long hair. There is something about him. Something not quite right. I don't believe he is a boy. Why doesn't he drop his trousers? Put the matter to rest?"

"Chota, leave it," another relative said. "You honestly want this boy to drop his trousers right here in the sitting room, in front of all of us?"

"What if a lady comes in?" someone else chimed in. "You would like one of your daughters to see Kiran's pee pee?"

"You *know* Kaka in America has two children. This is the younger. You have seen so many pictures ever since he was born. What is this nonsense, Chota? Stop teasing the poor fellow."

Chota Kaka clicked his tongue and shook his head side to side. "Oh, sorry, sorry. Nothing meant. I see now, he is not a girl." With some difficulty, he rolled out of the rattan chaise, woven cane snapping beneath him. On his feet, he almost tumbled forward, stumbling his way over to the wooden ladderback chair where Kiran sat. He stood behind Kiran, lightly tracing a single index finger down the length of Kiran's hair, along his neck, and across his shoulder, before allowing it to float back down and rest on the back of the chair. He leaned over and whispered, his breath hot against Kiran's ear, "You are a gandu."

Kiran didn't know the word, but he didn't need a translation. Over his lifetime, he had heard the word *faggot* enough to recognize it in any language.

Kiran had bought the Superman journal in a moment of whimsy just before leaving for India. He had seen it on display in the bookstore at the airport, propped next to a Wonder Woman journal, which was the one he picked up first. But in the end he was seduced by Superman, in particular the lock of hair that curled in the center of his forehead. Only Superman had that lock of hair; Clark Kent didn't. Clark's hair was perfect, parted, combed.

Late that night—after having left Chota Kaka's place, Hero Honda tilting through the dark streets, and returning to his room at Bharat's house, the word Chota Kaka had called him still burning his ear—Kiran curled up in bed with the journal. His intention had been to keep notes about his experiences in India, though so far the only entry he'd written was on the eighteen-hour airplane ride over. He had noted the row upon row of old men and women in their Nehru hats and plain cotton saris, seasoned travelers, aging parents of American immigrants, shuttling back and forth between continents every couple of years. He had noted the way passengers, after dinner, impatient for the flight attendants—and perhaps thinking of them as mere servants—stacked empty food trays in the aisles, reclined their seats, belched. He had not noted the shame he felt at having to be fetched three weeks earlier, his father on his hands and knees in his sixth-floor walk-up, scrubbing. He had also not noted the apprehension he felt at having to see Bharat again, or worse, having to see Prabhu Kaka.

Kiran liked the interior marginal drawings inside the journal. In one, Superman is leaping over an art deco building. In another, Clark Kent is ripping off his shirt. In a third, Superman's back is turned and his cape is swirling behind him.

As a child Kiran had loved Superman, loved Batman and Spider-Man, too. Though he couldn't have named it, he instinctively understood the need to have dual identities, to keep secrets. But now he wondered, which was the true self, Clark Kent or Superman? Peter Parker or Spider-Man? Bruce Wayne or Batman? Which was the costume? Which was the disguise?

What Kiran loved most about his Superman journal was the hologram cover. Tilt it one way, he was Superman. Tilt it the other, he was Clark Kent. But from a certain angle, if Kiran held it just the right way, he was both at the same time.

Kiran closed the journal and set it down without having written anything about that evening. He went to the window to check on Pooja, relieved to find her beneath the peepal tree, a raggedy dog lying nearby.

How had Pooja known who she was? Kiran wondered. Later she would tell him the story of how she had been only ten when she left home and found Guru Ma. How had she understood so young? How had she been able to distinguish which was the disguise and which was the true self? Or was this very premise flawed? He wondered if the binary itself was false, duality an illusion. Perhaps the true self was always in flux, always in between. Perhaps the true self was like the hologram, simultaneously both and neither.

Kiran was not surprised to see the photograph of Neela Kaki, the same one in the alcove at the top of the stairs in his parents' house, here in India. He had already spotted it in two places: in the entryway, where everyone would see it immediately, and in the kitchen, where Neela Kaki had spent so much of her time while alive, and where Kamala Kaki now toiled (especially while Ameera was occupied with her pregnancy), her predecessor keeping watch over her. This echo of his childhood home was one he fully expected. But what he found that afternoon— wandering the rambling house, creaking open closed doors, poking in disused rooms, peeking in shut cupboards—shocked Kiran. He discovered the stash resting on shelves in a metal cabinet in a third-floor room. Although he recognized the objects instantly, he couldn't immediately process how or why they would be—of all places—here.

Yet here they were: The red Tonka truck he had thrown at his cousin-brother, the one who grew up to be an investment banker, causing a gash perilously close to his right eye (a quarter inch closer and he could have been blinded, the doctor had said), the scar still visible into adulthood, an indelible reminder of the World of Cousins long after they all drifted. The Etch A Sketch on which Kiran had learned to draw the basic outlines of his life: house, parents, sister, tree. Preeti's doll, the one with the dial on her back that shortened and lengthened her hair, and whose lacy nightgown Preeti had accidentally set on fire when she left it lying too long on a lightbulb ("I wanted it to get nice and toasty so she would feel warm in bed"). The A-frame dollhouse Preeti kept on a high shelf behind her bed and that reminded Kiran of the house of Chris and Amy Bell. And, perhaps most surprising of all: the tiger. That enormous tiger, not in the metal cabinet, but *on* it; perched, ready to pounce.

Later Kiran would learn that his mother, just as she had packed a bag of things for Kiran to bring to India, had done so for Bharat seven years earlier. For Kiran, it had been mostly old saris and salwars Shanti never wore. ("If relatives don't want them, drop them off at a temple. There are so many needy people in India.") And then of course there were the gifts— bottles of cologne and perfume; Timex watches; pistachios carefully measured out and sealed in Ziploc bags; L'Oreal and CoverGirl compacts and lipsticks in colors appropriate for subcontinental skin tones—accompanied by detailed instructions of which relatives were to receive which gifts. Shanti had hustled the three weeks Kiran was home, taking breaks from trying to soothe her suffering child in order to dash out and purchase what she could.

For Bharat, Shanti had packed many of the same items to give as gifts, but instead of her cast-off clothing, she had sent Kiran's and Preeti's childhood toys. "I'm sure you can find people who'll want them. Maybe you can keep some for your own baby," Shanti had said, winking. "Surely it won't be long." Bharat had not wanted the burden of carrying the extra luggage—particularly the enormous tiger!—cross-country during his two-week tour, but he wouldn't say no to his aunt. Shanti purchased an extra-large canvas bag that she packed herself, starting with the tiger, and then squeezing in additional toys wherever possible, wrapping them in Bharat's clothes for added padding. She had given Bharat money for any additional luggage charges he might incur.

Shut away in the metal cabinet, the toys looked to Kiran both imprisoned and displaced. Kiran had spent very little time in his Western New York home since going off to college; still, he wondered how he had not noticed these toys missing. Especially the tiger, which had once meant so much to him. It had been like a living thing to Kiran; all the toys had been. Here, now, they were dead. Or maybe they were just waiting for Bharat's baby to be born so they could come alive once more.

The previous year, 1997, had been the Year of the Two Dianas. It was the year Diana Hayden, Miss India—Indian despite what Guru Ma would say was a very un-Indian name—won Miss World. It was also the year Princess Diana died. Princess Diana's death happened first, though it would be some time before Pooja would feel its full effects, and when she did, it would surprise her that such a global event, owned and experienced by the entire world, would have such a singular and personal effect on her life, and especially on Guru Ma's.

As for the Miss World pageant, Pooja had not seen it when it first aired, but it played again and again on television; there was a period where it seemed like no matter the time of day, it was always on. She had seen it the first time at Guru Ma's house, Guru Ma spread out queen-like on her regal chintz armchair (a gift from an admirer; she did still have those), Pooja and her hijra sisters clumped on the floor at her feet. The second time, she had been alone one afternoon when Guru Ma went out and asked Pooja to stay, in case the grocer came by with lady fingers, Guru Ma's favorite. After that, Pooja caught bits and pieces of the program now and then; in Guru Ma's house there was infinite appetite for it. Over and over, Pooja watched Ricky Martin sing "Maria" and was mesmerized by the contestants in their satin sashes swaying like palms behind him. The pageant that year was in Seychelles, a place Pooja had never heard of but which sounded to her magical. In between competition rounds, the show cut to previously recorded footage of the contestants frolicking on beaches, posing in front of waterfalls, riding on yachts, smiling and waving. Smiling and waving. How much of their lives were spent smiling and waving? Pooja wondered. Pooja had never seen the ocean, wasn't even sure how far or in what direction the nearest shore would be. Her world was not much larger than what she could walk in any given direction in three days along dusty roads.

Of all the images of the pageant, it was the final one Pooja loved most. She wasn't alone in that assessment. Whenever the show was on, when it was time for Diana to be crowned, who-ever was watching would call into the street so that whichever of her hijra sisters happened to be nearby could gather around and watch: Diana in her white gown and white elbow-length gloves holding the crown atop her upswept hair while the pre-vious year's title holder, now in shadows, placed it. When Pooja was watching and when the final moment came, she did not call into the street as the others did; she wanted to savor the moment alone. Diana, after being crowned, took one final walk back and forth across the stage, smiling and waving, before set-tling into her seat—a white wicker throne threaded with white roses. Pooja knew that the path to that seat had not been easy for Diana, and yet it was where she belonged. The Diana wear-ing the crown was the Diana she was always meant to be.

* * *

Almost immediately after Pooja arrived, taking her spot beneath the peepal tree, the men started coming, sometimes three or four in a day. Young, thin-waisted men from the market, long leather belts looped one and a half times around, with extra holes crudely punched with kitchen knives. Married men with yellow-gold jewelry and gray in their chest hair, and polyester dress shirts that didn't breathe, that were redolent with sweat heavy with garlic and turmeric and ground coriander from the curries their wives cooked. Nice men and mean men. Ugly men and not-so-ugly men. Shy men who barely said a word to anyone: mice who, with her, became tigers. Rich men, not that anyone in this town was so rich, but men who sat in the back-seat of air-conditioned Marutis with tinted windows and drivers and dashboard altars to Ganesh.

Kiran sometimes saw the men from his window. He watched them arrive, watched Pooja lead them somewhere they could not be seen. They'd vanish around corners, duck into doorways, disappear down shadowy hallways and lanes. Sometimes he caught only the glint of some gold in the threads of Pooja's salwar, or heard the jangle of her bangles, but even with only these tiny clues, without even seeing her face, he somehow knew it was Pooja.

During the day Kiran would see them at the shop, the one that sold sundries, household necessities, on the main thor-oughfare around the corner from the house. He would see them loitering, looking at soap too long, waiting for Pooja to walk by. There was one man Kiran saw with particular frequency. He had yellow teeth and glasses with thick black rims, and lenses so thick that they distorted his eyes, made his pupils seem trapped, fish in an aquarium.

Kiran, too—those last, terrible weeks in New York—had had his own parade of men. Men in too-tight designer jeans. Fat men in heavy wool cable-knit sweaters the hems of which itched Kiran's forehead when he knelt before them. Men with wedding bands and hairy wrists and heavy watches they didn't remove. Young men fresh off buses from Kansas, Ohio, Indiana, still with their midwestern haircuts and vowels. *Young* men—Kiran knew better than to ask their ages. Broad-shouldered men like Chris Bell, like Matt and Rick from the water tower. Thin-chested boys like Jeffrey, boys like himself, boys like Shawn.

Then there was the man Kiran barely remembered, only that he had been very rough, had slapped Kiran's ass, had slapped his face, had pulled his hair, kept saying, *Is this how you like it, is this what you want?* and Kiran didn't know how to answer, didn't know what he wanted—he wanted all of it, he wanted none of it—so he stayed silent.

Tonight there were thick clouds, no moon, no stars, so Kiran couldn't be sure what he saw. But he knew what he heard: Pooja crying, not loud—even now she was careful not to draw attention—but crying nonetheless. The dog whimpering, barking. He heard a struggle, he heard, or thought he heard (could he really hear this from his window?), glass bangles jangling as her arm was grabbed and pulled. He heard (or thought he heard) slapping.

When he went down to the tree early the next morning before anyone was awake, Kiran confirmed what he could have seen from his window: Pooja wasn't there. He looked for clues—a broken bangle, a ripped piece of cloth, a lost sandal—but found instead, near the spot where she slept, a brown baseball-size rock, speckled like a bird's egg. It was nothing special, there were any number of rocks nearby; still, he picked it up as if it meant something, held its cool weight in his palm, closed his fingers tight around it. Back in his room he placed it on his bedside table and fell asleep. When he woke again an hour later he rushed to the window and was relieved to see Pooja asleep beneath the tree. He looked at the rock resting on the worn wood table: his only proof he had not dreamed it. He had gone down and she was not there and now she was.

The previous year, the day Princess Diana died, Pooja had not expected to find Guru Ma already awake. That's not the way it worked. Usually, one of the girls—they took turns doing this—would knock on the door; sometimes they'd have to knock hard, sometimes several times (Guru Ma was a sound sleeper), until Guru Ma answered. There were several locks to negotiate. Sometimes Guru Ma would accidentally close a lock she had already unlocked. Sometimes the girl, whichever girl it was, would stand on the other side of the door for a long time listening to the keys on Guru Ma's ring jangling, scraping against keyholes, bolts and bars and chains clicking this way and that. When Guru Ma finally swung open the door, her eyelids would be heavy, her sleeping sari disheveled, the room itself dark, the air in her one-room flat thick and stale. She would climb back onto her mattress while the girl made her way into the small kitchen at the back of the room and started preparing Guru Ma's breakfast: chai and dahi and hot rotli cooked fresh on the tava.

But today was different. When Pooja arrived, the door was unlocked, the curtains pulled open, and Guru Ma was sitting in front of the television, not on her chintz armchair but on the floor, very close to the screen, as if she had been magnetically pulled toward it. On the small television, a split screen. On one side: flashing lights bright against the faint gray-blue of early morning, police cars blocking off a narrow tunnel. On the other side: an official at a podium speaking in French, a voice-over translating in Hindi. When Guru Ma recalled it later, she said something, *someone*, had woken her early, had compelled her to switch on the television right away. She hadn't known then what it was, but she knew now: it was Princess Diana herself.

Of all her daughters, Pooja was the one Guru Ma had selected for the errand. Guru Ma would have liked to have gone herself; in fact, she knew she should go. Wasn't this errand more than an errand? Wasn't the errand itself an integral part of the devotion? But the thought of braving the bazaar on market day made Guru Ma shrink. She had never liked crowds, even when she was younger and it was easier to navigate them, before the weight gain and weak knees and before beedis had transformed her lungs into dark clouds. Now she saved her energy for performances, though those too were becoming increasingly rare. These days, her daughters did most of the heavy lifting. But occasionally she would turn out herself. On those days they were sure to collect at least double, sometimes triple the offerings. Guru Ma's powers were legendary.

Pooja kept the magazine clipping in her shoulder bag exactly the way Guru Ma had given it to her, sandwiched between stiff cardboard pieces and then wrapped in thin white cloth decorated with line drawings of Radha Krishna and red swastikas. (So small was Pooja's world, she was ignorant of how the ancient sacred symbol had been co-opted, corrupted by the Nazis, though of course that knowledge wouldn't have made her any less likely to use it or to wear it, just as it had not deterred anyone else around her.) Guru Ma had given her strict instructions not to remove the clipping until she was at the bazaar, in front of the merchant, picking out the frame. And then she was only to remove it to get the proper size and to select the perfect frame. Pooja was to ask Aravind Bhai to place the image in the frame, cutting a mat if necessary, but not cropping the image, not one single millimeter. Guru Ma had given Pooja not a small amount of money; she was to spare no expense.

Aravind Bhai had quite an array of silver frames that day, laid out on a red blanket on the ground. He had more in boxes behind him. "If you don't see what you want," he said, "ask." Pooja's hand had been instinctively resting on the bag, protecting its contents, and now she slid it inside and removed the parcel. She unwound the cloth and then lifted a cardboard piece. The image was reverse-side up, so at first she saw text from a magazine article in English she couldn't read. She flipped it over, and there she was, in all her beauty. Of the hundreds, no thousands, of images that had appeared in magazines over the past weeks, Pooja wondered why Guru Ma had chosen this one. It wasn't Princess Diana at her most glamorous, not in an evening gown or a crown, not standing straight, her head slightly turned, her neck long and regal. Instead, it was a close-up of a young Diana, premarriage but probably postengagement, judging from the pose, the quality of the photography, the lighting. And perhaps this was the reason Guru Ma had chosen it; it was the period in Diana's life when she knew she was to become a princess but before she'd actually become one. Unlike her smile in later pictures—her radiant smile, always radiant—this smile was real, or relatively real (were smiles in posed photographs ever really real?). Once the details of her unhappy marriage came spilling out, it was hard to see those later smiles as anything other than masks. But this smile was the smile of *arriving*, not of having already arrived and having realized that the ball was not at all what one had hoped.

Guru Ma had made it clear to Pooja: while she didn't want any expense spared, she also didn't want anything fussy. She wanted a frame like Diana herself: classic and modern. So Pooja selected a clean frame with neither engraving nor filigree, just an immaculate, burnished band of gleaming silver all around. She handed it to Aravind Bhai along with the clipping and the sum of money he requested. (Guru Ma had warned her not to haggle.) While Aravind Bhai readied the purchase—cutting the mat, centering the clipping, wiping down the glass—Pooja found a perch on an upturned crate outside a shop and sat quietly, watching the bustle of market day swirl around her. When Aravind Bhai finished, he handed her the package wrapped in newspaper and tied with string, and for added security Pooja wound it in the cloth Guru Ma had given her and put it back in her shoulder bag.

Pooja had not known what Guru Ma's intentions were. She knew—by the expensive frame and the careful way Guru Ma had handled the image—that it was destined for something greater than the patch of wall above her mattress covered with stills from *Stardust*: Madhuri Dixit and Kajol and Sushmita Sen. But Pooja did not expect that, upon handing the frame to Guru Ma, she would place it on her sacred altar, where she prayed every morning and night. How odd Diana—or Maha Diana, as Guru Ma would later insist she be called—looked sandwiched between Bahuchara Mata and Durga Ma, dark-haired, ancient goddesses, one riding a rooster, the other a tiger. Maha Diana: with her feathered blond hair and white teeth and blue, blue eyes.

Pooja needed a tent, Kiran decided. It wasn't safe for her to sleep like that, exposed under the peepal tree. So far, they'd been lucky not to have any rain since she'd arrived a few days earlier, but a briskness had already started creeping into the nights, and it was only going to get colder.

Ironic then that it would happen to be so hot the day Kiran—

with chilly nights on his mind—set out to find Pooja a tent. Kiran was stupid to have ventured out midday, and without even a hat or umbrella for protection from the sun. He had taken a bus from the thoroughfare adjacent to his house to the main market some kilometers away, but he had missed the stop and had gotten off too late, having to backtrack through the heat. He finally found the market and searched the stall and shops for someplace that might sell the item. He hadn't wanted anyone at home to know where he was going or what he was looking for, so he hadn't asked for help, hadn't learned the Hindi word for "tent," and even the shopkeepers who spoke English didn't seem to understand "tent" in English, so he relied on his bad drawing on a piece of paper he'd ripped from his Superman journal and his awkward charades—miming lifting the flap, stepping in, zipping the zipper, lying down to sleep—but he was met with blank looks and shrugging shoulders. He wandered around for what he thought was half an hour, but when he looked at his watch he realized it had been three. He remembered visiting only a few shops. How could it be possible that three hours had passed? It was already time to head back, and he hadn't found what he was looking for.

He was walking on the jagged sidewalk past shops on a long stretch of road with heavy traffic—a chaotic jumble of cars and trucks and bicycles, scooters and auto rickshaws, and the occasional camel or bullock—not quite sure where he was, searching for the bus he needed to return home. He choked down the exhaust fumes and reached into his satchel for a water bottle he could not find and could not remember if he had even brought. He noticed two small children, a boy and a girl, very dirty, following him, flanking him. The girl held one of her arms outstretched, her palm open. With her other hand she mimed eating, bringing the pinched fingers repeatedly to her mouth.

The first time Kiran had seen a beggar in India was just after he'd arrived, when Bharat fetched him from the airport in the nearby city to drive him to their town. Just a few kilometers from the airport, while their car was stopped at a signal, a disfigured beggar with only one arm had come and put his face right up to Kiran's window and stared at him through the glass. The signal seemed to take forever to change. Kiran went to open the window but Bharat barked, "No. It's best not to give to beggars. Others will follow and before you know it you'll be surrounded." Kiran looked away but couldn't help looking back, the man still staring at him.

Now the small boy was trying to get Kiran's attention. Kiran wasn't looking at him, and the boy started pawing at Kiran, scratching at him lightly. Kiran turned to the boy and said, "No," louder and more forcefully than he had intended. The boy continued to paw at Kiran, more insistent now; there was desperation in his persistence. Kiran looked at his filthy hand, black with dirt and soot and who knew what else, and Kiran said no again and pushed the boy hard. The boy fell to the ground, not quite into the street, but still a car driving too close to the edge of the sidewalk honked and swerved. Kiran had stopped walking now. He was looking at the boy who lay fallen on the ground, looking in his eyes, which were welling up with tears. He looked both scared and angry. The boy scrambled to his feet, scrambled, it seemed to Kiran, toward him. Without thinking, Kiran shot his leg out and with the sole of his shoes pushed the boy back onto the ground. Kiran looked, made sure the boy had not fallen into the street, saw the girl bending to help him up. Then Kiran ran. He ran as fast as he could in the sun and the heat, and when he finally stopped he was drenched in sweat, and he was panting and clutching the paper with the "tent" drawing, the ink now smeared on his hands and neck and face.

Eventually he found the bus and rode it back to his neighborhood. When he reached the busy thoroughfare where it intersected the quiet lane Bharat lived on, he did what he'd seen so many young men do—he jumped while the bus was slowing to a halt but still in motion. But Kiran misjudged the speed and he stumbled and fell hard onto the ground. The bus driver shouted something at Kiran he didn't understand. When he picked himself up off the ground, gravel embedded in his hands and forearms, dirt on his jeans, smeared ink marring his face and neck, Kamala Kaki, having just exited the small shop that sold sundries, was standing before him, watching. "I'm OK, Kaki," he said, adding, "Don't tell Bharat." He wasn't sure why he said it, only that he was embarrassed and didn't want his cousin to know how clumsy and stupid he had been.

If asked later why he had recoiled, lashed out at the beggar boy, Kiran would have blamed the heat, the hours of wandering. He would have said he was weak and not in his right mind, otherwise he never would have done it. He would not have been able to say that the boy and the girl, ragged and full of need, reminded him of his own self and sister. He would not have said how the girl's tattered dress reminded him of Preeti's ripped, soiled shirt that she held in one of her hands that evening their uncle brought her out of the woods, her small frame swimming in his brown sweater, the shirt she did not throw away as Kiran would have, but which she washed and mended in Home Ec and then folded neatly into a dresser drawer and never wore again.

Many years later it would be one of the things Kiran loved about having a dog (a two-year-old mutt he'd found tagless and terrified, starving in the woods)—how transparent and easily met her needs were, how gratifying to be the one to meet them. With a dog, how easy it was to bring happiness to another living creature. But the fierce need flickering in these children's eyes, he had no clue how to answer. He knew only to push them away and run.

There had not been much love in their household, or if there was, love was expressed in unusual ways. Was a slap across the face an act of love? Was Pooja's mother trying to teach Prakash something those nights she made him sleep outside? Was she trying to prepare him for the future? Was it her tough-love lesson about darkness and the dangers that lurked there?

In spite of the ways Pooja as Prakash had not felt protected, each fall he was presented a rakhi by his mother on behalf of his younger sister, until she was old enough to present it herself. Prakash's mother would tie the sacred thread on Prakash's wrist, a blessing from sister to brother, a promise of protection from the brother in return.

Prakash had not given these rakhis much thought. He didn't know the deliberate and painstaking way in which his mother picked out the rakhi each year. He didn't know how the salesclerks at the upscale gift shops looked at her when she came in, dirty from her day's labor. How the few rupees she would need to buy something special, something with gold thread or polished beads or a tiny, carved Ganesh, had meant planning, careful saving, and sacrifice.

It had been five years since Pooja had left home, and it was again that time of year, and she had been noticing rakhis on the wrists of all the boys and men in town. She'd noticed it on Kiran's wrist when he brought her rotis he'd swiped from his auntie's kitchen (the rakhi tied by Ameera Bhabhi; Preeti had given up the tradition even before converting to Christianity). She'd noticed it on Bharat's wrist (courtesy of the daughter of a close family friend) in the morning when he sat outside on the jhoola swing and carefully poured a few swallows of tea into a china saucer. She noticed them on the wrists of the men who lay with her each night, noticed one even on the man who had closed his hands around her throat as he slammed into her, and she thought—not in that moment, but later, when he slept briefly, his hand on her stomach—Someone loves this man; a sister somewhere is praying for him.

At first, when she was very young, Pooja had thought of the rakhis as jewelry, like the bangles or bracelets that she, as a boy, was prohibited from wearing. Later, she came to think of them differently: as markers of gender, pieces of string that, as long as they were on her wrist, would not let her forget that she was a boy. But they were also what reminded her (sometimes the only things that reminded her) that she was—in some small, difficult-to-decipher way—cherished.

The last rakhi she received as a boy was pink and mint green with faceted plastic beads and a gold foil medallion with tiny depictions of not one but three gods—Lakshmi, Shiva, and Ganesh—as if Prakash's mother knew that Pooja would need extra protection in the coming year. The medallion had come off within days, but the rest of the rakhi stayed intact for months, and Prakash was still wearing it when he left and walked the day's journey to Guru Ma's. Even there the rakhi remained on Pooja's wrist. She'd forget about it and then she'd be washing her hands or serving Guru Ma from a platter piled with afternoon snacks and she'd see the string—now faded and dingy, but still with the tiny beads that glimmered in certain light—and she would be reminded of the life she both wanted to, and did not want to, forget.

Eventually the rakhi left her. She didn't know when or how it had happened—if the threads had frayed and split and the rakhi had fallen off, or if she had thrashed about in her sleep and loosened it from her wrist. Just that one day in early spring she noticed it was gone. For a couple of days she looked for it, but with no luck. If she had found it she might have kept it: a memento of her former self, her life as Prakash.

Although Pooja didn't find the missing rakhi, it *was* found. A starling nesting nearby caught the glint among the grasses, swooped down and snatched it, and wove it among the twigs and straw of the structure that would cradle its hatchlings and shelter them until it was time for them to fly.

Earlier that year, not long before his unraveling, still living in his shared New York City apartment, the cruel sixth-floor walk-up, his bedroom a tiny closet of a space with a window that faced a brick wall, Kiran received two letters, one short, one longer.

The short one was from his mother in her unmistakable convent-school script, immaculate but written in pencil so light it was as if she were barely pressing. It was written on the back of a photocopy of a clipping from the local newspaper, an obituary for Shawn. The obituary didn't mention how he died, though Kiran had already heard through the grapevine. The obituary also didn't mention the string of drug-related arrests, the constant in-and-out of jail or court-mandated stints in rehab.

The photo accompanying the notice showed Shawn wearing a tuxedo and a bow tie and a boutonnière from what Kiran could only assume was his brother Greg's wedding the previous August, a wedding Kiran did not attend. He had received an invitation and debated going, not for Greg—he felt no particular tug of nostalgia for his childhood friend—but for Shawn. He both wanted and did not want to see him again. In the end, the cream-colored reply card sat unmarked and unreturned on top of the badly scratched chest of drawers Kiran and Penny had rescued from the sidewalk one trash day, humping it up the five flights.

In the photo, Shawn's eyes are half closed. A hand rests on his shoulder, someone who has been cropped out. Shawn is smiling his crooked, snaggletoothed smile. It is huge. He looks high on both liquor and life; genuinely, if fleetingly, happy. Or at least that's the story the photo seems to want to tell. As a photographer, Kiran understood how pictures could be made to lie. Brother of the groom, Shawn had certainly posed for more formal portraits that day. Kiran thought it was interesting that this—a candid shot during the reception on the dance floor or in some similar place—was the photo that was chosen to memorialize him.

Kiran flipped over the photocopy. His mother's letter—not a letter, more of a note—was just two sentences long: *He shot himself in the woods up Sherman Road where you kids used to play. You know the spot.*

Kiran had heard the details. In the dead of winter Shawn had wandered off into the woods. It was four days before anyone even thought to look for him. (His father, with whom Shawn still lived, said he disappeared all the time; he was a grown man and could do whatever he wanted.) And it was another three days after that before he was found in the Cathedral, his body frozen, a hole blown through his mouth clear through the back of his head.

Kiran imagined that final moment, Shawn's lips wrapped around the barrel of the gun. The woods in winter were so still. The snow, endless and deep, muffled everything. Shawn wouldn't have heard the secret sounds of the woods. Some thick-furred animal tiptoeing nearby. Water trickling far beneath the frozen skin of the creek. The blinking eyes of a red-tailed hawk perched like a Christmas tree star on top of a pine. Shawn wouldn't have been able to hear anything except his own desperate heart *thump-thump-thump*ing, calling out to be silenced. Had he thought of Preeti? Had he remembered lying naked with Kiran in the pine needles, his baseball jersey their blanket?

Three weeks after Kiran read his mother's letter, the second letter, the longer letter, arrived. Immediately recognizing the Mississippi return address, Kiran set the envelope aside, tossing it into a pilfered milk crate (stenciled "Thou shalt not steal") in the corner of his room already half full of unopened junk mail and bills, waiting for a moment when he felt brave enough to read it.

"We are special," Guru Ma said to Pooja one afternoon some years ago when Pooja had only been with her a few months. Guru Ma's flat was dark. Pooja, an hour earlier, had lowered the straw blinds for Guru Ma's nap, and while Guru Ma slept, Pooja swept the kitchen and wiped the pots and pans and utensils and started chopping vegetables for dinner. She was the only one who could do this quietly enough that it wouldn't wake Guru Ma. She wondered if it was because she was still new. In her old life as Prakash, she had learned the art of silence, of disappearance. She was so skilled people would often forget she was in a room. After she left her mother's for good, how long was it before anyone even noticed? Surely all of the girls, in their old lives, had learned the same art. But they had forgotten. In their new lives, they'd had to cultivate something different: dancing, singing, clapping, performing. To be hijra was to be—finally!—heard.

When Guru Ma woke, she called Pooja to the bed, her voice still heavy with sleep: "Beti, come." Guru Ma sat up, her back against the wall, and motioned to Pooja. Pooja, not sure she understood the gesture correctly, climbed onto the mattress, lay down, rested her head in Guru Ma's lap. Pooja's hair was still growing, no longer the close-crop cut of Prakash, but not yet the long tresses she'd always—even in toddlerhood—dreamed of. It was now a mop, a mess, shapeless and wild from the humidity. Guru Ma stroked her hair, her hand gentle on Pooja's forehead. Pooja had never been held like this.

Sounding far away, still with her big toe in the world of sleep, Guru Ma said, "We are special. We are *magic*. What they say about our powers: it is true. We see what others cannot. We know what others do not. And we can influence what happens."

Guru Ma took Pooja's chin in her hand and turned her around so Pooja was facing her. "*You* are special." She let go of Pooja's chin, put her hand on Pooja's head, one long, slow stroke, then a sigh, and Pooja knew without being told that the moment was over. Pooja wasn't sure what to make of what Guru Ma said. On one hand, she knew better than to doubt Guru Ma. But on the other hand, she had never experienced such things, had never heard a faraway voice, had never felt a gentle hand guiding her. And what was this business of being able to influence what happens? She couldn't imagine what powers she—ten years old, all but homeless, essentially a beggar—could possibly have, or how she could be capable of magic. She got up from the bed and lifted the straw blinds, sudden afternoon light hard against the laminate floor. She still had work to do.

Not long before Kiran received the two letters—one short, one long—he had sent a letter of his own, written on blue-lined paper ripped from a spiral-bound notebook, the frayed edges of which would arrive flattened when his mother, standing at the kitchen counter, opened the security-lined number ten envelope. Kiran had not included a return address on the envelope, but Shanti somehow knew right away it was from him. She knew this even before she looked at the postmark and despite the fact that she had no great familiarity with her son's handwriting—he had rarely ever written them a sticky note ("Out with friends"), let alone a letter. Kiran had used clear packaging tape to seal the flap—as if he didn't want them, or anyone else, opening it—so Shanti used kitchen scissors to carefully cut a slit along one of the edges of the envelope and slide the letter out.

Dear Mom and Dad,

I'm not going to beat around the bush. Surely, you've suspected. I'm gay.

I've known this about myself for a very long time, but it is only in the last few years that I've been able to accept it.

First, know that I didn't choose to be this way. Who would choose this?

Next, you'll want to find a reason. You'll wonder if it was something you did, or something that you could have protected me from, that made me gay. Was I born gay? I believe that I was. Regardless, as tempting as it will be, there is no point in your combing through the past looking for an explanation you'll never find. Things are the way they are.

Finally, I know you will worry about AIDS. I'll spare you the graphic details of my sex life, but please be assured that I am very careful. You have nothing to worry about.

I hope this hasn't come as a surprise to you. As Popeye says, "I yam what I yam." I hope you can accept that.

With love,
Your Son

What Kiran hadn't written in his letter was how he remembered his father watching Martina Navratilova on the television and mumbling, "She needs a good man to set her straight." Or the slight though perceptible way his father recoiled when an effeminate salesclerk in Suitings asked him if he needed help finding his size, the way he'd looked at Kiran afterward and rolled his eyes. Kiran also hadn't written anything about how he'd had to start the letter over several times, the words rendered illegible by his trembling hand.

When Nishit came home, Shanti, without a word, handed him the letter across the kitchen table and held his hand while he read it. Within the hour, Nishit telephoned his son.

"We read your letter."

Kiran, in the sixth-floor walk-up, lay on his belly on his frameless futon, his chin propped against the edge, the cordless phone in one hand, a finger from the other hand absently tracing a figure in the dust of the floor: an infinity loop, a sideways eight.

"We didn't suspect," Nishit said, speaking for both himself and Shanti, and Shanti—though she *had* suspected, had, dare she say, *known*—chose not to contradict him. Meanwhile, Kiran was thinking, If you didn't suspect, it's because you didn't want to see.

There was a silence, and then Nishit said, "We love you. Son, you are the apple of my eye."

Kiran heard the words and was truly grateful for them. But he also wondered why his father was crying. On the other end, Nishit didn't know why he was crying either, only that suddenly there seemed to be a gap between the life he had and the one he'd thought he had, a chasm between the life he thought he had given his son and the one Kiran was actually living. Nishit's foundation was shaken. It frightened him to think how often this might be the case, how often life appeared to be one way when in actuality it was really something else.

When the children were very young, Nishit read aloud to them, not Paddington Bear or fairy tales as Shanti had, but Shakespeare. Never mind that the storylines were too convoluted and macabre for young ears, Nishit wanted only the best for his children, and Shakespeare—hadn't the world agreed?—was the best. It wasn't until ninth grade, when Kiran read *Romeo and Juliet* in English class, that he realized his father had not in fact read them Shakespeare; instead, he had read them the Reader's Digest prose versions, essentially plot summaries of Shakespeare's greatest works. When he confronted his father about it, Kiran was angry—he had borne the hot blush of embarrassment in class—but Nishit couldn't understand his son's ire. Nishit remembered only how much he had loved sitting with the children, their monkey limbs wrapped around his trunk, and how he dreamed of bright futures for both of them: ages four and eight, and already they were learning Shakespeare! Neither of the children's lives had turned out anything like Nishit had imagined hunched over in his children's small beds, reading them Reader's Digest *Macbeth*.

A few days after receiving Kiran's letter, on another phone call with their son, Nishit said, "I just don't want your life to be hard." Shanti, sitting next to him, absentmindedly gazing at the Marilyn Monroe postage stamp on Kiran's envelope still sitting out on the kitchen table, silently mouthed "harder," because couldn't they all agree life was hard no matter what?

When the entire family was home one Thanksgiving some years later and the topic, uncharacteristically, came up, Kiran repeated himself: "This isn't a choice." Shanti instinctively understood what that meant. Shanti had not chosen to come to America, just as she had not chosen Nishit for her partner, not really. "Do you like him?" her mother had asked after their arranged meeting. "Do you want to marry him?" But Shanti understood even then that she didn't really have a choice. She could have said no, but who knew what the next prospective match might be like? Eventually her parents would have lost patience. She could practically hear her mother saying, "Some young women are lucky to have even one good match. Don't be greedy. You make what you can from what you are given." So many things in life had been chosen for Shanti. Why, Shanti wondered, were Americans so dogged in their belief that they could control things, that in this world they had perfect freedom of choice? Why could they not appreciate, as Indians did, the role of fate?

"I didn't choose to be gay," Kiran said that Thanksgiving, "but I *would*. If given the choice, I would choose to be gay every single time." *Who would choose this?* he had written in his coming-out letter. So much would change in the years that followed, and Kiran would realize that if being gay had made his life difficult in some ways, it had also come with invaluable gifts. But this was still many, many years away.

Kiran was lucky, he knew it. He had heard all the stories: dear friends who had been rejected from their families or tossed out of their homes at fifteen, made to live with sympathetic parents of friends or to find their own way on the streets, friends subjected to "Dear God, what have I done to deserve this?" or "As far as I'm concerned, I no longer have a daughter." Kiran was lucky; he was loved. Not that his parents were perfect, not that there weren't moments of fumbling, mistakes—past present and future—some major, and while Kiran often wondered if they were proud of him, he rarely doubted how much they loved him. But that love was both a blessing and a burden. It hurt to be loved. It hurt because it was paradoxically unconditional and loaded with responsibility. It hurt because he knew he didn't deserve it.

When Kiran arrived in India, Bharat had spoken to him of duty—dharma, a concept that looms large in Hindu culture. There was a period in one's life where duty was foremost. Once you'd fulfilled your duties—traditionally that meant getting married, raising children, taking care of your own aging parents and seeing them off to the next world—then your life was yours. Until then, you were bound.

What did all of this mean for himself and his sister— American born and raised? Surely there were not the same expectations. But there were expectations nonetheless. All parents had expectations of one sort or another for their children. And children, in turn, had expectations for their parents.

Kiran thought of his mother. She had done her duty. She had rejected Chris. She had stayed. What went into that decision, Kiran couldn't know for sure, but he knew one thing: he knew the look on her face the second after she kissed Chris, the second before she saw Kiran across the food court, peeking from behind the concrete pillar, a look he'd seen again when Chris slung his arm, big as a tree bough, across the back of their seats in the pickup truck and Kiran gazed up at his mother, a look he'd seen those two times and then never again.

In Kiran's mind, the equation worked like this: his mother had rejected her own desire to preserve the family. In reality Shanti's decision had been more complicated. But that's not how Kiran saw it, not now. He saw it only as sacrifice. Surely Kiran wouldn't be expected to make the same sacrifice, to reject his desire. But weren't there other sacrifices that were expected of him?

Now, on the line with his father, Kiran thought only of the sacrifices his parents had made for him and his sister. He heard not his father's words—*You are the apple of my eye*—but only the tears in his voice. He would rather his father shout at him than this, the certain sadness (so much worse than anger) that Kiran knew he had caused.

A week after tossing the unopened envelope with the Mississippi postmark into the milk crate, Kiran dug it out from under the additional junk mail that had since arrived. He was in his small room, sitting cross-legged on his secondhand futon mattress placed directly on the never-swept floor: a raft, grit and dirt and hair from Penny's cat gathering like flotsam at its edges. Unlike his mother's short note and his own letter, his sister's was not handwritten; it was typed, single-spaced. Even the envelope was typed. The only evidence of his sister's hand was her signature at the end, not just her first name, but her full name—first, middle initial, and last—no longer the bubbly loops of the girl who dotted the *i* in her name with a heart, but now the cold, clean lines of a woman who had no patience for frivolity.

Kiran read the letter by the light of the gooseneck desk lamp on the floor beside him.

Dear Kiran,

By now you must have heard about Shawn. I'm guessing that Mom sent you the same obituary clipping that she sent me. His death has stirred up emotions long buried, and I have been thinking again of the past, as I imagine you might be as well. I barely know where to begin, how to resume a conversation stalled almost two decades.

Let me start by saying I never blamed you. Okay, yes, I was angry. I was angry at you. I was angry at him. I was angry at myself. I was angry at Mom and Dad for not being there. I was angry at all those kids who saw me stripped naked, who kept coming back again and again, and who never once thought to go home and to tell their parents what was happening. At least I hope they didn't, because the possibility that one of them might have told an adult and that adult didn't come to help me is too horrible for me to contemplate. So, yes, I was angry. But I never blamed you.

Yet I have wondered over the years why you waited so long to bring help. I've wondered what you did in those intervening hours, where you were, what you were thinking, if you were thinking of me.

I am asking for God to give me strength to tell you now what happened that day, because for so long all I wanted to do was forget. But you need to know. Or I need to tell you. I'm not sure which.

He came to the house early that Saturday morning, throwing stones at my window. He told me that he was sorry, that he missed me, and that he had something to show me. I was glad to see him. We walked hand in hand up Sherman Road. We turned into the woods and made our way to the Cathedral.

I didn't know what was in his backpack until we were already there. He took out the Indian headband with the feather and told me to wear it. I did. He told me to twist my hair in two braids. I did. He told me to remove my shirt. I did not. He removed it for me. He held me against the tree. I struggled, but it was no use. He took the jump rope from his backpack and tied me up, all the while calling me Pocahontas.

The neighborhood kids started coming almost immediately. The first must have stumbled on us by accident, having come to the Cathedral for their own reasons. But then word spread, and soon it seemed every kid in the neighborhood had come and gone and, in some cases, come again.

When I saw you, my heart leapt. I thought, It's finally over. But you left, and it was hours before anyone came to help.

When I saw you, I had already been humiliated. But the worst was still to come. Soon after you left, the others followed suit. Shawn and I were alone again.

He whispered in my ear, "You are my Pocahontas. I am your Captain Smith." He put his hands all over me, he put his filthy fingers inside me. Even now, when I close my eyes I can still see the smirk on his face.

For years I felt those fingers inside me. My body was not my own. For years, I felt empty inside except for his hand.

When he was done, he disappeared, leaving me alone, still tied to the tree. I didn't know if anyone would come. I don't know how long it was after he left me before Prabhu Kaka arrived, but it felt like days.

I know this will be difficult for you to understand, but in spite of everything I don't regret any of it or wish it had happened any other way. Were it not for what happened, I may never have found God.

Kiran, I know you've never understood and I know you don't believe, and still I feel I must tell you the love and consolation I have found in the Lord.

After Shawn left me alone in the woods, I thought there was no point crying out, that no one would hear me. But I was wrong. God hears me. Not only that: He answers.

When I first started attending the Bible group at school and going to Ray of Light Ministries, I was attracted to how black and white everything was. Wrong or right, evil or good, there is no confusion, no shades of gray. We grew up with so much gray. Still, I wasn't sure I fully believed. I wanted a sign. And then I got it.

For Christmas, my friend Clara gave me a Verse-A-Day desk calendar. Each night I went to bed with a question. When I woke up, I flipped the page of the calendar. Every day for two straight weeks, the Bible verse directly answered my question. It was the sign I was looking for.

From that moment on, I have felt a deep and intimate relationship with Christ. I am never alone, just as I know now I wasn't alone when Shawn left me tied to the tree. God is always with me.

Kiran, I know you are struggling, I know you are searching. You don't know what you are searching for (that is the very nature of searching), but I do. I know what you're looking for, even though you don't: Jesus Christ.

I know something else, Kiran. I know what Shawn did to you. I knew it by the way he smiled at you when you came to the woods, and the way you slinked away. It was the same smirk I saw on his face later when he put his fingers inside me. I know that is why you are the way you are. I know that's why you are gay. I was your big sister. I should have protected you. I didn't. I will never forgive myself for that.

In the hospital every day, I see people suffering. I know what it looks like. I know you are hurting. Let God heal you. I don't want to preach, but my prayer, dear brother, is that you will one day find what I have found: an intimate relationship with Jesus. This world is too painful, Kiran. I don't want you to have to walk through it alone.

Love,
Preeti N. Meyers

Over the years Kiran would torture himself wondering why Shawn had hurt Preeti. After what he'd done with Kiran, was Shawn trying to assert some twisted sense of heterosexuality?

Was he trying to prove something to himself, and to Kiran? And why had he kept calling Preeti Pocahontas, when he knew they weren't that kind of Indians?

A friend of Kiran's told him she'd spent years trying to understand her own childhood sexual abuse before accepting that there was no answer. Abuse was beyond reason, she said, and to try to understand the abuser was to give him a kind of power he didn't deserve. Still, Kiran couldn't help wondering if he wasn't somehow to blame. Maybe if he hadn't followed freshly showered Shawn into his bedroom and shut the door, Shawn wouldn't have pursued Preeti, spending hours on the phone with her, Kiran in her lap. Maybe he would have never brought her to the woods.

That night after finishing reading Preeti's letter, Kiran drank until he could barely stand. Around one A.M., he stumbled down the five flights of stairs and started making his way crosstown to the Limelight, remembering Halloween two years earlier, the year he dressed as Princess Leia, marching in the Greenwich Village Parade, the sexy Jesus (there was always a sexy Jesus) and the *very* intimate relationship he'd had with him that night. At the Limelight, the thump of the techno house was loud enough and the drugs he procured strong enough to drown out Preeti's voice in his head, speaking her letter. The next morning, he wasn't sure how many men he had been with in the back room, but he imagined he could still feel their hands. Hands on his chest, on his ass, fingers *in* his ass, in his mouth. Hands on his stomach. Hands on his shoulders, on the back of his head as he sucked a cock. Hands pushing him down, holding him there. Hands that hurt. Hands that healed.

Aimlessly wandering the jumble of streets around his cousin's house, Kiran saw a man standing on the railed balcony of a concrete chawl. He was wearing nothing but a green lungi, his mouth closed around a cigarette. The man looked at him, and Kiran knew—he didn't know how he knew this, but he knew it with certainty—that inside the open doorway, deep in the shadows of the room, another Kiran, the Kiran whose father never immigrated to America, was lying on sweat-soaked sheets, trying to collect himself after having just been broken open.

Kiran had felt this sensation before. He would walk past a Dutch Colonial in Bethesda, Maryland, and would know that there was a Kiran who would live there, whose son, not yet born, would bounce a basketball against a garage-mounted backboard. Or he would peer from the sidewalk into a white-clothed restaurant in TriBeCa and know that the Kiran who got into Princeton and became a banker, the Kiran who was heterosexual and who married his childhood sweetheart, Kelly Bell, was eating seared ahi across the table from her.

Sometimes he could feel these other Kirans tapping at his shoulder, Kirans from other worlds, their hands having somehow slipped through the walls that separated this world from theirs, having found a crack in a window, curling their fingers underneath, prying it open. Sometimes they scratched at him. Sometimes they pulled at his clothes. But mostly when he felt them, they were gentle; he felt their hands pressing on his back. An infinite number of Kirans. It made him feel both inflated in a Walt-Whitman-Song-of-Myself-I-am-large-I-contain-multitudes kind of way and also tiny like a grain of sand. It made what this Kiran did in this world mean both more and less.

If it was true for himself, it was true for others. Somewhere there was a Prabhu whose wife didn't die. A Shanti who had stayed with Chris. A Bharat who fell in love with Maria and remained in America. A Kelly Bell who called in sick the day the towers were attacked. Somewhere there was a Preeti who never went with Shawn. A Shawn who never hurt her. A Kiran who didn't wait to call for help.

Other selves, other worlds. Was it possible? Kiran remembered hearing a theory that the universe was really a multiverse where any and every alternate self and outcome existed. In another model, the universe was like an origami object. Each facet, each plane, was a different world, a different point on the time-space continuum. But then it would flatten out and you would realize it was just one single flat piece of paper: the other selves, the other worlds, were really all one. Then as quickly as it had flattened out, the paper would fold itself into something new—a sailboat, a cat, a crane, a rose.

* * *

"You don't believe all that Maha Diana stuff, do you?" Kiran asked after Pooja had told him the story of Guru Ma's devotion. "That she is a goddess?"

It was evening. The two had become close in the week Pooja had been there. It happened quickly. They told each other their stories, though they hadn't needed to; they had known each other from the start. They were walking along the banks of the wide river, which seemed gentle, though Bharat had warned Kiran that the current was much more powerful and dangerous than it appeared. Earlier, Kiran had bought a double string of marigolds from a street vendor, and Pooja was now wearing the flowers in her hair, bursts of orange entwined in her black braid.

Kiran had watched Princess Diana's wedding when he was eight: 1981, the Year of the Mouse, the year his uncle Prabhu had come to live with them. In fact, the wedding had been just days before Prabhu Kaka's arrival, before everything was to change for all of them.

His mother arranged pillows and couch cushions and comforters on the green carpeting in the subterranean family room in front of the only color television in the house, and they slept there overnight. Shanti, Kiran, and Preeti: three burrowing creatures, huddling close. They had to wake up very early, and this way they would not have to go anywhere, would not have to climb stairs or fumble for house slippers, would not have to miss a minute.

Kiran marveled at the tiara, the ivory taffeta gown, the impossibly long train, *enormous*, everyone said, but it had to be long, Kiran thought, for surely such a colossally bright star would leave a glittering trail of proportional length. Kiran marveled, yes, but he was careful not to marvel too loudly, lest his mother and sister take note. He shouldn't have bothered trying to hide his emotions: Shanti and Preeti could feel excitement rising from him like steam. For her part, Preeti—who had already begun to experiment with the eye-rolling, too-cool-for-school posture de rigueur for the town's teenage girls, particularly for one on her way to becoming a cheerleader—was plainly awestruck. She audibly gasped when Diana first emerged from her glass carriage.

But it was Shanti who was most transformed. She was girlish in the way her hands fluttered and clapped when something exciting happened: the Queen making her appearance in a blue hat, or Diana gliding down the aisle, or the couple kissing their clearly passionless kiss on the balcony of Buckingham Palace, though who would have thought at the time that it was anything other than innocence and shyness. Shanti had not noticed it while watching the ceremony, but afterward the commentators made a big deal about how the couple had omitted the word *obey* from the vows.

After it was all over, Shanti served tea: not the chai she simmered with cardamom and cloves in a dented, handle-less stainless steel pan she lifted using metal tongs, but rather proper English tea, made weak for the children, poured from a porcelain teapot and served with the Nabisco Social Tea Biscuits she usually reserved for company.

Kiran asked Pooja, "You don't actually believe that Princess Diana sends—what's her name . . . Guru Ma?—messages, do you? You have to admit it's pretty far-fetched."

Pooja touched the marigolds in her hair. "In your world," she said. "Not in ours."

Watching the wedding with his mother and sister had been one of the last times Kiran had felt so close to them. Years later, he watched Princess Diana's funeral alone. He was moved by her younger brother's fiery eulogy; his excoriation of the press for hunting her; his coded criticism of the royal family. Her brother made a wish that her children, unlike their mother, would have a life not circumscribed by "duty and tradition" (Kiran remembered his word choice so vividly), but one in which their "souls" could "sing." He was so fierce in the way he defended his sister, continued to defend her, even after she was gone.

"We live in the same world," Kiran said.

"Don't be so sure."

The words coming out of Pooja's mouth were Guru Ma's, not her own, but even as she said them, she felt that—perhaps for the first time—she believed them.

Pooja removed one of the marigold strands from her hair and reached to put it in Kiran's.

"Don't," he said.

"But you look so lovely," she said. "And your hair is even longer than mine!" Kiran relented, and Pooja wove the garland into his hair. For a moment together they were girls giggling.

Pooja plucked one of the blossoms and popped it into her mouth, smiling.

"What does it taste like?"

"Sunshine. Joy." She picked another blossom and held it to Kiran's mouth. "Taste." At first he resisted. Then he closed his eyes and opened his mouth and let her feed it to him like prasad.

"So? Joy?"

Kiran looked at her. When he was her age, roaming the halls of his high school, he was invisible—ironic, since being one of the only brown-skinned kids, he should have stood out. But he'd been grateful to fade into the background. Camouflaged, he could keep his true self hidden. But here was Pooja, hiding nothing. He was beginning to understand how brave she was, how much she had to risk every day to be who she was, and how much she'd been forced to sacrifice in the process.

"Joy . . . ," Kiran said, ". . . dish detergent." He made a face. Pooja laughed, though Kiran knew his joke made no sense in Hindi.

"Brother, are you sure you even know what joy tastes like?"

If he had known that Chota Kaka was dropping by, if Chota Kaka had given any notice, Kiran wouldn't have stayed at home. To make matters worse, it was early afternoon and Bharat was still at work and Kamala Kaki was preparing dinner, so Kiran was left to entertain Chota Kaka on his own.

Chota Kaka was wearing another brightly colored kurta, this one an orange that made Kiran think of mango sherbet, though his uncle was anything but sweet. Still, his demeanor was a little different today. There was none of the chortling, with its scary dark edge. Chota Kaka was almost serene, sitting on the daybed, one leg folded below his fat belly Ganesh style.

"Dear boy, I have an important question to ask you," he said grandly while popping pistachios into his mouth, shelling them with just one hand, prying them open with a single thumb and dropping the shells onto the glass-topped cocktail table. Kiran waited for the question, but Chota Kaka was taking his time.

"I have known your father since he was a baby. I washed his dirty bottom more times than I can count. Which brings me to my important question." Chota Kaka inspected the nut in his hand a moment. "My, this is delicious pista! You brought this from America, didn't you?" Kiran nodded. "See, see, I know. You think I don't know, but I do." His voice lowered slightly. "I know everything.

"As I was saying," he continued in a louder voice, "I have known your father his whole life. I know lots of secrets, lots of juicy-juicy tidbits about your father, your mother, everyone. Someday maybe I'll tell you. But that's not what I want to talk about now. I want to ask you a question."

Kiran reached for a pistachio from the quickly diminishing stock, and Chota Kaka slapped his hand away.

"Your father loved India. He was such a happy boy. It wasn't easy for him to leave. But he did. Do you know why?"

"Because he was doing what his father told him," Kiran answered.

"Yes, true, but that's not the whole story." Chota Kaka didn't describe for Kiran the day Nishit had come to him and sat on the floor by his rattan chaise—as Nishit's father had certainly instructed his son to do—and asked for money to help with his journey to America, a journey that was supposed to benefit eventually the entire extended family. "Your father might have said no. He could have convinced his father. He was so charming, so persuasive."

Kiran had never thought of his father as charming. As a child, he'd only ever seen his father as embarrassing.

"He came for you. You and your sister. He thought things would be better for you in America. That's why he sacrificed, leaving the country he loved, leaving behind his own brother. Who knows how Prabhu's life might have turned out if your father had stayed? But he did it for you. So let me ask you: Was it worth it? To your father, was it worth it?"

At some point, without Kiran noticing it, Chota Kaka had finished the pistachios and moved on to a small glass bottle of Johnnie Walker Red Label that must have been hidden in one of the folds of his flowing kurta. The afternoon was wearing on, the heat causing Chota Kaka to slowly melt to mango syrup. But Kiran hadn't answered Chota Kaka's question, and Chota Kaka continued to call from the puddle he had become, his very voice liquid: cloying, clawing. "Tell me, gandu, what would your father say? Was it worth it?"

When Pooja told Kiran she had never had her picture taken, Kiran couldn't believe it. He had been inside, looking out the window, admiring the late-afternoon light bathing the yard in a warm glow, and he decided to come out with his camera to capture what he could of it. He'd brought his expensive camera with him from America, intending to document his experiences in India, though, as with the Superman journal, he had barely touched it. From inside he had not noticed Pooja, but now here she was, sitting on the ground with the dog he had come to think of as hers, and he asked her if he might snap a picture.

His Hindi being what it was, he was never completely sure he was saying what he meant or that he understood what he was being told; there was always the possibility of error. "Never?" he asked. "You have never had your photograph taken?"

"Never."

Kiran's own life had been documented in such a feverish and relentless way, starting from infancy: hundreds of photographs if not more, a dozen photo albums in the cabinets beneath the bookshelves in the family room, framed photos sitting atop credenzas and side tables and hung on the walls. After his parents acquired a video camera when Kiran was in high school, there were videos, too: Kiran, a selected participant for the Senior Waltz (chosen no doubt more for his contribution to "diversity" than for his grace or dancing ability), the video shot entirely in zoom, no wide shots to get the full effect of the choreographic formations, just five shaky minutes of close-cropped Kiran and Jodi Klinger stumbling through Tchaikovsky's "Sleeping Beauty."

He wondered how his parents had decided which of the hundred of photographs to frame, to hang. Did those pictures remind them of particularly happy moments? Did they reinforce some narrative his parents wanted to believe about their lives, about their children's lives? He thought of a snapshot they had enlarged and hung on the wall next to the stairs leading up to the bedrooms. In it, Kiran is five or six, hunched over homework, pencil in hand, his father sitting next to him, helping. Kiran looks like he is concentrating so hard, as if he is solving a difficult mathematical proof, though he couldn't have been doing anything more complicated than "Trace the dotted line to complete the letter A." There was another photograph of him reading *Time* magazine while sitting on the toilet, clearly posed. He must have been three.

Kiran thought of another framed photograph, this one the black-and-white, garlanded portrait of Neela Kaki in the illuminated alcove at the top of the stairs. The exact same photograph had greeted him when he first arrived in India. Even though it had creeped him out as a child, here it was a source of comfort; he had been looking into those eyes his whole life. The photograph was not a flattering image, and many years ago, when he asked his father why that particular image was chosen to remember her, he explained it was one of very few photographs that had ever been taken of her. Cameras were not so cheap back then, not in India, and many people didn't have them, not families like hers. They would have to go to a professional studio to have their pictures made, and where was the money for that? They were all lucky they had even this photograph to memorialize her, his father said.

"I want to take your photograph," Kiran said to Pooja again.

The light was beautiful. Kiran had come outside thinking he might photograph the dramatic peepal tree, half alive, half dead, or the potted jasmine with its delicate petals in the corner on the porch. But now he wanted something edgier, something human. In New York, he had seen an exhibit of Diane Arbus photographs—outsiders, people on the margins: dwarves and giants, circus performers, the transgendered, the morbidly obese—and he had something like that in mind for his portrait of Pooja.

Pooja fiddled with a crow feather. She wasn't sure it was exactly true that she had *never* had her photograph taken. She had performed at plenty of weddings and births. Surely someone had snapped a photo. But she'd never been asked, and she certainly had never seen a photograph of herself. She thought of the framed photograph of Princess Diana on Guru Ma's altar. She thought of the photographs of Diana Hayden in her tiara and her long white gloves.

Kiran lifted the camera. "No," Pooja said. "Not here, not now."

"Why? This is perfect."

"How? I am sitting in the dirt with a dog."

"But that's perfect. We'll never have light like this again, the way it is hitting your face. You can't see what I see. Trust me. You look beautiful."

Pooja felt her face get hot. Had he just called her *beautiful*?

"Brother," she said, "just now I am not beautiful. Tomorrow. Wait until tomorrow. Tomorrow I will show you."

Kiran didn't want to wait. This was the photograph he wanted. He already had an image of how the photograph would look hanging on the wall of his apartment in New York, not the sixth-floor walk-up, but a new apartment, a better one. He would enlarge it and frame it with a gallery-quality frame. Maybe it would even get him into a group show in Williamsburg or SoHo. He would title it something simple and descriptive: *Village Scene, Western India, 1998*. Never mind that this wasn't really a village (the place where he grew up in Western New York was a village). This was more like a small town on the outskirts of a large one. But "village" seemed right for the photograph.

"Let me snap a few now," Kiran said. "I have plenty of film. We'll do more later."

"No," Pooja said. She was not used to saying no, and it was particularly difficult to say it now. Of everyone in this family, Kiran was the only one who had shown her kindness, who had brought her food, who had smiled. They'd grown so close during their walks by the river. Was it right for her to deny him?

She said, as firmly as she could, "Brother, tomorrow."

After Guru Ma returned home after leaving Pooja at Bharat's house to wait for the birth, she immediately arranged for some things to be sent for Pooja with a friend she knew would be passing through town. Not much. A sleeping mat. A cotton blanket. A pink bar of Lux soap. Two changes of clothes. These simple outfits wouldn't do for Pooja's portrait. She wanted something special.

If Kiran photographed her from the waist up, she didn't have to plan a whole outfit. A beautiful dupatta draped modestly over her shoulders would do the trick. Guru Ma had taught her the art of illusion. No one who saw the photograph would know that beneath the stole was a dingy cotton blouse.

One of the men who came to see her at night owned a shop. She had walked by one evening and seen him standing on the steps and recognized his name on the sign: "Manoj's Saree Emporium." The men from the shops on either side of his were standing on their steps, too, and one of them said loudly to the others—"Do you smell something? Is there a wet dog trotting by?"—and the men laughed.

Pooja knew this game. It was the game people played with hijras. She was supposed to say something sassy in return, snap her fingers, clap her hands, maybe make a joke about their manhood. Her job, after all, was to entertain. Their job was to remind her that she was not one of them. But she had not wanted to play that evening. She looked at Manoj. He had been tender the night he was with her. He had stroked her hair afterward. Now he was laughing with the men.

When she and Guru Ma first came to the town on that very first day, on their way to the house where the baby was to be born, they had stopped at each of the stores and extracted what they could from the merchants as payment of sorts, as was their right as hijras. Sometimes it was money. Often it was merchandise: a scarf, glass earrings, a lipstick. They had already taken from Manoj what was due. Pooja couldn't now demand more. And the money she had collected from the men who came to her was not enough for the quality of dupatta she wanted. Besides, Guru Ma surely knew all about the men and certainly was expecting her cut.

She still didn't know how she was going to convince Manoj

to give her the dupatta when she arrived at the back entrance to his store, just as he was closing for the afternoon. Almost immediately she regretted having come the way she did. She should have come during regular business hours to the front entrance. Who knew if Manoj would have let her in, but she should have insisted. She should have picked out something simple, something she could pay for in cash. She should not have come scratching at his door like an animal.

Manoj smiled at Pooja, and she could not tell what kind of smile it was. Was it too late to change her mind? She wondered if she could still pull out her packet of folded rupee notes and be any other customer: a housewife, a dentist, a businesswoman, a servant girl.

Manoj put his arm around her, placed the palm of his hand against the small of her back, pulled her toward him. He took her hand and brought it to his crotch, which was already hard.

The several minutes she was with him, as he was pressing himself against her, she found her thoughts wandering—for reasons she couldn't explain—to her mother. She thought partly of what her mother had done for money over the years. Pooja had watched her mother carry rocks on her head from one end of the construction site to the other, imagined the ache she must have felt in her neck and shoulders and legs from the weight pressing down on her. It was Pooja's last image of her mother.

But mostly what she was thinking about was the portrait Kiran was going to photograph. She couldn't imagine a scenario that might lead to her mother's seeing it, but what would she think if she did? Pooja hoped she would recognize her, would see the ghost of ten-year-old Prakash inside fifteen-year-old Pooja, something about her eyes or the tilt of her head, something that in all these years hadn't changed, something only a mother might know. She wanted her mother to see the dupatta—silk brocade, an article so fine her mother never could have dreamed of such a thing for herself—and think Prakash was right to have run away. She hoped her mother would be proud of what Prakash became.

After it was over, and after she had explained what she needed it for, Manoj gave her a dupatta. Not the one she had wanted, not the one on display, but one from the stock in back, maybe not as beautiful as the one she had had her heart set on, but beautiful nonetheless. It was only for borrowing, he said. She must be very careful with it, he didn't want to see even the tiniest speck of dust when she returned it. And she must not, under any circumstances, allow anyone from town to see her in it; otherwise, he'd never be able to sell it. With his hand he cupped her chin and raised her head so that their eyes met. "Darling little dog, you'll look smashing."

"Try to act natural," Kiran instructed. Even as he spoke, Pooja was striking a pose, her head angled slightly away, her eyes directed coyly toward the camera.

When he'd come outside that evening, Pooja was already waiting for him. He had intended to wait until after the photo shoot, but on impulse he decided to give her the gift right then: a CoverGirl compact and lipstick his mother had sent for relatives. Pooja had been overwhelmed—"For me? Really?"—and sat in the yard applying the makeup immediately, peering into the tiny mirror of the shiny compact, despite Kiran's insisting that she didn't need any more makeup for the photo. When she was done, he lifted his camera, but Pooja protested and made him follow her fifteen minutes to a nearby garden on the riverbank. She was carrying a ratty cloth satchel, and when they arrived she withdrew from it a black plastic bag with gold letters that read "Manoj's Saree Emporium." Carefully she unfolded the silk dupatta and draped it over her shoulders, allowing part of it to cover her head.

"Natural," Kiran said again. "Try to pretend I'm not here." Pooja turned to a rose on the trellis she had insisted on standing in front of and brought the blossom to her nose, narrowing her eyes and dramatically breathing in its scent.

Kiran sighed. He didn't know what else to do. Fine, she could have it her way. Kiran would find a way to make the photo work. He let the shutter flicker rapid-fire, *click-click-click-click-click*, quick as a machine gun, and then he stopped to reload.

Her name was Zena, but Kiran had not known that, not when he first saw her the previous year in New York. There was a party on a barge and the song "Choli Ke Peeche Kya Hai" came on and the crowd parted and there was Zena, in a lime-green chaniya choli, performing a perfectly executed lip-synch-and-dance routine. A few months earlier, home for a visit, Kiran had sat with his father and watched the scene in the movie where the village women are taunting Madhuri Dixit—*What's beneath your blouse? What's underneath your veil?*—and Madhuri replies, surprisingly and triumphantly, *My heart.* In the movie, as in all her movies, Madhuri is ethereal, transfixing. Zena, on the barge, was no less so. Reenacting the scene from the movie, Zena's backup dancers sang the same questions, but Zena added her own twist. She lifted her skirt above her ankles, her knees, her thighs: *My heart!* The audience erupted in whistles and cheers.

Several days later, when Kiran spotted Zena seated at a bar, he almost didn't recognize him out of drag. As a woman, Zena had been strikingly beautiful, impossible to turn away from, at least while she was performing. But as a man, he seemed to

Kiran dumpy. Without makeup he had terrible skin, Kiran could see that even in the dim light. Were it not for a distinctive mole on his cheek and something about the way he moved when he got up to go to the bathroom, Kiran wouldn't have recognized him at all.

"I think I saw you perform a few nights ago? On a barge?"

"Yes."

"Kiran."

"Gaurav."

"You were . . . well . . . spectacular. I barely have words. How did you learn to do all that?"

Gaurav smiled. "You'd be surprised what you can learn from an older sister."

Not long after meeting Gaurav was the one and only time Kiran dressed in drag, not counting his Princess Leia Halloween costume, of course (Halloween didn't count). He and Penny were throwing a party, and they were worried that no one would come or that too many people would come or that they should have cleaned the apartment more carefully or splurged on higher-shelf liquor and fancier canapés.

Gaurav came over early to help Kiran dress. The week before, Kiran had asked him to accompany him sari shopping in Little India. He had hoped Gaurav might offer to loan him something, but he didn't, so they went together to the shop. The salesgirl—truly a girl, a bucktoothed teenager fresh from India (a *fob*, Kiran would have called her some years ago)—refused to believe that the sari was for Kiran, even when he emerged from the dressing room wrapped in it. She giggled from behind her hand. He couldn't afford any of the fine chiffons and had to settle for a gold-colored synthetic blend that didn't move the way he wanted and whose shimmer was five levels louder than Kiran would have preferred.

In order to allay their anxieties, Penny kept assuring, "It will be dark and everyone will be drunk. No one will care or notice anything." Gazing in his bedroom mirror just moments before the first guests were to arrive, Kiran hoped it was true. He had to admit it was a cheap-looking sari, and Gaurav, a genius with his own makeup, had been a little less successful with Kiran's. Still, looking at himself, Kiran did think, if only for a second, of his mother and his sister, even if he couldn't remember the last time he'd seen either one of them wearing a sari (had Preeti ever worn a sari?).

The length of fabric that covered the bodice and hung over the shoulder was dotted in small silver hearts, which somehow due to the draping ended up upside down. Gaurav said they could redo it, but Kiran liked it. To him the upside-down hearts seemed somehow appropriate.

He and Penny had been right to worry. The party was almost immediately a disaster. The boom box ate the mix tape Kiran had spent hours making. Penny, drunk before the party even started, burned the canapés in the oven, and, crying, tossed the blackened cookie sheet onto the coffee table, causing three people seated on the couch to startle and jump. Kiran hadn't practiced walking in heels, and the slippery hardwood floor proved too much of a challenge; he kept tumbling, knocking down guests, their drinks crashing to the ground.

Kiran was surprised and somewhat distressed to notice that in attendance was Timir, a popular boy of the queer desi scene into which Kiran was only beginning to find entrée. Though they barely knew each other, there was already bad energy between them, though Kiran wasn't sure why. Kiran spotted Timir and his best friend, Hasina, holding court on the couch. Timir had taken seriously the semiformal dress code. He wore a crisply ironed blue dress shirt of thick, luxurious cloth tailored to his trim frame. Around his neck was a beautiful silk tie knotted in a full Windsor. On his chest, the tie formed an upside down exclamation mark; the point was his perfectly proportioned face. But even as his tie was exclaiming, Timir was sulking. Everything in his body language indicated boredom.

Who could blame him? Kiran himself was bored. After it was clear the night was going nowhere, a friend said to Kiran, "Let's get out of here. We look too damn good to waste our time at this lame-ass affair." Just outside the doorway, they bumped into Timir and Hasina, now lingering in the hallway. Timir looked Kiran up and down. "Nice outfit . . . ," he said, and then to Hasina, in a voice clearly loud enough for Kiran to hear, ". . . for a hijra."

In spite of what Timir had said, Kiran felt fierce storming down the sidewalk, and then later sashaying around the dance floor at the Roxy. Gold bands winding snakelike around his upper arms made him feel like a gladiator, like a goddess. He thought of Preeti that day at the Fiesta Cantina in Myrtle Beach, her hair, nails, makeup hard as armor. He felt, tonight, powerful.

Pooja was quiet. As they walked back from the photo shoot on the riverbank, she had listened to Kiran tell of Gaurav, of Zena, of himself in the gold sari, the upside-down hearts; she had heard in his voice a lilt, a laugh. She had listened to him griping about the boy who tried to cut him down. (Kiran had not told Pooja that Timir called him a hijra, but he had not needed to.) She had heard him say, "And those heels! At the start of the night, I kept falling, but by the end I was stomping that runway like a real queen. I have so much respect for you. I don't know how you do it."

When they arrived at the house, Bharat was sitting on the

jhoola swing on the porch. He looked at them, looked at Pooja in particular, with an expression she recognized. It was the same expression on the face of the bus driver waving a tire iron, refusing to allow her and Guru Ma to board. It was an expression she had been seeing her whole life. Bharat shook his head and then got up to go inside.

"Something's wrong," Kiran said finally. "Tell me."

Pooja hesitated. She hugged the ratty cloth satchel, inside it the Manoj's Saree Emporium bag and the CoverGirl compact and lipstick. "Why did you tell me that story?"

"What do you mean? It's a fun story, right?"

"Do you think I'm playing dress-up? Do you think I'm trying on a costume?"

"No, Pooja. I don't think that. I'm sorry."

Pooja had to admit, Kiran was one of the better ones. At least he hadn't asked her about her genitalia, as so many did, whether she had had the ritual castration, their faces a mix of fascination and revulsion. Still, she had hoped for more.

"Brother, forget it."

"I won't," Kiran said. "I'm sorry."

"You can't trust her," Bharat said, his mouth chewing a big bite of roti sabji.

"Who?" Kiran asked.

"You know who. Don't play dumb."

Kamala slapped a steaming roti, fresh from the stove, onto Kiran's stainless-steel thali. She'd already fed Ameera and Prabhu, locked away in their respective rooms, Ameera busy tending the future, Prabhu the past. After the boys finished eating, Kamala would serve herself.

"They are liars and cheats," Bharat said, "not to mention unclean. You absolutely should not be associating with a hijra.

What would your parents say? Never mind yourself, you are bringing shame on us. *We* are the ones who have to live here."

"Kamala Kaki, what do you think?" Kiran asked.

Kamala had no experience with hijras. Still, dark-skinned and pinched-faced, she had been ostracized as a child and well into her young adulthood. Before being matched with Prabhu, she had spent more than her fair share of time sitting alone in the dirt.

"You are lucky to be getting hot-hot rotis. Your mouths should be chewing, not flapping," Kamala said.

Bharat squeezed extra ghee onto his roti, dispensing the liquid from a repurposed plastic bottle of Vaseline Intensive Care. "You're not from here," he said, "you don't understand. These people are desperate. They are capable of anything."

Kiran peered out his window into the night sky, the constellations a map of the past, the light having set out thousands of years earlier to reach them. There was a scene in a movie he had watched with Penny in New York. It occurs just before the movie's climax and cuts back and forth among four characters, all in different places, all looking up at the night sky. The four of them are so different and in the dark they yearn for such different things, but the stars above them are the same. Penny, an aspiring director, had said the filmic device was cheap. But Kiran was moved.

After he'd abandoned their party and things had begun to sour between them but before the worst of Kiran's downward spiral, Penny had called Kiran a brown dwarf. At first Kiran thought it was a swipe at his skin color and height (though he wasn't exactly a shrimp, Kiran could at least admit his height was below average). Penny explained that a brown dwarf was a failed star. "It never lives up to its promise. It doesn't have what it takes to be a star, so it masquerades as a planet. But it's not really that either. It's basically a fraud."

Kiran looked down at Pooja lying beneath the tree, the dog curled at her feet. He had fucked up. Not just with Pooja. He had fucked up so much, and he didn't know how to fix any of it.

It was too dark for Kiran to tell whether Pooja was asleep. Perhaps she was awake, he thought. Perhaps she was gazing at the same stars he was. Bharat and Prabhu Kaka. Maybe they were also sleepless tonight.

"It's time," Ameera said, standing in front of Bharat in the hallway. Her face opened before him like a present. He took both her hands in his, stood very close to her, and repeated, a broad smile on his face, "It's time?"

Ameera, returning Bharat's smile, nodded. "Mh-hm."

Gently guiding his wife through the hallway, Bharat moved slowly down the stairs, but inside his body his spirit was bounding. Kiran could see this clearly. He was sitting on the jhoola swing when they came onto the porch. Light leaped in Bharat's eyes, jumped to Ameera's, and back to Bharat's.

"We're headed to the hospital," Bharat said. "Tell my parents."

The excitement was contagious, but Kiran couldn't help remembering that the baby's arrival also meant Pooja's disappearance. The baby may have been ready, but Kiran wasn't.

Ordinarily he liked to develop his own film, but without access to a darkroom, he had to rely on a local photography studio. He had stopped in four shops before deciding, choosing the one with the clerk who seemed the most professional and spoke the best English and the one which displayed the best-looking samples. He'd have them print four-by-six copies, matte finish with a white border, two copies each so he'd have something to gift Pooja, but when he returned to America he planned to make his own prints from the negative.

When Kiran fetched the photos, the clerk eyed him, but said nothing. Over time the clerk had seen all manner of photos: vacation snaps, yes, but so much else. The rolls of film he processed were a window into his customers' private lives. He knew their secrets. Perhaps most significantly, he knew—not just from the subject of the photos, but the way the shots were framed, the perspective, the angle, the gaze—how his customers viewed the world. He saw what they saw, the way they saw it. The photos were a reflection of the photographers as much as of what they were photographing.

Kiran waited until he was outside to open the packet. A fat cow lying in the alley twirled its tail lazily and licked its nose. Someone dumped a bucket of water from a second-story window, and it splashed Kiran's pant cuffs; he looked with irritation at the fresh stain. Flipping through the prints, he was surprised. That afternoon, Pooja had looked luminescent, elegant, her delicate shoulders wrapped in the embroidered dupatta, her lips the rich red of the lipstick his mother sent. At least that's how he remembered it now. And that's how he understood Pooja saw herself. But the girl in the photo looked awkward and cheap. Wide-shouldered, and with light and shadows accenting her Adam's apple dusted with the tiniest bit of black fuzz, she didn't look like a girl at all: she looked like a boy in a dress.

In the evening, when they were sitting on the wall in the garden by the riverbank, the very place they'd shot many of the photos, Pooja asked Kiran, "Where are they? You got them today, right? I want to see." There was a pleasant breeze blowing across the river, carrying faint sounds of bhajans and bells from a temple somewhere in the distance. High above them the crows had taken to the air for their nightly show: fighter jets flying military exercises lest anyone forget their might. Pooja shook her hair back, a coquettish move Kiran had seen performed by any number of models, young women in music videos, and, years ago, his own teenage cheerleading sister.

In one world, Kiran would return to New York and make huge prints of the photos and exhibit them in a Chelsea gallery where, opening night, guests would comment on the images' grittiness, how *real* they were. Overnight he would become a minor art-world sensation, and his career as a photographer would be launched.

In another, he would rip up the images and place them at the bottom of a plastic bag, which he would then fill with vegetable peels and spoiled food and throw in the trash.

Kiran rested his hand on the thick envelope hidden inside his satchel. "We'll look at them later," he said.

"Later? Why? Let's see them now."

"Actually . . . sorry . . . I didn't want to tell you. I knew how much it all meant to you. But . . . they ruined the negatives."

"Ruined?"

"Yes."

"All of them?"

"All of them."

Pooja looked into the distance. Farther downstream on this very river—Pooja wasn't sure exactly how far down—was the shantytown where Prakash had lived with his mother and younger sister. Surely the hotel was finished by now; surely the shantytown was gone.

"I'll take more," Kiran said. "I've learned from our first photo session. Now I know the correct light and angles to capture your best qualities. These will be even better."

The sun was just rising when Kiran heard it, all at once, a cacophony outside: Hanu barking wildly; Pooja pleading, "No!"; hard open-hand slaps vibrating like tiny earthquakes across the yard; and Bharat growling in a voice Kiran had never heard, "I will kill you! I will fucking kill you!"

Kiran ran to the window. Bharat had taken hold of Pooja by the hair and was dragging her across the dirt. One of her hands was holding her hair, desperately trying to save her scalp, the other was struggling to keep her skirt down.

"You've done this, you goat-fucking whore! I will make you pay!"

"Brother, please, no!"

"Don't call me brother, you filthy cunt!"

Kiran saw Bharat turn and kick Pooja. She covered her face with her hands. Her body curled into itself. Hanu pulled at Bharat's pant cuff, but Bharat kicked him away. He raised his whole foot and positioned it over Pooja, bringing it down in a loud stomp. "It's your fault. *Your* fault!"

Kiran rushed to the other side of the room and grabbed the speckled rock from the bedside table. Back at the window, he took aim at his cousin. He heard Shawn's voice, "You throw like a girl. You throw like a *girl*." He hurled the rock at Bharat as hard as he could. He didn't stay to watch its sad arc, its limp landing in the dry bush. He raced down the stairs, three at a time, bolting out the front door, onto the porch past the jhoola swing, out into the yard.

The Dianas held vigil in the hospital room. Maha Diana, aka Princess Diana ("Diana, really, please, just call me Diana"), charmed all the orderlies and nurses. She wore a jade-colored salwar kameez, the scarf modestly covering her head, and folded her hands, bowing "Namaste" to everyone who entered, even the women squatting to empty the trash and sweep the floor. She drank tea not like a proper English lady, pinkie extended, but like an Indian, pouring the hot sweet liquid into the saucer, slurping it up. She planted herself bedside, holding and stroking the patient's hand; she barely slept.

Diana Hayden wasn't what anyone expected. She may have arrived in elbow-length white gloves, but she quickly shed them. She was the most down-to-earth, the one still *of* this earth. She was the first to recognize when a bedpan needed changing, a brow needed mopping, an IV drip needed replenishing, and when she couldn't find a nurse to do it, she did it herself.

Unexpectedly, and without anyone noticing, a third Diana arrived. Wrapped in a white tunic, she was luminescent, carved from moonlight. Grecian goddess, goddess of the hunt, Diana stood guard at the foot of the bed, a dog by her side, bow and arrows at the ready, slung over her shoulder. Goddess of birth, she brought with her a breeze no one could feel but her. It blew perpetually through her hair; its sound was the whisper of new beginnings.

Together the three Dianas formed an impenetrable circle around the hospital bed. Hours stretched into days. The dingy room reeked of ammonia and ointment. The walls, cracked, were further marred by ancient stains from splattered fluids. Fluorescent lights flickered. Each of the Dianas had her own way of rallying flagging spirits. Diana of the Hunt sang Judy Collins songs. ("To every thing, turn turn turn, there is a season, turn turn turn.") Diana Hayden told off-color jokes. ("How many beauty queens does it take to screw in a lightbulb? Beauty queens screw in hotel rooms, not lightbulbs!") Maha Diana needed to do nothing; she was serenity personified.

The days became a week. A week became two. The Dianas never left the hospital room.

After fifteen days, Kiran finally opened his eyes. At first, the light in the room was impossibly bright. He could make out only blurry outlines. Objects morphed, shape-shifted, started off as one thing and then settled into another. He saw, standing over his bed, first his mother. Then his sister. Finally, squatting in shadows in the far corner of the room, Pooja and her dog.

Bharat knew to stay away the day Kiran returned to the house. Kiran's parents had already collected his belongings and brought them to the air-conditioned hotel suite next door to the hospital, where they'd been staying since their arrival just two days after receiving Kamala's phone call informing them of Kiran's "accident," his subsequent coma, and the doctors' fears he might not awaken. Even Preeti had come, and she was with his parents now waiting in the hotel suite, three-year-old Sheila perpetually balanced on her hip; her newborn, Chance, back in Mississippi with his father.

Kiran's parents knew his injuries were the result of something other than his jumping from a moving bus, as Kamala had claimed. ("I'm sure it was just an accident? I'm sure he wasn't trying to hurt himself? Though you said yourself how fragile he was when you sent him.") They knew by Bharat's complete avoidance of them and by Kamala's and Prabhu's refusal to make eye contact during their solitary visit to the hospital—the same hospital where Ameera had died during childbirth—that there was more to this story, but, looking at each other, they'd made an unspoken agreement not to ask questions. One day, perhaps; not now. So it was with trepidation that they let Kiran return to the house to say good-bye and to do so alone, as he requested.

Kiran had been out of the hospital for a few days now. Tomorrow they were all heading back to America. He was still in recovery, but his parents wanted him to continue his healing in America, and the doctors said he was finally strong enough to fly. They had sprung for first-class tickets to make the long flight easier.

As the hired Ambassador bumped along, Kiran could feel, in his bruised and broken rib cage, every dip and divot in the road. The car turned from the busy thoroughfare onto the quiet lane. The stone house slowly came into view. Looking at the yard—seeing the familiar peepal tree, the dirt, the scraggly bushes—Kiran winced. The previous day, meeting him at an outdoor chai stall near the hotel, Pooja described to Kiran what had happened that fateful morning in the yard. She told Kiran about how not a molecule in her body doubted that Bharat was going to kill her. And that when Kiran bounded out of the house and threw himself on Bharat, trying to wrest him away from Pooja . . . well . . . she had heard the phrase "blind with rage" before, but she'd never actually witnessed it. "Whatever it was he was seeing, it wasn't me and it wasn't you. His physical body was here, but the rest of him was somewhere else. It was like the rest of him was in another world where the only thing that existed was his anger and his grief."

Pooja promised Kiran she had nothing to do with Ameera's death, and Kiran said, "I know. You're incapable of such a thing." Pooja had wondered whether Kiran meant incapable of such cruelty or incapable of magic, but she didn't ask. Much later, back in her own town with Guru Ma and her sisters in the run-down section of slums where they lived, Pooja would find that there was a tiny part of her—it shamed her to realize this—that felt proud that Bharat had finally believed in her powers, even if it meant he also thought she was a monster. She even wondered herself: there *had* been a moment—really, a blink-and-you-miss-it nanosecond—when she did wish harm on Bharat. Was it possible she somehow made it happen? The thought chilled her.

In the years to come, Pooja would come to believe that what we think, the invisible things we hold in our hearts, is what we ultimately manifest in the world, and wasn't that a kind of magic? It was not an easy thing to explain, and she didn't have it completely clear even in her own head, but this she believed: everyone was capable of curses, and everyone of miracles.

Pooja planned now to leave the same day as Kiran, returning to Guru Ma and her sisters. She would meet him one last time as he departed for the airport; she refused to leave even a second earlier. Despite the danger she faced by staying—especially after the horrible things Bharat had been saying about her to anyone who would listen—she insisted that Kiran needed her. Manoj had taken her in and had made a space for her in the stock room; and even though it was a potential threat to his stock, he looked the other way on nights when Pooja let Hanu inside to sleep with her.

After he entered Prabhu's room, it took Kiran's eye some time to adjust to the darkness; exactly how long, Kiran wasn't sure. Time in this room seemed to have little relationship to time outside it. Prabhu's room was its own world with its own logic, its own laws of physics: a windowless, interior room that must have been unbearable during the hot season. Even now the air could only be characterized as stagnant and dull; the listless ceiling fan was little help. A low-watt bare lightbulb glowed bedside; a diya flame flickered in the corner altar. With a nod of the head, Prabhu invited Kiran to take a seat on one of the ripped cushions positioned on the bare floor. If he was taken aback by Kiran's appearance—the bandage over his left eye and torn earlobe, the cast on his right arm, the bandages wrapped around his rib cage—Prabhu didn't betray it on his face. In some ways, the room reminded Kiran of his own dark room in the sixth-floor walk-up in New York, albeit a much cleaner version. Both rooms were spare and minimally furnished, with frameless mattresses floating raftlike on the floor.

After some silence, Prabhu said, "You're going back."

Kiran contemplated the word: *back*. It was the same word his father had used that summer. *We think you should go back to India.*

"Yes," Kiran said. "Tomorrow."

Prabhu nodded.

Kiran opened his mouth, closed it, tried again, three, four times—a fish out of water, choking on air. Finally he said, "What did you see when you found her in the woods?" Kiran didn't say his sister's name. He couldn't and didn't need to. "It was my fault. I'm to blame. So I need to know. What did she look like? What did I do to her?"

But Kiran was asking the wrong question. He didn't want to know the details; Preeti had already told him enough in her letter. What he was really asking, without even knowing it, was for Prabhu, the only adult witness to his deepest failing, to tell Kiran, *It's OK, you were just a child. It wasn't your fault, none of it was.* This dark room a confessional, Kiran hoped to be forgiven.

Prabhu looked at his nephew, recognized the pain on his face, the burden he carried. Prabhu had lived through enough tragedies: first his own wife's death; now Ameera's. Kiran's pain—no less, no greater than anyone else's—was his own to manage.

"Beta, darling, whatever it is you need from me, I can't give you."

Kiran watched the diya flicker in the altar, light lapping at framed images—Ganpati, Ram, Durga, Neela. A small insect skirted Kiran's cushion, searching for safe passage. Kiran's ankles pressed uncomfortably against the hard floor. The air hung around him in heavy curtains.

"It's time for you to go."

Even after Pooja would leave town (the same day as Kiran; she kept her promise and met him at the airport before finding her own way back to Guru Ma), the crows would remain, a reminder for folks that Pooja had been there. They watched from trees, sharp-eyed, heads able to articulate in every direction. They circled and cawed, swarmed and swooped. Bharat, seeing the crow-darkened sky or hearing their cries, would think not of Pooja, but only of what he'd lost.

It wasn't fair, Bharat thought. He couldn't believe in God—his very life began with his own mother's death, what God would allow that?—and he wrote off religion as superstition, but deep down he wanted to believe that the world wasn't random, that people got more or less what they deserved. But where was the justice in this? He had done everything right. He was a good son, all his life he'd done what he was told. He had even behaved toward his American cousin, who had humiliated him years earlier, with kindness and generosity.

Maybe this was why he had snapped. It wasn't true that he'd been blind with rage when he was trying to destroy Kiran. He saw Kiran clearly, perhaps more clearly than he had ever seen him. And he hated what he saw: the smugness, the selfishness, the privilege. It shouldn't have been Ameera. It should have been Kiran. If there were justice in the world, he'd be the one dead.

It wouldn't have helped Bharat to imagine—as Kiran sometimes did—that there was another world, one in which Ameera lived, in which they were still together, happy. He wanted her in this world.

The jyotishi his parents had consulted seven years earlier had said over and over, *It is written*. Was this written? What else did the future hold that he couldn't control? At least his daughter had survived, but he wondered how he could protect her. He cradled the baby in his arms, tucking her blanket tighter.

One day late in spring, suddenly and without anyone really noticing, the crows disappeared. They departed first in a flock, flying then turning, tilting extravagantly, the evening light silvering their wings. In the darkening sky they transformed into origami cranes. Back in college at the end of his freshman year, Kiran had left all the cranes he'd collected over the year in the dresser drawer. He intended the dorm room's next occupant to inherit them. Kiran had been miserable here, but at least this was some positive energy he could leave behind for the next occupant in hopes he would have an easier time. Kiran didn't realize that a cleaning crew would come through before then, charged with discarding whatever students had left behind, items they no longer wanted or would rather not bring back to their childhood homes for summer. The origami cranes were dumped into a trash barrel containing a ripped teddy bear, jeans that no longer fit, a dead lizard, a pink dildo.

Now, in India, the crows-turned-cranes scattered, each following its instinct in a different direction, looking for its next home, ready to unfold, smooth itself flat, fold itself into something new.

When Kiran returned from meeting Prabhu Kaka, taking the lift up to the air-conditioned hotel suite—two bedrooms attached to a sitting room with a kitchenette—he was dragging behind him, using his one good arm, the enormous stuffed tiger. Shanti was the only one who saw him. She was on the couch in the common room. Preeti and Sheila were in one bedroom, and Nishit was catnapping in the other.

Shanti recognized the stuffed tiger immediately. She had sent it with Bharat seven years earlier—"For your and Ameera's first baby!"—never guessing it would take so long for them to conceive, or that Ameera would die.

After leaving Prabhu Kaka, riding in the back of the bumping Ambassador, Kiran had spotted something in the abandoned lot near his cousin's house. He wasn't sure, but he asked the driver to stop and he got out and there it all was, among the ruins and the neighborhood trash—the A-frame dollhouse, the Tonka truck, the tiger—the peacocks picking their way around the mess.

"Oh, I remember *this* guy," Shanti said, trying to sound casual as she rushed to help Kiran, still struggling in the doorway. "You loved him so much." She lifted the tiger, hugging it a moment. The synthetic material itched her nose. She remembered when Chris had presented it to her at the food court in Elmira, the kiss that followed. She remembered afterward sitting in the hot car in the parking lot, crying, the creature in the trunk.

"Sheila will be over the moon."

"It's for Pooja."

"Pooja?"

"Remember Pooja? From the hospital?"

Shanti didn't immediately recognize the name. It took a moment for the image to fade in, like a ghost finally showing itself. It had been like that in the hospital, too. The first day she had not even noticed her, so focused was she on her son.

The second day, seeing the creature—that's how she thought of her—crouching barefoot in the corner, she assumed she was some hospital maid, a bai, a nameless woman there to empty the bedpans and sweep the floors. Finally, the third day, Shanti asked her who she was.

"Fr . . . friend," Pooja stuttered in English, even though Shanti would have understood her Hindi.

Shanti never asked her son about Pooja. She thought she knew the story. Sensitive soul, Kiran as a child brought home hurt birds, hoping to help them. Had she been honest with herself, Shanti would have seen this wasn't what was happening with Pooja. But she needed to believe this narrative about her son.

"Pooja needs it," Kiran said.

Shanti paused a moment, then said, "Well, you better hide it before Sheila sees it. Otherwise it'll be hers for sure." She helped Kiran wrestle the animal into the closet by the door.

Hearing the ruckus, Nishit came to check on his son. "You're back," he said, sounding relieved. "How did it go?"

"Fine."

"Did you say your good-byes?"

"Huh?"

"Isn't that why you went?"

"Yeah," Kiran said.

Nishit had wanted so much to accompany Kiran, not just to assist him in his infirm state, but to see his own brother one last time before he left India. He'd only seen him that once when he and Kamala had come to the hospital room; Nishit had been too occupied otherwise shuttling back and forth from the hotel to the hospital and caring for Sheila while Shanti and Preeti remained day and night in the hospital room. Who knew when he'd have a chance to see his brother again. But Kiran had been so insistent that he needed to go alone.

"Did he seem OK?"

"Who?"

"Prabhu. How was he?" Nishit noticed Kiran's eyes shift to the side and the muscles in his face tense.

"The same. He's always the same."

Nishit remembered Kiran slumped against the wall in the sixth-floor walk-up months earlier while Nishit scrubbed the apartment. He would protect his son; he would do what it took.

Sheila burst into the room, barreling into Nishit's arms. Nishit lifted her onto his shoulders; she squealed. He was grateful for the distraction, glad to be able to change the subject. "I'm famished," he said. "Who's hungry?"

No one wanted to leave the comfort of the air-conditioning, so they ordered room service. Biryani and curries for the four adults, cornflakes ("cornflaks," the menu read) with hot milk for Sheila. They sat around the wooden dinette table, eating. It would be the only time the four of them were ever all together in India, five of them counting Sheila. Kiran would make future trips, surprising his parents, considering his near-death first experience. Even more surprising to them, Preeti would also return, coming every couple of years to volunteer with her husband at a Christian mission hospital. Children in tow, she'd tell them each time, as if they somehow didn't know, "This is where your Nana and Nani are from."

Much later that night, Kiran, lying awake in the room he was sharing with Preeti and Sheila, his bed just inches from theirs, would think how strange it felt. Even as small children he and Preeti had always had separate bedrooms at home. There was the odd vacation here or there, the last being Myrtle Beach, 1991, but aside from that Kiran had no experience sharing a room with his sister. In the dim light of the bedside lamp Sheila insisted remain lit, he would look over at them. Preeti and

Sheila were curled into one another. Preeti had finally wiped off the makeup she persisted in wearing even in the hospital room. Her face was soft, slack.

Asleep, everyone was vulnerable—all breath and beating heart. Asleep, everyone was a child. Whatever armor protected them during the day was shed. Kiran thought of his own armor, the walls he'd erected, the way he'd betrayed and repeatedly pushed his family away. And yet they'd all come. Even his cousin-brothers abroad had made calls and sent cards. A couple even threatened to travel, though they didn't follow through. Still, one way or another they were all represented, every last minkey.

As they were finishing their room service, Sheila turned cranky, clinging to her mother and crying into her shoulder. "There, there," Preeti said, patting Sheila's back with one hand and trying to finish her food with another, but Sheila's wails only intensified. Preeti couldn't blame her. She'd been cooped up for so many days and no doubt missing her father and her life back in Mississippi.

"I know," Preeti said. "I know what will make you feel better. How about we play . . ." She paused dramatically. Sheila's eyes widened, waiting for her mother to finish the sentence. ". . . musical chairs!" Sheila squealed and clapped her hands, her eyes still wet from crying. How easy it was to turn her desperation into delight! She hopped down from her mother's lap and toddled over to a wooden chair, struggling to drag it from the dinette set to the empty space in the center of the room. Preeti popped up from her chair, repositioning it near Sheila's, and Kiran followed suit.

"I don't think it's a good idea for you to play," Shanti said to Kiran. She looked at him pointedly. "Your injuries. You're still so fragile."

"It's musical chairs," Kiran said, "not tackle football."

"Kiran," his mother pleaded.

"Don't worry, Mom. I'll be careful." Ameera had died. Kiran himself had almost died. He'd been given another chance. He was going to do it all right this time. He wasn't going to sit anything out.

Shanti sighed.

"I'll do the music," Nishit said. He'd already sunk into the small couch and had no intention of moving. He started whistling a romantic Kishore Kumar song he knew none of his children would recognize, but after a couple of bars Shanti looked over at him, once she'd caught the melody, and flashed him a smile. Her hair was cut short, as it had been for many years, now dyed a chestnut brown light enough that she was sometimes mistaken for Hispanic. He remembered when she'd first cut it, not long after Prabhu returned to India. He knew how close he'd come to losing her that year. Since then, how often had he told her he loved her? Not often enough, not nearly enough. He watched her chasing her granddaughter around the chairs, looking so joyful. He had not done everything right, he knew that. He was so young when he came to America, younger than Kiran was now, and he knew no one. He'd had to find his own way. But Nishit believed he had done his best, and look, here they all were; they had come together when it really mattered. As a father, as a husband, was there more he should want?

They played several rounds. Not wanting anyone else to lose, Shanti was always the first one out. "Oh, I'm no good at this," she'd say, flopping happily on the couch with whistling Nishit. They made sure that Sheila always won, but for second place Kiran and Preeti fought fiercely, Preeti tucking her hair behind her ear, Kiran trying unsuccessfully to leverage his injuries for sympathy. All the while Sheila shrieked and laughed—leaping, skipping, dancing, even as her eyes never left the chairs.

It was a game they all knew. Round and round and round you go. Where you'll stop, nobody knows. Now you're in someone else's chair. The music starts, the music stops. Chairs disappear. Before you know it, the chair you thought was beneath you isn't. You're out. Someone wins. Someone loses. Eventually, it all starts again.

Acknowledgments

THANK YOU to Nat Jacks, agent and friend, for your enduring faith and for being so superb at all the stuff I stink at.

Thank you to Rakesh Satyal for believing in this book when it was only a page long.

Thank you to my editor, Terry Karten, for asking all the right questions, and for gently but firmly guiding this book toward the best version it could be. And thank you to Jillian Verrillo and all the other wonderful folks at HarperCollins.

Thank you to Susan Morehouse for being the other member of our Writing Group of Two. You helped nurture and shape this book at every stage; it simply wouldn't exist without you.

Thank you to the other readers of various drafts of this book for providing valuable feedback and needed encouragement and support: Janet Iafrate, Mel Gilles, and BFF extraordinaire Erin Brooks Worley.

The son of a librarian, I grew up in libraries and consider them to be sacred spaces and librarians themselves to be protectors and brave warriors. Much of this book was written in libraries. Thank you to the David A. Howe Library in Wellsville, New York; the Lovett and Chestnut Hill branches of the Free Library of Philadelphia; and the Grand County Public Library in Moab, Utah.

Thank you to the canyons and creeks and sunsets and creatures—human and otherwise—of Moab, Utah, for providing perspective and that crucial last bit of heat to help this book finish baking. I am especially grateful to Mike, Wendy, and Sugar Newman; Mathew Gross; and again Mel Gilles.

Thank you to the Big Blue Marble Bookstore in Philadelphia and to all the independent booksellers across the country for carrying the torch.

Thank you to Monday Night Sangha.

Thank you to Kimona, whose canine brain likely will never comprehend just how much she's helped me and how much she is a part of this book.

Thank you to Kunj Mehta, Nalini Mehta, Nimish Mehta, Kim Cross, and to my nephew and niece, Jay and Mia (great sources of joy!), and to all of my uncles and aunts and cousins and their little ones who are such a big part of my life. I couldn't ask for a better family.

Thank you to the Lambda Literary Foundation, the Asian American Writers' Workshop, and the San Diego Multicultural LGBT Literary Foundation for all your fierce advocacy for queer writers and writers of color. Keep fighting the good fight.

Thank you to my students at the University of the Arts, and to my colleagues, especially Elise Juska and Zach Savich.

Thank you to Michael Sledge and Brian Leung for encouragement and support.

Thank you to Jane Hirshfield for your amazing work and for kind permission to use your remarkable poem. You are an inspiration in the truest sense.

Thank you to George Saunders for superhero levels of mentorship and generosity, and for providing a shining example again and again.

And thank you to Robert Bingham for being my everything and more.

About the Author

RAHUL MEHTA's debut short story collection, *Quarantine*, won a Lambda Literary Award and the Asian American Literary Award for Fiction. His work has appeared in the *Kenyon Review*, the *Sun*, *New Stories from the South*, the *New York Times Magazine*, the *International Herald Tribune*, *Marie Claire India*, and other publications. An *Out* magazine "Out 100" honoree, he lives in Philadelphia with his partner and their dog, and teaches creative writing at the University of the Arts.